NEW YEAR, NEW ROMANCE

"You can't leave now—it's almost midnight. Stay and have some fun, Madelyn. That's what New Year's Eve is all about."

She hesitated, knowing she ought to tell him good night. Instead, she raised the glass to her lips and took a long, slow sip.

Time flashed past, their glasses disappeared, and she was in his arms, her head spinning as they whirled to the music, their bodies pressed close in a way she should never have allowed.

The band played a drumroll to signal the twelve o'clock hour was only moments away. Everyone stilled in a jubilant hush, then began to count backward from ten in a loud, boisterous chorus.

". . five . . . four . . . three . . . two . . . one . . . Happy New Year!"

Colorful balloons and gaily striped confetti rained from above as horns tooted and the band swung into a brassy rendition of "Auld Lang Syne." Amid the glitter and spectacle, people embraced and kissed.

Zack turned her to him, cupping her face in his hands as he smiled down into her eyes. "Happy New Year, Madelyn."

He leaned down and covered her lips with his.

Also by Tracy Anne Warren

TRACY ANNE
WARREN

THE LAST MAN ON EARTH

A SIGNET SELECT BOOK

SIGNET SELECT
Published by the Penguin Group
Penguin Group (USA) LLC, 375 Hudson Street,
New York, New York 10014

USA | Canada | UK | Ireland | Australia | New Zealand | India | South Africa | China
penguin.com
A Penguin Random House Company

First published by Signet Select, an imprint of New American Library,
a division of Penguin Group (USA) LLC

First Printing, January 2014

ISBN 978-0-451-46600-6

Printed in the United States of America
10 9 8 7 6 5 4 3 2 1

For Tony and Mimi
The new kids on the block

ACKNOWLEDGMENTS

Cheers to Wendy McCurdy for letting me do a little creative time traveling, and to my wonderfully persistent agent, Helen Breitwieser, for never giving up—good things really do come to those who wait!

With love to my friends Dorothy McFalls and Jim Johnson on the arrival of baby Avery, their newest "edition."

CHAPTER ONE

"You no-good, low-down, scurvy dog!"

The door to Zack Douglas's office flew back hard on its hinges, striking the wall with explosive force. Madelyn Grayson stood framed in the entrance, hands on her hips, her blue eyes bright with rage.

Zack looked up from the storyboard he'd been making changes to and arched one dark eyebrow.

"You self-serving piece of scum!" she continued. "You underhanded bottom-feeder! You trough-dwelling, swill-eating pig!"

He leaned casually back in his leather executive chair and let her insults run off him, harmless as rain. "Good afternoon to you too, Maddie."

What a firecracker, Zack thought, watching her practically crackle with anger as she walked toward him, shaking one well-manicured finger his way.

"Don't you dare 'good afternoon' me, you lowlife. Not after the stunt you pulled today. You must think you're pretty clever, engineering things the way you did. And don't call me Maddie. The name is Madelyn or Ms. Grayson to you."

Holding back a grin, he took a moment to enjoy the sight of her. She was wearing a plain, pearl gray skirted suit that would have looked dowdy on anyone else but seemed only to increase her attractiveness. Her breasts rose and fell beneath a long, tidy placket of ivory-colored shirt buttons, the effect as sexy as a Hooters girl in a tight tee.

He lifted his eyes so he didn't get caught staring and noticed the wisps of red hair that had come loose from the librarian bun she always kept it in. He pictured threading his fingers into the whole luxurious mass, popping and pulling at the pins until her hair came free around her shoulders. After that, he'd go to work on those shirt buttons—

Careful, he warned himself, interrupting the thought. *Don't get distracted.*

"So, Madelyn, what terrible crime have I committed now?"

He was quite familiar with her less-than-glowing opinion of his character. She didn't approve of him or his reputation, the more titillating particulars of which had spread like a raging viral infection through the office grapevine within hours of his arrival at Fielding and Simmons, one of New York City's leading advertising agencies, some eight months before. Generally he found her reactions amusing. There was nothing quite like watching Madelyn Grayson—all neatly starched, five feet seven inches of her—get completely worked up.

Especially when it was over him.

She glared. "As if you don't know."

"Sorry." He shrugged. "I'm at a loss."

"Stop with the innocent act! What you did was sneaky and conniving, and I deserve an apology."

"I rarely give apologies, and certainly not for wrongs I didn't commit. You'll have to be more specific."

She planted her hands on the edge of his desk. "Specific? You want specific? *Specifically*, it's about your parading that overgrown jock through my fashion event, knowing he would monopolize everyone's attention. It was totally contemptible!"

"Karl Sweeney is a sports superstar. He can't help the way his fans behave."

"Exactly my point. You knew how people would react and deliberately chose that time of day to leave the building."

"If you mean I deliberately chose lunchtime to take a client to lunch, and deliberately decided to walk through the lobby on the way out of the building? Then, you're right. That's exactly what I did."

"Yes, but you set it up. You timed your exit from the building so you and your basketball star would just happen to meet up with Fielding at the perfect moment. A moment designed to get you an invitation to the executive level for lunch."

His eyes widened. "Is that what I did? Engineered lunch for myself in the executive dining room with our CEO? Whoa, that was genius!" He paused, his eyes moving beyond her for a moment. "You might want to close the door, by the way. We're starting to attract an audience."

Madelyn whirled around and saw one of the copywriters walking ever so slowly by in the corridor. She pinned him with a frosty glare, then shut the door. She turned back to Zack. "Now, you were saying?"

"I wasn't, actually, but look—the meeting with Sweeney ran a lot longer than expected, okay? He insists on providing his own creative input, and his agent and I managed to work out an arrangement that keeps us all happy, especially Sweeney. We decided to conclude our discussion over lunch and couldn't help but notice your fashion show in the lobby on our way out. It's only natural that Sweeney wanted to stop for a closer look."

"Oh, I see," she said sarcastically. "It was all Sweeney's idea."

"Once he got a look at the implants on some of those runway models, I couldn't pull him away."

She crossed her arms defensively over her own very real breasts. "While you, of course, shielded your eyes."

Madelyn was well aware of Zack's penchant for eyeing anything in a skirt, especially a tight one.

"A man can't help but look at what's put right in front of him," he said with a straight face. "Anyway, one thing led to another, Fielding showed up, and you know the rest. There was nothing calculated or premeditated about it. Nice job, by the by, on the campaign you put together for Evaan. Very slick. It should double his sales."

"It'll triple his sales. I suppose you expect me to thank you for the compliment now, right?"

He stood and came around the front of his desk to stand beside her. "Only if you want to. I'm not always the villain you make me out to be. The comment was honestly meant."

Sunlight streamed in through a modest side window,

highlighting the strong lines of his jaw and the beginnings of a five-o'clock shadow. He'd taken off his suit jacket, leaving him in a white shirt and a pair of tailored charcoal gray pinstripe pants. At thirty-two, he was impossibly handsome, beautiful even, with a smile that could melt ice, and hearts. A woman would have to be dead to be immune to his charms. And Madelyn was very much a living, breathing female, though she did her best not to acknowledge it in his presence.

His kind words left her feeling churlish. She cleared her throat. "The fact remains that you took shameless advantage of the situation."

He leaned against his desk. "If you're talking about the invitation to dine upstairs, what would you have had me do? Refuse Fielding and drag away his favorite sports hero? Just between you and me, I'd like to keep my job.

"Look, Madelyn, you do great work, keep the clients happy, and earn the company a bundle. That's what's important and what everyone will remember. Not the fact that you missed out on lunch in the penthouse."

He lowered his voice as if to share a secret. "To be honest, you're better off. A meal up top is nothing but a lot of dry talk and heavy food." He tapped a fist to the center of his chest, mimicking heartburn. "A little of that French stuff goes a long way."

"Maybe so, but I deserved the chance to decide that for myself. I was entitled to that invitation."

Today was supposed to be my day, not yours. Why was it lately that he was the one receiving all the accolades?

"You're right," Zack agreed. "You were entitled. And likely you would have received it if Larry Roland didn't turn into a quivering puddle every time one of the top brass looks at him for more than two seconds in a row. But that's bosses for you. You'll get another chance—don't worry."

He smiled broadly, flashing her a glimpse of his perfect white teeth. "Are we square now?"

A weak, traitorous need to say yes ran through her. She choked it down.

Square? With Zack Douglas?

Her fiercest competition?

Her chief rival?

The only person who stood between her and the promotion that by rights would have been hers by now if he hadn't come along?

The man who'd been an aggravating thorn in her side from the instant he'd walked through the door?

The man who exuded charisma as if it were fine cologne and didn't mind taking advantage of that fact?

No, she'd never be square with him.

Still, the outrage that had propelled her into his office moments ago had largely evaporated. "I'll consider a truce; it's the best I can offer. A very short, very temporary truce."

"That'll do," he said. Then, in a move that surprised them both, he reached out and gave the curl lying against her cheek a gentle tug, his fingers brushing her skin. "For now," he added.

Sensation burned like a line of fire where he'd touched.

"Wha . . . what was that?" she said, stepping quickly back and lifting a hand to tuck the loose hair behind her ear.

"Loose curl," he murmured, meeting her eyes.

"Oh." She took another step away. "Well, I should get back to work."

"We both should. Glad we had a chance to talk this out, Red."

Red? She blinked and opened her mouth to correct him but found herself at a loss for words. She turned and yanked open the door.

Once she'd gone, Zack returned to his chair. What had he been thinking, playing with her hair like that? Touching her? At least he hadn't given in to the impulse to kiss her, an idea that had definitely crossed his mind. But kissing a woman like Madelyn Grayson could have serious repercussions. The sort that might lead to long-term complications a man like him didn't need. God knows, the failure of his one and only marriage years ago had taught him that lesson well. Never let a woman get too close; that was his motto. Enjoy them, appreciate their beauty, then wave good-bye before they have a chance to curl their claws around your heart and squeeze.

But enough of that. He and Madelyn worked together, end of story. Besides, if the rumor mill was right, she was all but engaged to some rich international financier. He'd seen the guy's picture—tall and blond with a perfect toothpaste-ad smile—sitting on her office credenza. According to the other women in the office, *blondie* was as close to a knight in shining armor as any flesh-and-blood man could get.

He rolled his eyes at the ridiculous notion.

No, he'd done the right thing.

The wise thing.

Especially since he hadn't told her about the Takamuri account. Once Madelyn found out about that, she'd be furious, leaving them both back at square one.

Shrugging over what he couldn't change, he picked up his pen and resumed work on his storyboard.

Madelyn was still trembling in reaction to her confrontation with Zack when she reached her office. She closed the door behind her and sat down at her desk.

What in the hell was that? Even now, her cheek tingled where he had touched her. She reached up and fingered the curl that had come loose again. *Damn him,* she thought. *And damn me for responding.*

Bad day; that's all it was. Bad week, actually, but she didn't want to dwell on that now. She dug a small mirror out of her purse and used it as she ruthlessly combed her hair back into place, every last strand.

After taking a long pull from the eco-friendly water bottle she kept on the edge of her desk, she reapplied her lipstick—a pale shade of pink called Strawberries and Cream that managed to complement, instead of clash with, her red hair.

Much better, she thought, tucking the lipstick and mirror away again in her purse. Her confidence was restored, her control once again in place. At least that's what she was going to tell herself.

She was gathering up materials to review with her assistant, Peg Truman, when the telephone rang.

It was her mother. "Hello, love. How was your morning? Just had to call and find out."

"Hi, Mom." Madelyn resumed her seat. "It was fine."

An image of Zack Douglas flashed into her mind. She pushed it away.

"Only fine?" Laura Grayson questioned. "Did something go wrong? Oh, I hope not. I know how hard you've worked on that fashion campaign." She paused. "One of the models didn't fall off that makeshift runway you had built, did they?"

Madelyn smiled. Her mother had such a wonderfully dramatic imagination. "No, no one fell off the stage. The show went fine—great, in fact. The client loved it, said he had orders flying in before the show was even half through."

"Well, that sounds marvelous. So what's the matter?"

That was the trouble, Madelyn thought, when you were speaking with the person who'd once dusted powder on your naked baby bottom, patched your skinned knees when you fell off the monkey bars in first grade, and took flash pictures of you in your prom dress until you thought you might be blinded—they sensed everything.

"Nothing," Madelyn said. "I'm tired, that's all."

There was a long pause. "Well," Laura said, "I'm not surprised, working yourself to the bone the way you do. If you ask me, those people you work for don't appreciate you enough."

After the day she'd had, Madelyn had to agree, though she didn't say so out loud.

"If I had my way, you'd have come to work for me a long time ago," Laura said. "You'd make a terrific planner—you know that."

It was an old argument. Madelyn opted for the path of least resistance. "So, how *is* the wedding business?"

"Busy, frantic, wonderful. That's why I'm calling you at the office. I've got another half hour; then I have to leave for the Richardson rehearsal. The wedding is scheduled for tomorrow morning and sure to be spectacular. Five hundred guests, two dozen white swans, flowered luminaria, and a twenty-piece orchestra from the Boston Philharmonic. Lord, it's going to be a madhouse."

Madelyn chuckled. "And you'll love every minute of it."

"You're right; I will. I thrive on insanity. Must be why I married your father, had you four children, and became a full-time wedding consultant," she declared. "I just wanted to confirm that you and James will be here tomorrow night around seven and that you're bringing the olive tapenade with you. The one from that delightful shop in the Village, and some of those delicious little cheese biscuits to go with it."

Drat, Madelyn cursed in silence. What with everything happening this past week, she'd completely forgotten about her mother's Last Gasp of Fall party. If there was one thing Laura Grayson loved, it was a party—attending one, hosting one, didn't matter so long as she was part of the excitement.

Madelyn picked up a pencil, twirled it between her fingers. "Um, Mother, about that—we may not be able to make it."

"What do you mean, not make it? Of course you're going to make it. A weekend in the country is exactly what you need, both of you."

"Connecticut isn't exactly the country, you know."

"It is compared to where you live. Now, I won't hear another word. You're coming and that's that. You can help me pick out new sample invitations and James can get in a round of golf with your father and brother."

Madelyn tapped the pencil against her desk mat a few times, then tossed it aside. "All right, I'll be there. But about James, he . . ."

"Yes?"

She didn't want to discuss this. Not now. Actually, not ever, if she had her druthers, but she knew it would have to be done sometime. She drew in a deep breath. "James and I aren't seeing each other anymore."

Laura Grayson chortled. "Not seeing each other? Whatever do you mean? Has he gone on a trip somewhere? I know he was talking about acquiring some property in Asia. Hong Kong, I think, despite the Chinese taking it back and all. Although it isn't like him to simply run off without a word. He's never been the thoughtless type. Such a dear boy; I couldn't love him more if he were my own."

Leaning her head back against her upholstered seat, Madelyn closed her eyes. Yes, she knew.

The "boy"—who'd just turned thirty last month—was everything her mother said. Kind, thoughtful, charming. Incredibly handsome, intelligent, and rich. The epitome of everything any red-blooded American woman could desire in a man. Added to that, he and Madelyn were friends. They had been since the day fifteen years earlier when her family purchased the house next to his and they'd met as hesitant teenagers over the hedge in the backyard. Everything had been fine between them. Great, in fact. Until last Saturday. The day he'd asked her to be his wife.

"Mother, James and I broke up."

There was a long silence on the other end of the

phone. "I don't understand. You and James . . . Well, the two of you . . . you've been together forever. Did you have a fight?"

"No, not exactly. He proposed."

"But that's wonderful!"

"I didn't accept."

"Didn't accept? Why not? The two of you have been practically engaged for years."

Madelyn picked a microscopic piece of lint off her skirt. "Maybe we have, but . . . please just leave it alone, Mother."

"But, sweetheart, you love James," her mother sputtered, helpless confusion plain in her voice.

Madelyn sighed. "You're right; I do love him. But not enough. Not the way I should. Not the way a wife should."

"Pish-tosh! Cold feet—that's all it is. I see it all the time in my profession. Give yourself a little room to reconsider and you'll snap out of it."

"There's nothing to snap out of."

"Of course there is. The two of you are wonderful together and you couldn't ask for a better man. Besides, dear, despite all your hard work and dedication to your job, I know how much you want a family. What about that?"

"What about it? I can have a family and work too. You do."

"That's not what I'm saying. I'm thinking of your age."

Madelyn bristled. "I'm only twenty-nine."

"Soon to be thirty," Laura reminded her. "It's time you were starting your family. With you settled on James, it wasn't such an issue. But now . . ."

"Women are having babies well into their forties these days. I have time."

Laura sighed. "Perhaps you do, biologically speaking, but from a practical standpoint, I've always wondered about these women who wait so long. I know the kind of energy it takes to raise children. And let me tell you, the older you get, the harder it gets. So when these thirty- and forty-something-year-olds finally have their babies, I can't help but think they're too tired to keep up, too exhausted to enjoy what they've waited so long to have. I don't want that to be you, Madelyn. I want you to be able to have fun with your children and still have enough spark left over to enjoy life once they're grown."

"I will, Mom. Don't worry. I'll find someone."

"The way I see it, you already have found someone and his name is James Jordan. Who is it you're waiting for? Prince Charming?"

No, not Prince Charming, Madelyn thought, *just a man.* A real, human man who would one day lock eyes with her across a crowded room and make the rest of the world fade into nothingness. Whose most casual touch would send her heart skipping as fast and hard as a smooth stone across the surface of a calm summer lake.

Madelyn shook her head. Maybe her mother was right and she was being fanciful. A stupid, idealistic fool throwing away the best thing she was ever going to have. Perhaps she should call James, beg his forgiveness, tell him she'd reconsidered. He'd take her back—she knew he would—in spite of the hurt she knew she would see in his blue eyes.

But she'd done the right thing. When James had proposed, her refusal had come rushing from her lips before she'd even thought out the answer. It wasn't right for her to settle, not for James or for her. He deserved a woman who adored him. Not one who would always see him first and foremost as a very dear friend.

And she deserved . . . Well, she didn't know precisely what she deserved. All she knew was that there had to be something more, something deeper. Love with a man who would take all she had to give and offer her more than she could ever imagine in return.

"Look, Mom, I've got to go, okay? I'll see you tomorrow evening."

"All right," her mother sighed. "We'll talk about this later when we both have more time. Congratulations on today's ad launch."

"Thanks. Good luck on your swans."

With a chuckle, her mother hung up.

Madelyn slumped in her seat, desperate for a moment's peace.

And a moment was all she had before her e-mail beeped to let her know she had six new messages, her telephone rang, and someone knocked on her door.

"That man is the bane of my existence," Madelyn declared. It was several days later, and she was gathered around a small table in the bar of a trendy midtown restaurant with her three best friends.

The crowd was heavy, especially for a Wednesday night, the atmosphere thick with a haze of heat and noise, glassware chinking softly in the background.

"He should be drawn and quartered," she fumed. "And once that's done, his head should be stuck on a pike."

"Ooh, kinda like that poor guy Mel Gibson played.

You know, the one who got it at the end of *Braveheart*."
Suzy Katz's brown eyes widened at the gruesome idea.

Peg Truman, vivacious and brunette in a red miniskirt
that barely covered her legs, and copy editor Linda Hernandez, who'd long since resigned herself to knee length
after the birth of her second child, exchanged knowing
looks. Suzy, a production assistant and the youngest of
the group at twenty-three, had a habit of saying whatever popped into her head, which usually provided welcome comic relief.

Madelyn, too sunk in her own misery, didn't even
crack a smile at Suzy's guileless observation.

Linda scooped a handful of pretzels out of a bowl in
the center of the table and set to munching.

Peg took a swallow of her vodka gimlet. "It wasn't a
sure thing to begin with anyway, Madelyn. The fact that
they decided to give the account to Zack might not have
anything at all to do with that lunch."

"It has everything to do with that lunch," Madelyn
said. "I'd bet my boots on it. Takamuri Electronics was
supposed to be mine. Everyone knows I'd done the prep
work, the initial concept planning, and then suddenly
they go and give it to *him*. Rotten, conniving creep. He
worked it just right." He'd worked her just right too,
hadn't he?

"Maybe it wasn't his idea at all," Peg countered. "You
know how management can be. As much as we women
like to think we've earned our equality, things still run
along pretty traditional lines. I mean, look at what Zack
works on, cars and sports products. You, on the other
hand, primarily get handed fashion and cosmetic accounts. They probably wanted a man for the Takamuri

deal since electronics targets so heavily with the male consumer."

"Which is exactly why they should have given it to me. The company, the industry in general, needs to broaden its appeal with women. And I could have offered that to them, tapped into a market with real growth potential. Brought them the woman's point of view. I thought they agreed with that. I thought they were going to give me the green light. And they were until Zack oh so conveniently got himself invited upstairs for a tête-à-tête with the company's CEO. No, he planned it, executed it, and got exactly what he wanted."

And like a fool she'd let him. What bothered her most was that she hadn't seen it coming. Instead she'd stood there in his office last week like some dewy-eyed fawn and let him bamboozle her. He'd talked such a good line she'd believed him in spite of her own better judgment. All that garbage about how much he liked her work. Yeah, right, and he had a nice bridge for sale at a rock-bottom price too.

"I don't know, Madelyn." Peg twirled the toothpicked olive from her drink through the air for emphasis. "As hungry as Zack is to move up, it doesn't sound like something he'd do. He's more direct than that. I'm not claiming he's a saint, but if he wants something he goes straight for it. He doesn't sneak around from behind."

"How do you know he doesn't? The man's a manipulator, plain and simple. Why, my God, he's even got you wrapped around his little finger."

"He does not." Peg stiffened. "Just because I don't think he's the devil incarnate like you do doesn't mean I'm in league with him."

Madelyn apologized. "I know. You're a good, loyal friend and I didn't mean to imply otherwise. It's just . . ."

"Just what?" Peg asked.

"It's just that everyone likes him so much!" Madelyn said with exasperation. "How can so many people be taken in by a pretty face? There's more to a person than their looks, you know."

"True, but when you look like him, well . . . it's hard not to be swayed," said Linda. "Especially when he turns on that smile."

"I know," sighed Suzy. "He's so positively yummy. All that thick dark hair and those gorgeous green eyes. Have you noticed his lashes? They're as long as a girl's."

"Yeah, and that body ain't so bad neither," Linda drawled, wiggling her brunette eyebrows up and down in her best Groucho Marx impression.

They all laughed. All except Madelyn.

She scowled. "Hey, would you three snap out of it? This is exactly what I'm talking about. So he's hot. So what? There is such a thing as character, stability, morals, and he's got none of the above. Did you hear the latest, about that clerk in accounting? I understand they were found together in the third-floor copy room doing a lot more than making copies."

Peg waved a hand. "I know the one you're talking about. From what I hear she's a total tramp. Wears her skirts even shorter than mine."

"Is that possible?" Linda quipped in mock seriousness.

Peg's eyes flashed; then she retaliated, flicking a drop of her drink across the table at the other woman using the end of her plastic olive skewer. Linda squealed, swerving sideways on her chair as she tried to duck.

Suzy ignored them, leaning forward to share. "I heard he had her shirt off." She paused, then sighed dreamily. "I'd let him take my shirt off."

"In the copy room?" the other two exclaimed.

Linda and Peg cracked up.

Madelyn waited until they'd settled down. "Yes, well, the point is that Zack Douglas is a complete tomcat."

Linda snapped a pretzel in half. "Maybe, but there're other men in the office with reputations just as bad or worse than his. And at least he isn't married and cheating on his wife like most of them." She paused. "You know what the problem is between the two of you? You're too much alike."

Madelyn's mouth fell open. "Excuse me, but I can't have heard you right. Zack Douglas and I are nothing alike. I don't know how you could even suggest such a thing."

"You're both intelligent, ambitious, highly creative people who happen to be in a position to get in each other's way. My guess is if you weren't so competitive toward each other, you'd like him better. And you'd be able to see what other people see in him."

Madelyn gave a self-righteous snort. "I'd see exactly what I see right now. A devious, unprincipled jerk who manipulates people with his good looks and charm. He's even managed to manipulate you guys. I will never, ever find anything good to say about the man."

Peg sipped the last of her drink. "Nothing? Not even one single tiny thing?"

"Not so much as a microscopic speck."

"And why should you?" Suzy defended. "Not when you've got James, that sweet, gorgeous guy of yours. He's loaded, kind, brilliant, and built, plus he practically hangs on your every word! We should all be so lucky."

Linda and Peg murmured their agreement.

Madelyn gave a false smile, then buried her face in her frozen strawberry daiquiri, taking a long, slow sip that sent a jolt of cold straight to her sinuses. She hadn't told them yet, not even Peg. She knew she needed to soon. But right now, she couldn't handle the inquisition that was sure to follow.

She twirled the straw in her half-empty glass and decided the moment demanded something stronger. She flagged down a passing waitress.

"Hot fudge sundae, please, with the works."

CHAPTER TWO

Light flakes of snow drifted out of the sky, lazy and fat, a halfhearted reminder from old man winter that the first day of January was but a few short hours shy of its birth. Although not enough to stick to the streets and sidewalks, the small weather event had nevertheless given the awnings and treetops a wonderland effect, as if they had been sprinkled with a light coating of powdered sugar.

From high above, Madelyn watched, inside, where it was dry and a little too warm. The atmosphere was noisy with the press of people desperately trying to wring a few more drops of fun out of this last special night of the year. Behind her the elegant New Year's Eve party was revving into high gear. The room glittered, linen-lined tables crowded with platters of food: hors d'oeuvres and salads, entrées and sweets.

And champagne, lots of champagne.

Tables, each with a holiday-themed centerpiece, ringed

the outer walls. A ten-piece band played in the far corner, the lively music encouraging more and more people to join the growing crush of dancers. And above everyone's heads, suspended inside a clever series of mesh nets, were hundreds of colorful balloons and masses of curling streamers

Madelyn kept a smile on her face, even though she couldn't really say she was enjoying herself.

She had dressed for the occasion in a full-length evening gown made from a clever combination of crushed gold velvet and sleek bronze satin. The square-cut neckline was low enough to show off some cleavage. As usual, her hair was pinned onto the crown of her head. Tonight, though, she'd softened it with a few curls left down to frame her face.

She always went out on New Year's Eve. It was tradition with the Grayson clan, who never failed to ring in the holiday with gusto. But this year was different. This year, for the first time since she'd been a naive girl, she was out on the town without a date.

"Champagne?" A white-jacketed waiter stopped near her shoulder, a tray of filled glasses at the ready.

She accepted one with a grateful nod.

She'd danced a bit earlier in the evening, fending off one obscene proposition from an owl-eyed drunk who even now was staggering around the room, hoping to get lucky. The odds weren't in his favor. From what Madelyn had seen, nearly all the people in attendance were paired up, arriving two by two, male and female, like mated species boarding a symbolic Noah's ark.

When she'd originally agreed to meet her brother, P.G., and his wife, Caroline, for the evening, she'd still been dating James. The four of them had often gone out when her brother and sister-in-law were in the city.

P.G. had offered to set her up with a friend of his, a fellow architect who'd recently ended a long-term relationship of his own. Madelyn had declined, figuring it would be preferable to go solo rather than be stuck for an entire evening with a guy who was still moping over a recent breakup.

Now that she was here, she wasn't so sure. What she ought to have done was canceled and stayed home. At this very moment, she could have been lying on her sofa, wrapped snug and comfy in her rattiest robe, eating popcorn, and watching a sentimental old movie on TV.

Thanksgiving and Christmas had been less than jolly times for her this year too. She'd been forced to endure a constant barrage of questions from her multitude of relatives over her breakup with James and his absence from the festivities. For the first time ever, she'd used work as an excuse to leave early.

As she sipped champagne, she watched her brother and sister-in-law as they whirled by in the sea of dancers. Laughing, their eyes locked, they seemed aware of no one but each other, so very much in love. After almost ten years of marriage, they were as happy now as they'd been on the day they'd wed.

Crazy in love.

Was it so wrong of her to want that for herself? To crave more than friendship, however deep that friendship might run? Before she had time to ponder the question, a familiar figure stepped into view across the room.

Zack Douglas.

He had clearly just arrived, bits of melted snow glistening in his dark hair. She was used to seeing him in expensive, tailored suits at work. Tonight, though, he was wearing a black tuxedo with a satin cummerbund and a crisp bow tie.

He looked . . . amazing. For an instant, she felt a wave of pure, unadulterated feminine lust.

Then she came to her senses.

What in the hell is he doing here? This wasn't a business-related function.

She turned quickly on her heel and headed into the crowd, hoping he wouldn't notice she was there.

Zack noticed Madelyn Grayson almost immediately, a flash of gold and red drawing his eye, the fiery glint of her hair unmistakable.

No doubt she'd arrived on the arm of her upper-crust boyfriend, a man you could tell at a glance came from privilege and wealth. Old money, they called it. Zack watched Madelyn weave her way through the thick clusters of people but saw no tall, golden-headed male waiting for her in the wings.

His own date had received an emergency page just as the two of them had been walking out the door for the party. Rather than cancel, Sheryl had told him to go on without her. She'd join him as soon as she was free. Well before midnight, she'd promised. This was her crowd, not his, and he'd figured he'd be bored until she arrived.

But now that he'd seen Madelyn Grayson, well, that changed everything.

Madelyn took refuge at the farthest corner of the room, near the canapé table. P.G. and Caroline were still dancing, so she didn't want to return to their table and sit alone.

Deciding to take advantage of the party fare, she picked up a plate and helped herself to a selection of succulent-looking hors d'oeuvres, the better to blend in. She'd skipped dinner, and with the hour hand at half past ten, she was more than a bit hungry. Just as she was about to sample a mushroom cap topped with crab meat, she heard a familiar voice close behind her.

"Hello, Madelyn."

She set the uneaten appetizer back on her plate. *So much for hiding in plain sight,* she thought. Resigned, she turned to meet Zack Douglas's shrewd gaze. "Zack. What a surprise. I didn't know you were going to be here tonight. Somehow this doesn't strike me as your kind of party."

"You're right about that. All flash and little action. Slow, definitely slow."

"Not slow. Dignified. But I can understand that this might not be the sort of entertainment you prefer."

"And how would you know what sort of entertainment I prefer?"

Madelyn shrugged. "One hears things."

How could she not? There was always some story circulating about him. Last New Year's Eve, as one tale went, he'd attended a wild, raucous party at the home of a well-known rock star. The theme had been Old Morocco and the event had boasted, among other excesses, a mosaic-tiled fountain overflowing with champagne, exotic music, soft Persian rugs, lush pillow-strewn tents, and a bevy of half-naked dancing girls. Zack never admitted whether the rumors about him were true. He never bothered to deny any of them either.

"Listening to gossip? Shame on you, Madelyn." He chose a toast point, spooning a healthy serving of two-hundred-dollar-an-ounce caviar on top.

"So what are you doing here, then?" she said. "Did one of F and S's wealthier clients die and leave a grieving widow in desperate need of escort?"

Zack raised an eyebrow. "Actually, my date hasn't arrived yet."

"Oh, had one last set to finish at the strip club, did she?" She popped a canapé into her mouth.

"No, she was called in to perform emergency heart-bypass surgery. She's an attending over at Mount Sinai."

Madelyn choked.

He gave her a strong pat between the shoulder blades. "You okay?"

She nodded, tears stinging her eyes as she tried to draw a breath. She fell into a paroxysm of coughing, completely unable to speak.

"Here, try a little champagne. Just a sip."

"Thanks," she whispered, accepting the glass and taking a sip.

"Better?"

She nodded again.

"You need to be careful when you eat this rich, fancy stuff. Easy for it to go down the wrong way."

She looked at him through her lashes and drank a little more champagne, trying to decide whether he was teasing her. Gradually, her breathing returned to normal. That's when she became aware of his hand on her back, moving in gentle, soothing circles, his palm warm and large. She suppressed an urge to shiver with a kind of pure, almost feline pleasure. Slowly, she eased away.

His hand dropped to his side. "Where's the Viking to-night?"

"Who?"

She watched him scan the throng of partygoers.

"I figured he'd have been over here like a shot. What with you choking and all."

She gave him a puzzled look.

"Your boyfriend. The big blond who couldn't be pried away from your side at the company picnic last summer."

Surprised, she realized he meant James. Just barely, she kept herself from rolling her eyes. Even people who didn't know James asked after him. Although Zack's interest didn't sound terribly friendly. "He ... uh ... he isn't here. Business overseas."

She figured her excuse wasn't a total lie. As an international financier, James often had business overseas. He very well might be ringing in the New Year in another part of the world. She didn't know.

"You're here alone, then?"

Her back straightened. "No, I came with my brother and sister-in-law. Something wrong with that?"

Zack set down his empty plate. "Not at all. Most women would have stayed home, or else found themselves another date. Your loyalty is commendable."

She considered telling him the truth, but she'd had more than enough conversation on the subject already. She was tired of cross-examinations. Besides, it really wasn't any of his business.

"Considering that my date hasn't arrived yet and you don't have one for tonight, how about a dance?" He held out his hand, palm up in invitation.

"With you?"

He made a show of glancing around. "I don't see any-one else asking, do you? Come on, it's only a dance. I don't think one dance would compromise company rules about fraternization."

That would be a first, she thought, Zack Douglas con-cerned about policies on fraternization. "Be that as it may—"

"Unless you're chicken. Is that it, Red? Afraid to dance with me?"

She gritted her teeth.

Annoying SOB.

"You want to dance, Douglas?" she said. "Then let's dance."

She stalked ahead of him onto the dance floor.

He followed.

Turning, she slapped her hand into his. "And don't call me Red. You got it?"

He wrapped his arm around her waist and pulled her close. "I got it. Red." He winked and swept her into mo-tion, making several extravagant turns that revved her pulse into high gear.

The pace of the music soon slowed, the beat growing throaty, sultry, with a bluesy sort of jazz. Zack tucked her close, pressing her palm against the flat expanse of his chest. Warmed by his body heat, the expensive fabric of his dress shirt smelled faintly of starch and clean, healthy male. He wore no cologne. He didn't need to. Zack Douglas unembellished was better than any fragrance could ever hope to be.

Wait, where had that thought come from? Zack Douglas was the enemy. Her chief rival and archnemesis.

Beating her out of clients and accounts. Cheating her at every turn.

Too much champagne—that must be it. Well, she wouldn't drink another drop, she assured herself, not a bit more tonight. And as soon as this dance was over, she'd ditch him and forget he was even in the room.

She slipped her hand from beneath his, curling it into a fist to wedge a tiny space between them. "So . . . um . . . when is your date supposed to arrive?"

There was an intent look in his eyes, almost smoldering.

Green fire.

She couldn't remember ever seeing that particular expression on his face before.

"She wasn't sure," he murmured absently. "I told her if she hadn't made it by eleven, I'd call."

"It must be getting close to that now."

"Hmm, I suppose."

The music ended. The two of them moved apart, along with the other couples on the dance floor, to applaud the band, whose leader announced there would be a fifteen-minute intermission while he and his fellow musicians took a break.

Madelyn traced a seam on her gown. "I'd better get back to my table. My brother and sister-in-law will be wondering what's become of me."

He slid a hand beneath her elbow. "I'll walk you back."

"That's okay." She moved out of his reach. "Go phone your date."

He hesitated, then nodded. "Thanks for the dance, Madelyn."

"Sure. Happy New Year."

"Happy New Year. See you at work on Tuesday."

She made her way across the ballroom and was relieved to find P.G. and Caroline there, sharing a plate heaped with an array of desserts.

"Who was that?" Caroline asked as Madelyn took a seat. Her sister-in-law looked sweet and pretty in an aquamarine silk dress that went perfectly with her fair skin and tawny hair.

Madelyn picked up a fork and nipped the end off a piece of chocolate cake. "Who?"

"That man. The one you were dancing with."

"Oh, an acquaintance from the office. No one important."

Half an hour later the band was in full swing once more, the dance floor packed with couples whirling away the final minutes of December. Madelyn watched them, wishing she hadn't sworn off the bubbly. It wasn't as if she were driving home. And since the dance with Zack Douglas, she hadn't caught so much as a glimpse of the man. His date must have shown up. They were probably out there somewhere right now having a fabulous time. She sighed, wishing she were doing the same.

She was debating whether to indulge in her own personal tour of the dessert table—something sweet to go with that glass of champagne she just might change her mind about—when her brother appeared at her elbow.

"Madelyn, I'm sorry, but we've got to leave. Caroline just called home to check on Brian, and he's sick, running a fever. It's probably nothing serious, but we should go."

"Of course you need to be with Brian. You go on."

"We will, once we drop you off."

"I live in the opposite direction. Taking me home will add another hour to your trip, and it's nearly midnight now. No—you two go back to your hotel, check out, and get on the road. I'm a big girl. I know my way around the city. I'll take a cab. Don't worry; I'll be fine."

Uncertain, P.G. buried his hands in his pockets. "You sure? I don't like leaving you alone."

"You're not. Look around—there must be three hundred people here. Besides, you're forgetting which one of us is the eldest. I am. So do what your big sister tells you and go."

He made a face. "Big sister my foot. Just because you're ten minutes older than me doesn't make you the boss." It was an old argument, one they'd indulged in as twins for as long as each of them could remember. P.G. hesitated for a fraction of a second more, then gave in. "All right, but call us tomorrow. Promise?"

She stretched up on her toes to brush a kiss over his cheek. "I promise." She gave him a light shove toward the door. "Now, get out of here."

"Happy New Year, Madelyn."

"Happy New Year, P.G. Drive safely. There are a lot of weirdos on the road tonight."

He grinned. "This is New York City. There are always a lot of weirdos on the road."

Roughly two minutes later, dejection set in as she stood alone, feeling lost and more than a little sorry for herself. She checked the time on her wristwatch. Fifteen minutes to midnight. Stay and watch the balloons drop? Or call it an evening and look for a cab?

She'd taken three steps toward the door when a hand lightly touched her shoulder.

"Was that your brother and his wife I just saw leaving?"

Madelyn turned and tipped her chin up to look at—who else?—Zack Douglas. With the mellow glow of the ballroom light playing over his swarthy skin and dark hair, he reminded her of a fallen angel.

"What?" she murmured.

"Your brother. Did he just leave?"

She lowered her eyes to collect herself. "Yes. He . . . um . . . he and Caroline had a family emergency. Their son is ill."

He scowled. "Didn't you arrive here with them?"

"I did, but I told them to go on without me. I can see myself home just fine."

He opened his mouth as if to argue, then closed it. With a smile, he folded her hand over his elbow. "Good, then it seems I've got you all to myself."

She tried to pull her hand away, but he refused to let go.

"Where's your date, the doctor?" she asked.

"Still in surgery. Another emergency came in and she was needed to assist. I spoke to her nurse a few minutes ago. She'd been asked to convey Sheryl's apologies. Long and short, my date has stood me up."

"I'm sorry."

He shrugged. "It's not a big deal. We haven't been seeing each other very long."

"Actually, I was about to go home."

"You can't leave now—it's almost midnight. Stay and have some fun, Madelyn. That's what New Year's Eve is all about."

"I've had my fill of fun for one night."

"Surely not."

He released her long enough to snag two glasses of champagne from the tray of a passing waiter. He handed one to her. "Drink up—the night's young."

She saw his eyes twinkle. His face was a dream—far, far too beautiful for any woman's own good.

She hesitated, knowing she ought to tell him good night. Instead, she raised the glass to her lips and took a long, slow sip.

Time flashed past, their glasses disappeared, and she was in his arms, her head spinning as they whirled to the music, their bodies pressed close in a way she should never have allowed.

The band played a drumroll to signal the twelve o'clock hour was only moments away. Everyone stilled in a jubilant hush, then began to count backward from ten in a loud, boisterous chorus.

". . . five . . . four . . . three . . . two . . . one . . . Happy New Year!"

Colorful balloons and gaily striped confetti rained from above as horns tooted and the band swung into a brassy rendition of "Auld Lang Syne." Amid the glitter and spectacle, people embraced and kissed.

Zack turned her to him, cupping her face in his hands as he smiled down into her eyes. "Happy New Year, Madelyn."

He leaned down and covered her lips with his.

His kiss was electric, sending sparks whizzing through her body, head to foot. Her blood burned, singeing her nerve endings one by one. She shuddered and gasped and, unable to form a single rational thought, let him take more. The world narrowed down to just the two of them, leaving her aware of only Zack and the way his lips moved on hers, how warm his hands were against her face.

He drew away, slowly, reluctantly; their lips clung for a long, last second as if the flesh itself didn't want to be parted. Then he tucked her close and turned them once more into the dance.

Her heart thumped in hard, quick beats, so hard she wondered if he could feel it where their bodies met. She rested her cheek on his shoulder and closed her eyes, needing a few seconds to get her head screwed back on straight, since at the moment the top of it felt as if it might blow right off.

What on earth was she doing? She didn't even like Zack, so why had she let him kiss her? Worse, how could she have let his kiss affect her so strongly?

'Cause, wow, had it ever!

At the next break in the music, she excused herself and headed for the ladies' room.

Once inside, she held her hands under a stream of cool tap water, then blotted a few drops over her face and along her throat.

She studied her reflection in the mirror.

Cheeks flushed, eyes sparkling, lips reddened—she looked like a woman who'd just been thoroughly kissed.

I have to get out of here.

She knew a rear hallway ran behind the ballroom. If she slipped around that way, she figured she could retrieve her coat and be outside and into a cab in a matter of minutes.

She pushed open the door and stepped into the corridor.

Zack unfolded himself from the opposite wall, where he'd been waiting.

She stopped short, flustered. "Do you often loiter outside the ladies' room?" she said, going on the defensive in order to cover up her discomfort.

"Not generally, but something told me I might not see you again tonight if I didn't."

There were times, she thought, when he could be way too perceptive. "As a matter of fact, I was just heading out."

"Without a good-bye?"

"I didn't think you'd need one, a big boy like you."

He laid a hand on his chest and made an exaggerated face. "I'm wounded."

"To the bone, I'm sure," she said sarcastically. "But if a good-bye will make it all better, then good-bye and good night."

She started forward, but he caught her before she could take more than a couple of steps. "Don't go. Not yet. I mean, has it really been so terrible tonight? Spending time with me?"

She considered lying, knew she probably should.

"No," she answered honestly, "it hasn't."

And maybe that was the problem. She'd liked being with him, far more than she should.

Christ, she really needed to get out of here.

"Look, it's late and I've had way past my limit of alcohol," she said. "I need to be going."

"Okay, sure, then I'll take you."

"Oh no. That's not necessary. I'll be fine in a cab."

"If you can get one. It's New Year's Eve, remember? I wouldn't feel right unless I made sure you made it home safely."

He took her elbow and steered her toward the ballroom. "We'll grab your coat, take a brief detour upstairs to get mine, then be on our way."

"Upstairs?"

"I booked a room, a suite. I often do for holiday parties I know will run late. It's convenient having a place close when I'm ready to call it an evening. Beats dragging home through heavy traffic in the dark and the cold." He stopped in front of the coat check. "Do you have your ticket?"

Madelyn retrieved the stub from her small beaded handbag and handed it directly to the woman in the booth instead of passing it to Zack.

She waited until the clerk moved out of earshot. "I am not going up to your hotel room with you."

"Why not? Afraid I'll put the moves on you the moment the door's closed?"

She returned his look with a firm one of her own. "It's not out of the realm of possibility."

"I promise nothing will happen that you don't want to happen. Okay?"

"Okay," she said.

For some inexplicable reason, she believed him.

He handed her coat to her and smiled. "Ready when you are."

CHAPTER THREE

Clean and attractively furnished, the hotel suite was decorated in a muted collage of blues and grays. A conversational grouping of plump upholstery and wood— sofa, chairs, coffee and end tables, and an armoire—took up the majority of the main room. A narrow Pullman kitchen and wet bar stood off to one side. And on the far left there was a central doorway that presumably led to the bedroom.

Zack switched on a table lamp, the light giving the room an easy amber glow. "Have a seat. I'll be right back."

He disappeared into the other room.

She sank down onto the sofa cushions, aware of a mild buzz from all the wine she'd consumed. Relaxing back, she gave herself over to a rush of sensations, in- cluding a sudden wave of tiredness.

Zack returned a minute later, a black wool coat folded over his arm. "You know, I was thinking," he said, "maybe we should wait here for a little while. With all the parties letting out, not to mention the tourist crowd drifting up from Times Square, the traffic's bound to be horrible. And the line for a cab even worse. Why don't I fix us a cup of coffee and let the rush clear out some before we head out?"

Madelyn frowned.

"It's only coffee." He gave a rueful laugh. "You really don't trust me at all, do you?"

"Not especially. We work together, remember?"

His smile faded. "We do. And you shouldn't assume things are always the way you believe them to be."

"Really? Why don't you enlighten me then, starting with—"

"Let's not talk shop tonight, okay?" he said, cutting her off. "The evening's been much too pleasant to end it with an argument. How about a temporary truce? With the caveat, of course, that you can tear a strip off me the moment we get back to the office." He offered her his hand. "Deal?"

She considered his offer for a moment, then shrugged and shook his hand. "Deal."

Zack draped his coat over the back of a chair, then shrugged out of his tuxedo jacket as well. "How do you take your coffee? Black or with cream?"

"Cream. And sugar, please. Want some help?"

He strolled into the tiny kitchen. "I've got it covered, thanks. I'm not much of a cook, but I can brew a decent pot of coffee."

Madelyn leaned her head back against the couch cushions and let her eyelids drift shut. . . .

"You asleep?"

Blinking slowly, she opened her eyes and looked into his amused green ones.

"Half," she murmured.

"Here's your coffee, to wake up the sleepy half." The cup and saucer made a little chinking sound as he set them on the end of a nearby table.

She struggled to sit up straight. "Sorry. I'm not much of a night owl."

"*Whoo* would ever have known?" He smiled, tiny lines fanning out at the corners of his eyes.

"Are you making fun of me, Douglas?" she said, picking up on his bad joke.

He sat down next to her, propped one leather-shod foot onto the opposite knee in a loose, all-male sprawl.

"Me? Make fun of you, Grayson? Never." He blew on the steaming brew in his cup, took a careful swallow. "Although I might be guilty of a bit of teasing now and then."

"My father likes to tease. He says it's good for character development and personal growth. Builds grace under pressure, a sense of humor, that sort of thing."

"What does your father do?"

"He's a developer, residential construction."

Zack paused for a long moment, mental wheels clearly clicking. "As in Graysco Limited? Luxury homes for the rich and famous?"

"He might take exception to your description, but yes, that would be Dad."

"And your brother's an architect. I think I saw an article about him recently. He won some award for his environmentally friendly housing designs, right?"

"P.G. would be humbled. He didn't think anyone besides family, friends, and industry insiders even noticed that piece. Guess he owes me twenty bucks."

"You had a bet going?"

"Yeah, we do that sometimes." Madelyn sipped her coffee. She yawned and scrubbed a hand over her eyes. *"Ouch!"*

She set down her cup.

"What's wrong?"

"Eyelash, I think. Caught in my eye. *Ow!*" She blinked rapidly.

He scooted close. "Here, lean back and let me see. Look up," he ordered. "I see it, right there. Hang on a minute." Gently, he manipulated her eyelid. "I think I've got it. Better?"

"Yes, much." She blinked again. "Thanks."

She met his gaze and grew abruptly still, unable to look away. His fingers were resting on the curve of her cheek, their tips warm and slightly calloused. He was close. So close that it would be as easy as drawing her next breath to lean forward and touch her lips to his.

No sooner had the thought entered her mind than he was pulling her into a kiss. Or maybe she was pulling him; she couldn't say for sure.

Her thoughts scattered the instant their lips met, her senses jolting as if she'd been hit by a high-voltage electrical charge. The kiss they'd shared at midnight had been potent, but this one was so much more.

Powerful.

Raw.

Filled with a hunger so intense that it seemed to burn everything else to ash.

He began pulling the pins out of her hair, letting them

fall where they would. The thick strands cascaded to her shoulders like a vibrant curtain of fire. He thrust his fingers into it, using its mass to hold her steady as he kissed her again.

Her own fingers clutched the fine fabric of his shirt. He tasted delicious—of coffee and wine and man. A dark, sinful combination that left her craving more.

Zack brought a handful of her hair to his face. "It smells so good. Feels so soft, softer than I'd ever imagined."

"What?" she murmured.

"Your hair, it's beautiful. I've wanted to touch it like this for a long time."

He nuzzled her neck, finding a spot that made her legs shift restlessly beneath the heavy material of her skirt.

"I've wanted to touch you like this for a long time."

His mouth locked with hers once more, wrenching a pleasured cry from her throat. Even so, some fraction of his words filtered through the haze surrounding her.

What was it he'd said? That he'd wanted her for a long time?

He had?

The idea startled her, enough that she began to pull away.

"What are we doing? Maybe we should stop."

"Why?" He reached behind her, insinuating his hand between her back and the sofa cushions to unzip her dress.

"Be-...because ..."

Because why? she wondered, knowing there ought to be a reason.

His lips and tongue moved over her neck, so pleasurable she could barely think.

"Because you said you wouldn't try anything tonight," she said weakly.

He unhooked the clasp of her bra, then traced delicate patterns over the sleek length of her naked back and shoulder blades, making her shudder.

"I did? I believe I said I wouldn't do anything you didn't want me to." He pressed a hot kiss to her lips. "Are you saying you don't want this?"

He pushed her dress to her waist and bared her breasts, cupping one of them in his hand as if testing its weight and shape. He rubbed his thumb over a nipple, then bent to take her breast in his mouth. He sucked on it. Hard.

Madelyn groaned and fought to pull one of her arms out of its sleeve. Once free, she drove her fingers into his hair and pressed his head tighter against her aching flesh.

She felt him smile as his tongue flicked against her. Closing her eyes, she let the fire sizzle through her veins.

Suddenly he stopped, then stood her abruptly on her feet. She could barely stand as he pulled down her dress, letting it fall to the floor.

She watched as he took in the slight of her, his pupils dilating as he surveyed her slim, shapely body dressed in nothing but a lacy garter belt, hose, and a pair of panties so pale a pink they were virtually see-through. On her feet were three inches of golden high heels.

He groaned with clear appreciation, then drew her down so that she straddled his lap. His mouth found hers for a wild kiss. He pulled her closer, moving her hips so they fit more tightly against him. He was as hard as steel between her legs as he rocked them together.

"I can't wait," she gasped, shocked that she was already poised on the edge of an orgasm.

"Then don't," he murmured, his breath fanning hot in her ear.

He bumped them together. Once, twice, three times more. Rhythmically insinuating the sexual act, he slipped his fingers down and around to touch her intimately.

She cried out the instant he touched her, her fingernails digging into his arms. Crazy pleasure burst through her, and she was soaring, shaking, quivering helplessly.

As she hung over him, limp and half-delirious, he stood up, lifting her with him, and carried her to the bedroom.

The sheets were cool against her back when he lowered her onto the bed. Within seconds, he had his clothes off. He reached next to pull off her shoes, tossing them over his back, where they landed with two small thumps. Then he slid the last delicate scraps of cloth from her body.

Another moment passed as he paused to put on protection. She watched him as he stood silhouetted in the silvery moonlight filtering through the window, tall, deep-chested, and all male. It struck her again how very beautiful he was.

Then she couldn't think at all, her body taking control as he came down over her. He slid inside her, levering his weight onto his forearms as he drove deep.

Madelyn cried out. He drank in the sound as he claimed her mouth with the same intensity he was taking her body.

She gripped him hard, wrapping him in her arms, his flesh hot and slick beneath her hands. His muscles were bunched and trembling as he thrust into her again and again. She quaked, a fresh cry rising in her throat as he brought her higher, then higher still.

She called out his name on a near scream, light flashing behind her eyelids as she came for the second, glorious time that night.

She felt him find his pleasure moments later, shuddering hard and heavy against her.

Together, they collapsed, locked tightly in each other's arms.

A faceful of sunlight awakened Madelyn the next morning.

Still half-asleep, she rolled over, snuggling deeper into her pillow. Her nose twitched as something faintly ticklish pressed against its tip. It brushed her lips as well. Warm and solid, soft, yet ever so slightly rough. A curious study in contrasts. The something smelled nice too, she thought, a tad earthy with a dash of spicy-sweet tossed in. Ripe and very male. Very Zack.

Very Zack?

Her eyes popped open, giving her a close-up view of the strong, hair-dusted forearm stretched across the center of her pillow. She jerked her head back, then wished she hadn't, as a quick stab of pain shot through her skull.

Gradually the discomfort eased. Once the pain subsided, she slowly sat up, the sheet and blanket falling to her waist, exposing her bare breasts to cool air.

She was naked.

She never slept naked.

Memories of the night before came flooding back.

Oh my God, what have I done?

Zack lay sprawled on his stomach, still mercifully asleep, his long body taking up a great deal more than his fair share of the king-size bed.

He could have it, she decided. All she wanted to do was get dressed, go home, and try to forget. If she was very careful, perhaps she could slip out without awakening him.

Mouse quiet, she shifted sideways, ignoring the little aches and twinges that bit at her muscles and several intimate areas that hadn't had a workout in a good long while.

Boy, oh boy, they'd gotten one last night. Several times. And once this morning in the predawn hours as the first rays of light colored the sky.

No wonder he was sleeping like the dead. He had to be exhausted. On the other hand, maybe he always slept like that. Undoubtedly, awkward mornings after would be nothing new to him. He'd probably had so many they'd stopped being awkward at all. But this kind of experience was far from the norm for her. For all she knew, there was some sort of etiquette for moments like this.

How might the conversation go?

Good morning. You want room service? Eggs? Orange juice? No? Well, hey, thanks for the sex. It was fun. See you around.

She had to get out of here.

Chagrined, she discovered getting dressed wasn't as simple as it should have been, her clothes scattered throughout the suite like pieces of driftwood on a beach. As rapidly as she could, having no choice but to tiptoe around stark naked, she gathered up her dress and bra and shoes.

That's when she realized the worst.

Her most intimate undergarments lay on the floor.

On his side of the bed.

Directly under the long male arm dangling off the mattress.

She ground her teeth in frustration.

Creeping closer, she watched, waiting to see if he was about to wake. But his face remained serene, relaxed, and younger looking despite the heavy shadow of sexy black stubble covering his cheeks and chin.

She managed to slide free her hose and garter belt, draping the scanty delicates over the bundle of garments in her arms.

Her panties were another matter.

Zack stirred and shifted. For a hopeful second she thought he was going to roll over onto his side. Instead he stretched farther out on his stomach, lengthening his spine so that his arm dropped a fraction of an inch lower. His fingers now rested on the sheer garment, literally pinning it to the carpet.

Silently she cursed. If she couldn't retrieve her panties, she'd have to go home without them. A perfectly dreadful prospect, she decided. Yet somehow the idea of waking him up and having to confront him seemed even worse.

Defeated, she padded into the bathroom.

He hadn't moved, not even an inch, by the time she crept back into the room, fully dressed. Or rather, nearly dressed, she was reminded as a faint draft of air wafted up beneath her skirt. The sensation was immodestly disconcerting. As for her hair, rather than take the time to find her hairpins, she'd simply brushed it and left the strands to fall in loose waves around her shoulders.

Presentable-looking enough, she believed. At least as presentable as a woman could look, traveling home alone, at ten o'clock in the morning, still rigged out in full evening attire. It was New Year's Day. The odd hour wouldn't seem so remarkable, she assured herself, especially in New York City, where you had to look a lot stranger than she did to even get noticed.

Glancing at him one final time, where he lay sleeping like some enchanted fairy-tale prince, she pulled on her coat, grabbed her purse, and quietly let herself out the door.

The lock clicked ever so softly, the slight sound awakening Zack.

Instantly he realized he was alone.

Regrettable, he decided. He'd been looking forward to lazing away a few more hours with Madelyn, after calling the front desk first to request the latest checkout possible.

His fingers brushed against a silky something on the floor.

Fabric.

He curled a hand around the item and discovered Madelyn's abandoned lingerie dangling from his fingertips. In spite of his tiredness, his body responded, her scent drifting to his nostrils, evocative and utterly female.

He groaned, wishing she were here in this bed with him.

He'd see her tomorrow at work, he supposed. And when work was concluded, he'd see more of her.

A lot more, he promised himself.

He laid the thin scrap of pink on the nightstand, then rolled over. Eyes closed, he drifted back to sleep.

CHAPTER FOUR

Madelyn dropped a thick set of layout sketches and photographs onto the already overflowing top of her desk. Generally she managed to keep her work better organized, divided into neat stacks designed to make everything easy for her to locate.

But today had been a bear—as first days back after a holiday usually were—what with back-to-back meetings and barely enough time for a bathroom break in between. Lunch had been a chicken sandwich eaten on the run.

She glanced at her wristwatch. Five thirty p.m.

Rush hour would be at its unpleasant worst. Rather than sit idling in traffic, she decided to stay and make another attempt at scaling the Everest-high mountain of work looming on her horizon.

She was standing at her drafting table ten minutes later, flipping through a stack of storyboards, when a broad pair of hands slid around her waist from behind. Warm lips settled against a highly sensitive spot behind her ear.

She jumped, nerves tingling with surprise as she collided with a wall of solid male flesh.

"I thought this day would never end," Zack said. "I've been waiting for a chance to do this since I got in this morning."

He reached inside her suit jacket and palmed one of her breasts, his gifted fingers rubbing her through the delicate silk of her blouse.

A pleasured shiver raced through her. She closed her eyes to steady herself. "I've been busy," she told him.

"We've both been busy." He feathered kisses over her cheek, along the curve of her jaw. "How about we knock off and grab some dinner?"

"I can't." She forced herself not to react to his touch. "I have work to do."

"All right," he said. "Why don't I bring back some carryout? How about that great new Chinese place a couple blocks over?"

She crossed to her desk. "I . . . um . . . I know the one you mean. But not tonight."

"You have to eat," he countered.

"I'll eat later."

"All right, tomorrow, then?"

"No, sorry, I have plans." She picked up a report and leafed through the first few pages, seeing none of the words and graphics printed there.

Zack crossed his arms. "Um-hmm. And the night after? Do you have plans then too?"

She refused to meet his eyes, kept her tone deliberately cool. "Actually, my schedule is pretty full right now. I hope you'll understand."

"Oh, I understand completely." His voice was cool now as well, but laced with irony.

"If I can't interest you in dinner," he continued, "perhaps I can tempt you with something else?"

From the corner of her eye, she saw him reach into his trousers' pocket, pull out a swatch of pink silk and lace. She felt her face flush as he dangled the familiar scrap of lingerie from the end of one finger.

"Give me those."

She made a grab for the panties and missed.

Zack lifted them well out of her reach.

"Uh-uh," he scolded. "Not until you tell me why you ran out on me yesterday morning."

"I didn't *run out*." She crossed her arms over her breasts. "I needed to get home. You were sleeping. I didn't see any reason to wake you up."

"You should have gotten me up anyway. We could have shared breakfast."

"I wasn't hungry." She straightened her shoulders and looked into his face, determined to be firm. "Look, Zack, what happened between us ... it was ... well ... it was a mistake. That night should never have happened."

His look darkened. "But it did. Seems to me we had a good time. A *very* good time."

"Yes, well, maybe we did, but it's over now."

"It doesn't have to be over."

"Yes. It does." She held out her hand. "Now, give me back my underwear."

He grinned and tucked the lacy scrap into his pocket.

"I'm trying to remember the last time I heard those words," he mused. "High school, I think. Or was it college?"

Infuriating bastard.

She made an attempt to grab the panties out of his pocket, moving fast.

But Zack was faster.

He grabbed her wrist. "I want you, Madelyn. And whatever this is between us, it isn't over."

"What about your lady surgeon? The one you've been dating?"

"What about her?"

"Well, I can't help but wonder if you're planning to see both of us at the same time."

He frowned as if he hadn't considered that point. "If it bothers you, I'll drop her. But I expect you to do the same and give what's his name—Jeff?—the old heave-ho."

"James," she corrected, suddenly aware that she hadn't thought of him once, not since she'd seen Zack the other night.

"Right. *James.* Tell him it's finished between the two of you." He traced a thumb over her lower lip. "I don't share."

She knocked his hand aside. "I don't give a flying flip whether you share or not, since you and I are over."

His eyes turned glacial. "No. We aren't."

"*Let me go.* Someone might come in."

"Most everybody's already left for the evening, or they're on their way out. But you're right, we should make sure we're not disturbed.

He released her and went to lock the door.

"That's not what I meant," she said.

He came back, walking toward her with an athletic grace.

She took a couple of steps back, stopped when her hips bumped up against her desk. She gripped the edge hard with both hands.

"Honestly, Zack, I'd think you'd be relieved. No recriminations, no messy, tearful scenes, no responsibilities. Just a night of dancing and drinking and great sex."

"You're right," he agreed. "The sex *was* great. I want some more. Don't you?" He lowered his head, angling his face close to the curve of her neck. "Have I mentioned how fantastic you smell? Been sampling some new fragrance products?"

"No, and stop distracting me."

"Is that what I'm doing?" His breath whispered against her cheek. "Distracting you?"

"Yes, and it's not going to work. I've told you I'm not interested in seeing you again. Please respect that."

"Who said anything about seeing each other? Maybe sex is all I want."

"And maybe it's not what I want."

"Shall we put it to a test?"

She lifted her hands to push him away, but before she could, he captured her mouth in a hard, blatantly sexual kiss that left her in no doubt of his wishes. Madelyn groaned, partly in protest, partly from desire, and made one last try to stop him.

But even as her hands closed over his shoulders to shove him away, she found herself pulling him closer instead, opening her mouth wider to take more of his kiss, to seek out more of his tongue.

What was it about him that made her want him so

much? She didn't understand this crazy attraction between them. It made absolutely no sense. Yet the pleasure was almost mind-blowing, so intense she couldn't
seem to help herself, wanting him more than she'd ever
wanted any man before.

Glad now that he had locked the door, she began un-
doing the buttons on his shirt, practically tearing them
off in her haste to find and feel his bare skin against her
own.

Zack was busy too as he lifted her up onto her desk,
shoving her skirt high as he ran his hands up the length
of her thighs. Spreading her legs wide, he stepped between and fit himself against her, then reached up to
open her blouse.

He sucked her lower lip into his mouth, gave a gentle
nip that made her shudder. He released her breasts from
her bra, then bent his head to work his magic on them.

She moaned and dug her fingers into his hair, urging
him on.

The telephone rang.

The pair of them startled apart.

Madelyn stared blankly at the phone, offering a silent
prayer of thanks when her voice mail picked up. Body
throbbing, she made a vague attempt to straighten her
clothes.

"Let me down," she demanded.

"All right, after you tell me whose apartment we're
going to. Yours or mine?"

"Neither. We're not doing this."

"We just about did it, right here on your desk. I'd be
happy to continue." He pressed himself to her again.
"More than happy."

"Get off me."

"What's wrong with you, Madelyn?"

"What's wrong with *you*? Do you really expect me to put out whenever you like? I won't be just another one of your conquests."

He raised an eyebrow. "My conquests? You make it sound as if I'm assembling a harem."

This time she shoved at him in earnest, pushed him aside, and climbed down off the desk.

"You might as well be." She tugged her skirt into place, fastened her bra, buttoned her shirt. "Everyone knows the way you flit from woman to woman like some bee on a mission to pollinate the earth. My God, you can't pass by anything with a pair of breasts without taking a second look. Or a third."

"Phyllis Schrenk has breasts and I never look at her."

"Phyllis Schrenk must be at least eighty years old." She smoothed her hair. "If I start sleeping with you, it will be the talk of the office. I refuse to be fodder for the rumor mill."

She poked a finger his way. "An affair between us could put my career in serious jeopardy. I won't take the chance for a few meaningless nights. And if you say one word about New Year's Eve, I'll . . . I'll . . ."

"You'll what?"

"I'll deny it. I'll tell everyone you made it up to spite me."

"You could. Of course, the damage would already have been done, the seeds of suspicion planted. I have an alternate suggestion."

"I'm not interested in any of your suggestions."

He continued as if she hadn't spoken. "Obviously we

both want each other, at least for now. I propose we keep what's between us out of the office. We'll see each other in secret. No one will have to know but us."

"That will never work. One of us will slip up and word will get out. Nobody can keep a secret around this place."

"I can. I have."

"You've done this before? Seen someone in the office without anyone finding out?

"I didn't have an affair, no. Contrary to your poor estimation of my character and taste, I generally prefer to see women I don't work with. The secret involved a completely different matter. No one has ever known but me and the person I shared it with."

"How do I know I can trust you? How do I know you aren't lying?"

His eyes narrowed dangerously. "You don't."

She watched him fight aside his irritation.

"It's late," he said. "You must be hungry. Why don't we meet somewhere, your choice, and talk this over."

"I don't think there's anything to talk about. I don't think I can do it . . . fool people."

"Of course you can." He smiled reassuringly. "Just glare at me like you always do; ignore me the rest of the time. It won't be so difficult." He stroked a thumb along the curve of her cheek. "You know you want to say yes," he coaxed.

Damn him. He was right. She did.

A longing more dangerous than any she'd ever known before rose inside her. As unlikely as it seemed, she was actually considering his plan. "I don't understand this, any of it. I don't even like you," she said, not sure who she was more exasperated with—him or herself.

"But you want me." He slid his hand around the back of her neck and caressed her, drawing a shiver. "That's the only thing that matters, Madelyn. That's what really counts."

They met at a bowling alley a few miles outside Paramus, New Jersey.

The smell of sweaty shoes, disinfectant, and beer greeted them as they walked through the entrance's smeary double glass doors. The alley stood at partial capacity, busy for a weekday.

Half a dozen lanes had been appropriated by an amateur bowling league, players in starched shirts chatting in good-natured competition as they swung at pins and shared insulting remarks about the team they were due to crush that Friday night.

Other couples, some seemingly dating, some apparently married, dotted the landscape, racking up gutter balls and pitiful scores, while a handful of juveniles in danger of earning curfew violations roamed in unruly packs, hoping to relieve their boredom with trash talk and video games.

The steady thunder of rolling balls and falling pins diminished as Madelyn preceded Zack into the alley's restaurant. An occasional victory shout drifted upward from the lanes.

She chose a booth and slid onto one of the worn red vinyl seats, the scent of sizzling hamburger heavy in the air.

Disapproval plain, Zack hesitated for a long moment before he took the seat across from her.

"I hope I don't ruin my clothes in this grease pit," he

said. "Of all the places we could have gone, what on earth made you pick this one?"

"It's the only spot I could think of where I could be sure I wouldn't meet anyone I know."

"No chance of that."

The restaurant was nearly deserted, only two of the dozen available booths occupied, one by a bushy-browed old man who looked as if he might pass out in his soup any second. In the other sat a middle-aged salesman, his sample case open in the center of the table, a cell phone attached to his ear.

Madelyn planted her forearms on the scarred Formica tabletop and leaned forward. "I'd never have pegged you for a snob."

"I'm not a snob," he denied. "Just far too knowing." Places like this reminded him uncomfortably of his youth, how he'd spent it and where. "Next time, I'm doing the choosing," he told her. "Your pick of rendezvous spots leaves something to be desired."

"*Shh*, the waitress is coming. And I haven't decided for sure if there is going to be a next time."

He reached across the table and clasped her hand. "Of course you have or you wouldn't be here with me now."

With a sinking sense of resignation, she realized he was right.

"Evening, folks. Name's Nell and I'll be your server." The gray-haired waitress slapped two flexible plastic menus onto the center of the table. "You both want somethin' to drink?"

"*Hmm*, yes, I'll have tea. What varieties do you—"

"We'll both have coffee," Zack interrupted. "Cream and sugar for the lady."

Nell eyed the pair of them, then turned to Madelyn, the older woman's chin set in a stubborn square. "That okay with you, sweetie?"

"Yes, it's fine."

Nell shrugged. "Specials are clam chowder and tuna melt on whole wheat. Be back with that coffee in a jiff."

Madelyn waited until she'd gone, then turned on Zack. "That was incredibly rude. Are you always like this when you're in a bad mood?"

"Only saving you the misery of lukewarm water and a stale tea bag. I've seen that fancy loose-leaf stuff you drink. Believe me, you're better off with the coffee, especially since I noticed the waitress putting on a fresh pot when we came in. I'd steer clear of the specials as well." He turned her hand over to stroke the soft skin on her palm.

"Sorry if I was overbearing." He lifted her hand and pressed his lips to its center, raising his eyes to hers. "Forgive me?"

A funny little flutter rose inside her, her palm tingling where he'd touched it. Slowly she drew her hand from his, curling her fingers over the spot as if to hold on to his kiss. "I . . . uh . . . I suppose we should look at the menu."

He smiled. "Sure, let's look."

They both ordered hamburgers, although Zack predicted dire consequences for the health of their digestive tracks. While they waited for their food to arrive, he brought up the subject on both their minds.

"When should we meet? Friday?"

"No, Friday's no good," she said, shaking her head. "I'm trying to finish up the TV spot for Kincaid Brothers this week, and it's going to be a race to get it done. By the time this weekend arrives, the only thing I'll want to do is go to bed."

She caught the look in his eyes.

"Alone," she added. "And of course you're still working on Takamuri."

An edge had crept into her voice that Zack couldn't help but notice.

"Madelyn, about that account—"

She showed him the flat of her hand. "I don't want to talk about it. Apologizing now won't make things better."

"Good, since I have nothing to apologize for. But to set the record straight, I didn't want that account. Fielding insisted I take it."

"Oh, of course, Fielding insisted. No doubt while the two of you were swapping fish stories and making deals over lunch in the executive dining room. You'll remember I didn't receive an invitation to that particular event."

Zack reached for her hand again, refusing to let go when she tried to twist it away. "I know you wanted that account, and between the two of us you should have gotten it. You did a lot of work, good work that deserved to be recognized. I argued with Fielding about it, tried to convince him to give you the nod instead, but he wouldn't budge."

"And why should I believe that extraordinarily creative line of bull?"

"Because it's the truth. And old man Takamuri's the one who didn't want you, not Fielding or anyone else in management. You were slated to head the account. As I understand it, everything was green-lighted. Then Takamuri called Fielding, said he wanted someone else, said he wanted a man. I'm sorry, Madelyn."

Her face fell as his words sank in. "But Mr. Takamuri told me he liked my ideas. He seemed pleased with the concept, the budget, everything. I don't understand."

"He's old-school—traditional and very Japanese. From what Fielding said, he doesn't believe a woman has the skills required to make important leadership decisions. He said you're very bright but he couldn't entrust you with that sort of responsibility."

Affront heated her cheeks. "Doesn't have the skill? Can't entrust me with that sort of responsibility? What an idiotic, sexist pile of . . . Fielding should have told him he was wrong and given the account to me anyway. I would have done a wonderful job and made everyone a huge bundle of money."

"No doubt you're right. But to give Fielding his due, I think he did try to keep you. At first. They threatened to pull the account, Madelyn. It was simply too much money to risk."

Her eyes sparkled a touch too brightly.

"Well, it looks like I'm the one who owes you an apology this time," she said.

"That's not—"

"Not necessary? I think it is. I assumed you'd deliberately gone behind my back to steal that account. I considered you an evil, devious, blackhearted creep, one of the lowest forms of life to ever crawl on the planet."

"All that? It's a wonder I can look at myself in the mirror to shave in the morning."

"Apparently I misjudged you. I'm sorry. Usually I'm much better at assessing people's characters."

"Well, don't make my halo too big. We're still prime

competitors and I'm not one to let an opportunity pass. Not even for you."

"I'd never have thought otherwise."

"So how about Saturday?"

"Saturday?"

"To meet. You can sleep a couple extra hours, then meet me in the afternoon."

She considered his plan. "All right. Where?"

"I'll figure something out."

He creased the edge of his cheap paper placemat and tore off a piece of it. He slid the scrap toward her along with a pen. "Here, jot down your home phone number. I'll give you a call."

She hesitated, her hand poised over the pen in a final moment of uncertainty; then she picked it up and began to write.

CHAPTER FIVE

"*Phew*, what a week. Over at only"—Peg flicked a glance at the clock on the wall—"eight fifteen. I don't know about you, but I need a drink, a meal, a hot bath, and a soft bed. Preferably with a big hunk of man in it."

She ran a set of flame-tipped nails through her artfully styled brunette curls, then shrugged out of the businesslike plaid jacket she'd put on that morning. One that concealed a seductive little black dress underneath.

"Luckily for *me*," she continued, "I'm about to get my wish since it's Friday night and Bruno's on his way over to pick me up."

"Bruno?" Madelyn crammed a handful of drawing pencils into an oversize mug on her office drafting table. "What about Eddy?"

"Ancient history. I thought I told you we broke up. Well, never mind, Bruno's my latest. Met him last week at a bar. He's a bouncer there. Not the sharpest knife in the drawer, I admit, but one look and who cares? A very prime cut of beef, if you know what I mean."

Madelyn shook her head. "You are completely shameless."

"Of course I am. It's the only way to go."

They shared a grin.

"I suppose there's no point in my telling you to be careful?" Madelyn asked.

"*Me?*" Feigning astonishment, Peg raised a hand to her fine display of cleavage. "I'm always careful. I just make sure it doesn't interfere with my fun."

There was a quiet movement in the hallway.

Madelyn swung her head toward the sound. "Todd? What are you still doing here?"

Todd March, a lanky, dark-haired young man who didn't look old enough to have a paper route let alone a position as a copywriter, came to the doorway. His eyes moved instantly to Peg and riveted there like he was an adoring puppy.

The object of his adoration opened her purse, searched through it. Oblivious to her audience, she pulled out a lipstick and applied it to her lips, painting them a ripe cherry red. Smacking them together to set the stain, she checked the result with a compact mirror.

Madelyn repeated Todd's name twice before he transferred his attention to her. She asked him again why he was still at work.

"W-wallet," he said, finally finding his voice. "I f-forgot my wallet. And now I've missed my train."

"Oh, how awful. Is there another one soon?" Madelyn asked.

"Not for a while. Thought I'd come back and hang

around here for a couple of hours. I hate taking the bus."

"Everyone hates taking the bus." Peg snapped her purse closed. "Bruno and I were going to splurge on a cab. You're welcome to share if you're going that way. Where do you live?"

Stuttering only twice, Todd spit out the address.

"That's perfect," Peg said. "Come on, I've got to get out of here. You too, Colonel Grayson. Time for all the troops to head home, even those in charge."

"I've just got a couple more—"

"You've always got a couple more." Peg picked up Madelyn's briefcase and purse and held them out to her. "Whatever it is, it can wait. Todd, lights out."

Dutifully, he did as he was told.

It wasn't until Madelyn was in her car driving home that she realized Peg had been right to hustle her out. Stalling—that's what she'd been doing. Using work as an excuse to take her mind off what she was about to begin tomorrow with Zack Douglas. Or rather what she was about to continue, she amended, remembering New Year's Eve.

What did she think she was doing getting involved in a torrid office affair? She, who had been with only two other men in her entire life.

Her first was in college, a guy named Brice. He'd been a self-centered creep who'd revealed his true colors after a handful of dates and one miserable night crushed under him in a narrow twin bed.

Her second was James, a caring and considerate lover. Sex with him had always been satisfying and sweet. Not the wild, mind-numbing tempest, the animal hunger, she'd shared with Zack.

She must be crazy. Crazy in lust, she decided ruefully.

Despite the path her hormones were practically shoving her down, she knew she should call off her rendezvous with him before she got in too deep.

As her mother was always pointing out, she wasn't getting any younger. If she had any hope of finding her one right mate, the man who would complete her, body, mind, and soul, who would share her life and make a family with her to last all their days, shouldn't she be out searching for him? Instead of wasting her time with Zack?

On the other hand, maybe it was time to borrow a page or two out of Peg's book, learn to walk on the wild side. Simply live and enjoy herself for once in her life.

She'd never been given to impulse, content to do her chores and her studies. Satisfied to accept responsibility, driven to prove herself and succeed, both as a child and as an adult. Her parents hadn't insisted; it had been all her. A quirk of her nature. Doing things strictly for fun had never been one of her priorities.

No doubt about it, having an affair with Zack Douglas would be fun. But temporary. She had no illusions their interlude would last beyond a few meetings. Why not grab hold of the reins and enjoy the thrill ride while she could?

When she let herself into her apartment half an hour later, she was still waffling. Her indecision continued through dinner—a quick bowl of oatmeal with hot milk and honey—and through the washing up.

Afterward, she took a shower, then climbed into bed to watch a few minutes of television. She was just about to switch off the light and go to sleep when the telephone rang. "Hello?"

"Hi."

With just that one simple word, spoken in Zack's low, sexy rumble, she knew who it was.

"I didn't wake you, did I?" he asked.

"No, I was just about to go to sleep."

"Then you're in bed. Me too."

An image popped into her mind of him stretched out, as long and sleek as a panther, sprawled between a set of snowy white sheets, his skin and muscle golden in the dim glow of a bedroom lamp.

"Which means you must be dressed for bed," he continued. "So what are you wearing? Something sexy, I hope?"

"Sexy enough, if flannel turns you on."

He barked out a laugh. "I suppose it's one of those granny gowns? Heavy as a tent and twice as big."

"How'd you know?"

He laughed again. "Does it keep you warm?"

"Yes, it's very cozy."

"Well, you won't need it tomorrow since I'll be keeping you plenty warm myself."

Her heart rate hurried faster. "So . . . um . . ." She cleared her throat. "Why are you calling? I thought we'd agreed to meet at the hotel."

"We did. I wanted to make sure you weren't having second thoughts. You will be there tomorrow, won't you?"

Here was her opportunity to tell him. Yes, she would say,

as a matter of fact she was having second thoughts. And third ones and even fourth ones, and since that was the case she'd decided to back out after all, before it was too late. He wouldn't like it. He might argue with her, try to coax her into changing her mind, but in the end he would have to respect her decision. And that would be that.

But when she opened her mouth to say the words, something entirely different tumbled out. "Of course I'll be there."

Of course I'll be there? Had she really just said that?

"Good. I was all but certain you were going to renege, and I'd be forced to spend half the night convincing you to change your mind. I was even prepared to come over and help change it for you in person."

"You'd better not come over here," she warned. "We agreed we wouldn't meet at our apartments in case someone we know should happen to drop by."

"A rather unlikely possibility, especially at this time of the night. But seeing as it's not an emergency, it's okay."

"An emergency? My not showing up would be an emergency?"

"Damn right it would. I've been waiting all week to get my hands on you again. Seeing you here and there around the office, not being allowed to touch, it's been driving me insane."

She knew the feeling but wasn't about to admit it. Then another thought occurred.

"How do you know where I live?"

"I did a little research. It's extraordinary what you can find out on the Internet these days."

"But I'm unlisted."

"I wasn't looking in the online white pages. Remind

me to show you a couple tricks for keeping your vital statistics private."

"Thanks, I'll do that."

A natural lull surfaced between them, easy and companionable. Nice enough that the novelty of it came as a surprise and a pleasure.

"Well, it's getting late," she said. "I suppose we should go."

"Yes, I suppose we should." His voice deepened to a velvety growl. "Or I could break the rules and come over there now. Fifteen minutes and we could get started on our weekend."

He was smooth, very smooth, like a warm glass of brandy on a raw night. Madelyn's toes curled beneath the sheets, his tempting offer stirring her blood as she imagined him slipping into her bed and then, a breathless time later, into her. But no, she cautioned, one misstep and the news would be out, her reputation and credibility shattered along with it.

"We'll start on it tomorrow," she told him firmly. "I need my sleep."

"You will. I plan to keep you very, very busy. Sweet dreams, Red."

"Don't call me Red."

He chuckled, hung up.

Slowly, Madelyn returned the receiver to its cradle, then clicked off the light. Sliding farther beneath the covers, her body tingling, she wondered how she'd ever be able to sleep. Rolling over, she hugged her pillow, closed her eyes, and willed herself to relax. A few short minutes later she found oblivion.

*   *   *

Madelyn awakened amazingly well rested the next morning for her drive north to the Hudson River Valley.

Zack had booked a room for them at a quaint historic inn that boasted original heart pine plank floors and a working fireplace in each one of its thirty-odd guest rooms. Highway traffic was surprisingly light and she made good time, zipping along the roads in her shiny BMW like a little blue bullet.

She arrived only a few minutes past two p.m. check-in time. Shouldering her small leather overnight bag, she forced down the flutters in her stomach and walked into the lobby.

For a long, nervous moment she didn't see him. Then he climbed to his feet, unfolding himself from the recesses of a comfortable-looking upholstered wing chair.

Powerful, masculine, he had movie-star appeal in a chocolate brown, long-sleeve merino wool sweater, form-fitting black jeans, and black winter boots. She so rarely saw him in casual clothes, the sight of him robbed half the breath from her lungs.

Zack stole the rest as he stepped forward, bending to claim her mouth in a hearty kiss of welcome. "You made it."

"Didn't you think I would?" she murmured once she was capable, her lips tingling.

"You could still have changed your mind. I've learned never to count on something until the deal's closed. Lock, stock, and barrel."

"What an amazingly cynical attitude."

"No, just realistic." He lifted her bag and slung it over his shoulder. "We're all checked in. Shall we go to the room?"

She nodded, suddenly feeling a little shy.

He grabbed his own suitcase and led the way.

The room was charmingly old-fashioned, with a large four-poster bed, matching cherry end tables, and a tall two-door chest. Deep armchairs flanked a fireplace neatly laid with wood, the mantel above decorated by a pair of gleaming brass candlesticks and a delicate porcelain shepherdess herding her flock of two. On the floor lay a huge braided rug in a rainbow of colors, sunlight streaming across it through a set of sheer-covered, double-sashed windows.

"Oh, how lovely." She sighed.

He put down the luggage and shut the door. "You approve, then?"

She spun to face him. "Yes, very much. It's wonderful."

"I hoped you'd like it. Although when it comes to ambiance, it can't hold a candle to the bowling alley. Lacks a certain je ne sais quoi, don't you think? No burger grease or cheap perfume hovering in the air."

"Very funny."

Zack wandered over to the bed and sat down, bouncing once. "Comfortable."

"Is it? I . . . I think I'll go freshen up."

He leaned back onto his elbows, his sweater pulling taut across his chest. "Sure. Take your time."

Madelyn disappeared into the small connecting bath, breathed deeply in hopes of releasing some of the tension collected in her shoulders and neck. She was as jittery as a bride on her wedding night, and it was only—she glanced at her watch—2:35 in the afternoon. If she couldn't get through the first hour, how was she ever going to make it through the rest of the weekend?

Why was she so nervous to start with? It wasn't as if it was their first time. Maybe that was the problem. Their first time had been so spontaneous, so uncontrolled, without the need for thought or reason. Only action and reaction and pure, unfettered desire. Everything here was agreed upon and planned, structured.

Perhaps the solution was to simply unstructure it.

Before she gave herself too much time to think, Madelyn began to strip off her clothes. She was down to her underwear and bra before the nerves set in again.

What was she doing? Was she really going to walk back out there naked? What would Zack think? Somehow she didn't imagine he'd mind a full-fledged peep show, but she couldn't go all the way. Appearing in her skivvies was as daring as Madelyn Grayson got.

She took a few minutes more to use the commode, wash her hands and face, and drink a glass of cool water. She finger combed her hair, leaving it loose the way he'd asked her to.

Spine straight, shoulders back, she took a deep breath and opened the door.

Zack stood at the window, looking out. The click of the lock drew his attention. "You want to get a late lunch?" He turned and froze, eyes growing wide, lips parted in genuine astonishment. "I guess you don't."

Despite her lingering shyness, his reaction gave her a nice boost of confidence, a feeling of genuine feminine power. She could tell she'd surprised him, and he wasn't the sort of man who surprised easily or often.

She strode toward the bed. "I think we should just get on with it. I'm nervous. And I hate being nervous. Once the sex is over and done, I'll be able to relax." She turned back the coverlet, folding it to the foot of the bed.

"You make it sound as if you're about to be tortured."

"No, that's not it at all. It's just . . . it's . . . it's . . ."

He crossed his arms. "Yes . . . What is it?"

Stricken, she met his look. "I'm ruining everything, aren't I? I'm sorry. It's just that I'm so . . . so . . ."

"What?"

"Nervous."

"Do I make you nervous, Madelyn?"

"Horribly," she confessed.

"That's not my intention." He walked toward her.

"I know. It's me, not you. I'm usually far more poised and in control. I've never had this problem in the past. It seems to come over me every time I'm in a room with you. And I wish to hell I hadn't just told you that."

He took her hands in his. "I'm not. It's actually very appealing. Shall I let you in on a little secret of my own? You make me nervous too."

"I do not."

"Here, feel." He placed her right hand against his chest, over his heart, and held it tight.

Beneath her flattened palm, she could feel the muscle beat, hard and quick.

"See how fast it's pounding?" he said. "Just like a drum."

"That doesn't prove you're nervous."

"It proves I want you, and that's enough to make any man nervous."

He caught hold of her other hand and brought it up

to join its mate, flattening them both against the soft wool of his sweater.

"Why is it," she murmured, "that I always end up in my underwear when you're still completely dressed?"

"Happy coincidence. But the next time I come out of the bathroom, I promise I'll be in my briefs. Or better, nothing at all. In the meantime, why don't you help me rectify the situation?"

"Undress you, you mean?

He released her hands and spread his arms wide. "I'm all yours. Please be gentle."

She laughed, a bit of her tension easing. "I'll do my best."

Slipping her fingers beneath the waistband of his sweater, she pushed the garment up and over his head, tossing it sideways onto one of the armchairs.

Drawn as if by some magnetic force, she ran her hands over his beautifully sculpted torso. Next she traced his muscled arms and broad shoulders, admiring their width and masculine grace. He shivered when she moved lower and touched his flat stomach before heading south to the snap of his jeans. Heat rose from him, pure male animal and something else, something totally, uniquely Zack.

She bent to unlace his boots, drawing them from his feet, and afterward his socks. She set them neatly aside.

His eyes were blazing by the time she straightened.

"Do the rest," he ordered, his tone gruff, the rock-hard bulge in his pants proof of his response. "Do it now."

She eased open the zipper, then slid her hands inside, connecting with warm flesh as she shoved his jeans and briefs off his lean hips, down his thighs. He kicked the denim aside.

His hips bucked when she took him into her hand, finding him as hot and sleek as velvet. As she touched him below, she leaned forward to kiss his chest, his nipples.

Groaning, Zack clenched her hair in his fist and pulled her head back, savaging her lips, turning her world to flame. She heard something rip and realized with a wild kind of shock that he was tearing her underwear from her body. Shredding the material, bra and panties both, into useless scraps.

Then she was naked and there was no time to think at all as he pulled her to the bed and down. His hands were everywhere, touching her with an impatient fury she matched with a mindless savagery of her own.

Lifting her up and over, he impaled her, driving himself deep, deeper than she'd thought it possible to go. And then they were surging together, flesh beating against flesh, sounds of their breathing harsh in the air as they struggled to find completion.

It took her first, the climax, with a cry she heard but didn't recognize as her own, slamming her up and back in a brutal undertow that left her dazed and quivering as she came down on the other side.

He kept up the rhythm, giving new life to the tiny aftershocks reverberating inside her body, bringing her along and once again to completion.

Only then did he find his own.

Panting, replete, they settled in a tangle of limbs while they waited for the world to stop spinning.

With a smile on her lips, she gradually sat up. Astride him, she stretched her arms over her head, twisted at the waist, then leaned forward to plant her hands against the flat of his chest.

"Guess what?" she said.

"Can't. My brain's too fried," he muttered, eyes closed.

"My nerves are settled, just as I figured they would be. In fact, I feel great." She bent down and kissed him with a lusty sweep of lips and tongue. "How soon do you think you'll be ready to help me settle my nerves again?"

He pinned her with an arch look. "Sooner than you might imagine if you keep bouncing around like that."

Madelyn laughed and bounced some more.

It was full dark before they came up for air. And food. Both of them ravenous.

The inn had no room service, so they forced themselves to get dressed and wander down to the restaurant for a meal. Then it was back to their room to sleep and make love, which they tackled with eager enthusiasm.

Sunday afternoon arrived in what seemed the blink of an eye; then it was time to go home.

Packed and checked out, Zack walked Madelyn out to her car.

Taking her keys, he opened her car door and loaded her bag into the backseat. "I guess I'll see you at work tomorrow. We have a department meeting, don't we?"

"Yes, ten o'clock."

She'd had the freedom to touch him at will during the past twenty-four hours. It was going to feel odd slipping back into their old routine.

As if he read her mind, Zack told her, "Just steer well clear of me, like you always do. And if it can't be avoided, give me that look. You know, the one that could strike a cockroach dead at a hundred paces. No one will suspect a thing."

"It isn't people in general I'm worried about. It's Peg. She has a real knack for ferreting out information, and she knows me way too well. If I suddenly stop complaining about you, she'll wonder what's up."

"Then don't stop."

Madelyn thought about it for a moment and smiled. "All right, I won't."

"You don't need to look so pleased by the prospect." He took her hands, rubbing his thumbs over her palms as he brushed her lips with a kiss. "Until next weekend, then."

She nodded. "Yes, next weekend."

But that time already seemed so far away. Too far away. She hadn't had nearly enough of him, not yet.

She surprised them both a moment later when she dragged his head down and crushed her mouth to his for a long, intense kiss that left her breathless.

"Wow." Zack took a moment to steady himself. "Sure you don't want to check back in? We could both call in sick tomorrow."

Tempting, she thought, *definitely tempting.* She stroked a palm over his smoothly shaven cheek and gave him one last, lingering kiss. "Bye."

She turned, climbed into her car, and drove away.

CHAPTER SIX

"Here, try this." Peg placed a paper napkin containing a thin, oval-shaped wafer near Madelyn's elbow.

Madelyn eyed it, deciding the color looked nasty enough to take a bite out of *her*. It was a particularly virulent shade of yellow, bright enough to outshine a fleet of school buses.

"What is it?" she questioned in a wary voice.

"The new product from Carmichael Foods. That's part of the sample they sent over."

Madelyn picked the thing up with the same care she might have exercised around a letter bomb, then turned it over slowly, front to back to front.

She lifted an eyebrow. "Cracker?"

"Chip."

She gave it a tentative sniff. "Really?"

"That's what the package said."

"Have you tried one?"

Peg had on her poker face. "Yes, but I want your un-biased opinion."

"Why do I get the feeling I'm being set up?"

Peg settled into the visitor's chair next to Madelyn's desk, her expression still giving nothing away.

Madelyn braced herself. "Well, here goes." She popped it into her mouth and chewed.

Her gag reflex kicked in a second later.

Peg passed her a napkin.

Madelyn took it and spat, going so far as to wipe off her tongue before she grabbed the bottle of water she kept on her desk. She drank and drank, wondering if the taste would ever go away.

"My God," she gasped, "that's the worst thing I've ever tasted."

"That was my reaction too," Peg agreed.

"And you let me eat it!"

Peg gave a mildly apologetic shrug. "I wanted to make sure it wasn't just me."

"It wasn't, I assure you. Did they test market these things?" She couldn't bring herself to call them chips; they were an insult to corn and potato products everywhere.

"Yes, according to the information forwarded with the sample, they were well liked, particularly by males aged twelve to sixteen."

"I don't believe it. Rats wouldn't eat that stuff. Or even teenage boys. And I'm supposed to come up with an ad campaign? I can see it now." Madelyn lifted a hand to frame her imaginary slogan. "New! Ipecac in a Bag— the crunch will make you lose your lunch. Oh, or how about this? A bulimic's best friend, no fingers required. I should have known there was a catch to having this account handed to me, since Mark Stinson lands most of the snack food and soft drink stuff."

"I know. Funny how his schedule became mysteriously overloaded."

"Yeah, right. Well, we're stuck now." Madelyn slumped back in her chair. "Obviously someone should tell Carmichael Foods their product's a disaster, but if we do—"

"The client will be unhappy," Peg finished.

"Exactly. And if we proceed with the ad campaign and the product tanks, which it will—"

"The client will be unhappy."

"Not to mention the lead balloon response here at F and S."

The two of them shared a moment of gloom.

Peg tapped a polished nail on the corner of Madelyn's desk. "Larry should be the one to tell them."

Madelyn snorted. "Larry wouldn't tell a mouse it was brown unless it snarled and held him at gunpoint."

Peg snickered. "That sounds like something Zack would say, only cleaner."

"Please, don't make this worse by mentioning that man. Don't even so much as whisper his name in my presence."

The first of the ads for Takamuri Electronics had hit the airwaves a few days before and were an acknowledged triumph. Rumors were percolating that Zack was in line for a substantial bonus.

"Sorry, Madelyn."

Peg looked so remorseful that Madelyn felt a stab of guilt. She hated lying, especially to Peg. Although thinking about that particular account did raise her blood pressure to dangerously high levels.

Not because of Zack, though; not any longer. Since their revealing discussion about the Takamuri deal, she'd absolved him of any wrongdoing. Still, she couldn't afford to share her change of heart with Peg. A few well-chosen questions from that direction and the jig would be up, her affair with Zack out in the open.

"Hey," Peg said, "I know what you need. Why don't we all go out for drinks? I'll call Linda and Suzy. It's been weeks since the last time."

Eight weeks precisely, Madelyn thought, since before Christmas, since before Zack. "That sounds like fun, but I can't, not tonight."

"What—? You got a hot date or something?"

Or something, she thought, since she couldn't exactly call what she and Zack did together dating. More like hot bouts of incredibly satisfying marathon sex. And if she was going to be ready for another round tomorrow night, she needed her rest. "No . . . um . . . my cat, Millie, she's sick. I have to take her to the vet."

"Oh, I hope it's nothing serious. She's such a sweet kitty."

"She's been off her food a little lately. It's probably nothing, but I want to make sure."

"Well, of course you do. We'll make the rounds another night."

"Definitely."

Jesus, Madelyn thought after Peg left, *now I'm lying about my cat*—another source of guilt, since she barely saw the poor animal these days.

Lately, she'd taken to dropping her off at a neighbor's apartment for the entire weekend so the cat wouldn't be lonely. Luckily Mrs. Strickland, an elderly widow who loved animals but whose son discouraged her from keeping any, delighted in entertaining a furry houseguest.

What had this affair with Zack done to her?

She'd always been such an honest person. Now she was a liar and a sneak. Frankly, she'd never expected their liaison to last this long. Five weeks—six, if you counted that first time on New Year's Eve. You'd think they'd be getting sick of each other by now.

But Zack seemed as hot for her as ever. And when she was with him . . . well, there was no other place she wanted to be.

In fact, the longer they were together, the more they seemed to want each other. Just thinking of him now, and the weekend to come, had her glowing with anticipation.

At five o'clock she left for home, detouring briefly to pick up a load of dry cleaning. Once inside her apartment, she made dinner and, while it cooked, spent some quality time with Millie, eliciting long, rumbling purrs of contentment.

She was just sitting down to eat when the phone rang. "Hello?"

"Hi. It's me."

Zack. His voice was as familiar as her own these days.

"Hi, me," she teased. "What are you doing?"

"Packing."

"For tomorrow?"

"Unfortunately, no. I was ready to head home tonight when I got pulled into a last-minute meeting. Apparently there are some problems with the Rhinebeck shoes ad. I won't bore you with the numbing details, but the long and short is I have to fly to Dallas tonight. Chances are good I'll be there through the weekend. I'm sorry, Madelyn. I'm going to have to cancel our plans."

"Oh."

"Believe me, I wish I didn't have to go, but it can't be helped."

"I understand," she said, hiding her disappointment. "It's fine. Rhinebeck is a major account. If there's a problem, then of course you need to take care of it."

"It was my week to make the arrangements for us. I'll switch them around for next weekend, if that's okay?"

"Sure, that'll be great. What time's your flight?"

"Nine thirty."

"La Guardia or JFK?"

"Kennedy. They have a nonstop that goes straight to DFW."

"Oh, well, good." She could offer to take him to the airport, she thought. No, she couldn't. They didn't have that sort of relationship, and it would violate their agreement to keep what existed between them a secret.

"Have a good trip, then," she said.

"You'll be okay?"

"Why wouldn't I be?"

"Ruined plans for the weekend, that's all."

"I'll recover. I have plenty of things I need to take care of."

"All right, then. I'd better be going."

"Yes, you don't want to miss your flight."

"I suppose not. I'll see you when I get back."

She listened to the drone of the dial tone for a few seconds, then hung up.

Her dinner was cold—curried chicken and rice sitting in a congealed yellow lump in the center of her plate.

She considered warming it up but tossed the unappealing glob down the disposal instead, turning the switch on, then off again with an irritated snap.

She wished now she hadn't refused Peg's offer for a girls' night out. Friends and conversation were exactly what she needed.

Opting for the next best thing, she pulled a quart of ice cream out of the freezer—caramel chocolate fudge— and plowed ferociously into it with a long-handled spoon. Whoever'd said you had to drown your sorrows in booze had never eaten this.

The package arrived at four thirty in the afternoon on Wednesday by special courier. Her thoughts elsewhere, Madelyn carelessly scribbled her name on the signature line to accept the delivery.

She nearly set the envelope aside to open later, then changed her mind at the last second. She didn't get a lot of packages by courier, and her curiosity was piqued.

There was no return address. She flipped it over, but there was nothing remarkable on the reverse—it was just an envelope, small and plain.

Its inside was a different story.

The envelope contained a key card, the plastic kind that opened an electronic door lock, together with a note.

Meet me at the Hyatt. 7:00 tonight. Room 2511. I can't wait until the weekend.

The note wasn't signed. It didn't need to be.
Zack was back.

Excitement raced through her bloodstream. She hadn't heard from him since he'd left for Texas last week, and hadn't really expected to.

Word was, problems with the shoot—primarily issues with the Olympic track star hired to run in the ads— were taking longer to solve than expected. She'd even started to think he might be held up for another weekend, but obviously he'd managed to resolve the situation and return home.

And the first thing he'd done was arrange to rendezvous with her.

Technically, he'd broken the rules, the ones the two of them had agreed to follow. From the start, they'd said there would be no personal contact between them at work. No notes or e-mails. No phone calls or smoldering glances. If they didn't do anything suspicious, there would be nothing for anyone to notice.

Yet she felt no irritation that he'd contacted her at the office. She couldn't wait for the weekend either. Not now that he was back.

Madelyn glanced at her watch.

Four forty-five.

If she left the instant the hour hand hit five, she should have time to dash home, take a quick shower, feed the cat, change into something attractive—and far more comfortable than the navy skirted suit she was currently wearing—and still make it to the hotel by seven.

She slipped the key card into her purse, then wondered what she should do with the note.

Shred it was the obvious answer.

But someone might wonder if they saw her shred one

tiny piece of notepaper. She'd dispose of it at home, she decided.

Her mind made up, she tucked the note into her purse as well, then sat down at her desk to wait for the final minutes to tick past.

Zack was standing at the window, gazing out at the city lights that winked and shimmered below, when he heard the snick of a key in the lock.

He turned around and watched as Madelyn walked into the room.

She shut the door, then flipped the security lock. She smiled and sauntered toward him.

He grew instantly aroused, his eyes raking over the slim curves of her body. She was dressed in a form-hugging twin set of some soft material—cashmere, he supposed—its icy blue color a perfect foil for her beautiful red-gold hair.

He cleared his throat. "I see you received the parcel I sent."

She nodded. "It arrived late in the day. I almost didn't open it."

"I thought of that possibility but decided to take the chance. Seems it paid off."

"What time did your flight get in?" She toed off her shoes.

He noted the move, his lips bending upward into a slow smile. "Around two this afternoon."

He remembered the landing, how his mind had been awash with vivid thoughts of her. Thoughts strong enough to nearly drown out the roar of the hydraulic brakes, the shuddering in the cabin, the whining squeal of airplane tires as they bumped and burned against the tarmac.

Safe on the ground, he'd been consumed by an over-whelming impatience to see Madelyn, to feel her, to be with her the way he'd wanted to be every day since he'd been gone.

He began unbuttoning his shirt.

"How was Dallas?" Madelyn peeled off her sweater, stretching her arms high over her head. Carelessly she tossed the expensive garment onto the back of a nearby chair.

With appreciation, he eyed her lace-covered breasts. "Hot and dry, especially for February." He stepped out of his shoes and loosened his belt buckle.

She shimmied out of her slacks. "And did you settle all the problems with the ad? Everybody happy now?"

God knew he was about to be, he realized, as he yanked down his zipper and let his pants drop to the floor. He swallowed as he saw her reach back with both hands to unfasten her bra, the movement arching her chest forward.

"Yeah," he answered, "with some pull from the account executive who manages Rhinebeck and a lot of arm-twisting by Tanner's agent."

He sent his shirt flying, then stripped off the last of his clothing.

"Tanner's the track star, right? I take it he wanted more money." She stepped out of her underwear and straightened, completely naked. She set her hands on her hips to wait for his answer.

"Right. Money." He reached out and caught hold of her wrist, pulling her to him. "Now, enough with the twenty questions. We've got more important things to discuss."

She glided her hands over his firm shoulders and arms, then down his chest, burying her fingers in the dark mat of hair that grew there, rubbing her thumbs across his flat male nipples. She leaned near and laved her tongue over his collarbone.

"Such as?" she teased.

Zack growled and lifted her into his embrace, high enough for her to wrap her arms and legs around him.

Slowly, he walked them across the room. "Such as whether you want to be on the top or the bottom."

She smiled and crushed her lips to his in a ravenous, openmouthed kiss.

"How about both?" she invited, her tone husky.

In complete agreement, they tumbled onto the bed.

It was ages later before they broke apart, flushed and replete, their bodies all but humming from a near overload of sensory pleasure. Stretched out side by side across the tangled sheets of the wide king-size bed, they lay with eyes closed, hands clasped.

Madelyn gave a luxuriant purr. "*Umm*, that was amazing."

"Amazing, huh?"

"Definitely worth staying up late for on a Wednesday night."

"Well, they don't call it hump day for nothing, you know."

She gasped and rolled her head toward him. "My God, Zack, you are outrageous. And incredible."

She started chuckling.

"No doubt the reason you can't resist me."

She shifted to lean her forearms against his chest. "Incredibly awful is what I meant," she said.

He gave her a light pinch on the bare flesh of her thigh.

In retaliation, she pressed her fingernails into his side.

He sucked in his stomach and arched away. "Hey, watch where you put those things."

"Or what?"

"Or else," he growled playfully. "That's what."

"Now, now, don't start anything you can't finish." She rolled away from him.

"Who says I can't finish? I finish everything I start." He lunged across the bed after her.

"Not now, you don't," she laughed, eluding him. "I'm hungry and I demand to be fed."

"Food, is it?"

"Yes, a big thick steak and a salad, I think. Followed by a towering slice of cheesecake with cherries on top."

Now he was getting hungry. "I suppose I could eat." He tucked his hands behind his head. "Call room service and order something for us."

She bounced out of the bed and onto her feet. "No, *you* call room service. I'm going to shower."

"Slave driver," he complained. "All right, but then I'm coming in after you."

"No way. I want my dinner and it'll end up getting cold if you join me. Remember what happened the last time we showered together?"

He did, fondly. "I promise I won't do anything but wash."

She pinned him with a knowing look. "*Nuh-uh.* That's

what got us in trouble last time, since I'm the one you washed. I'm locking the door behind me."

"You're cruel, you know that?" he called to her retreating back.

Grinning, he picked up the receiver to dial room service. He was hungrier than he'd thought and ended up ordering steaks and salad for them both, cheesecake, a pitcher of ice water, coffee for him, and tea for Madelyn.

While she showered, he tugged on his pants, then straightened the rest of their clothes, hanging them neatly in the closet.

Their meal arrived just a couple of minutes before Madelyn padded out of the bath, wrapped inside a large fluffy white robe. She hadn't lied about being starved, and dug enthusiastically into her meal. Zack ate his own dinner at a more moderate pace.

Halfway through, though, she slowed and leaned back in her chair, pushing her plate to one side.

He pointed a fork toward her partially eaten steak. "Aren't you going to finish that?"

"I'm leaving room for dessert."

"Waste of a damned fine piece of meat, if you ask me."

"Would you like it?"

"At these prices I would." He stabbed the expensive cut of beef and transferred it to his plate.

"I had no idea you were so frugal." Madelyn ate a bite of her cheesecake, taking a moment to savor the taste. "You know, it just occurred to me, I really don't know that much about you, even after all these weeks."

He shrugged, finishing his own steak and starting in on hers. "What's there to know?"

"Well, basic things, I suppose. Where you grew up, for instance."

"Pennsylvania, near Pittsburgh."

"What was it like, your hometown?"

"Small. Blue-collar. Nothing special, just a town."

"And college? Did you attend one in Pennsylvania?"

"No, I went to NYU. At least that's where I finished up. Did a tour in the army first, right out of high school. I was stationed over in Germany. It gave me the chance to earn some money, take a few classes, and see a little of the world."

"Now, that's exactly what I mean. I had no idea you'd done any of those things."

"And what about you, Madelyn? Which one of the Seven Sisters did you attend?"

She paused for a long, telling moment before she confessed. "Wellesley, but we're not discussing me."

He smiled and ate another slice of steak.

"How about family? Any brothers and sisters?" she persisted.

"One. A sister."

"And?"

"And what?"

"Is she older, younger? What's her name?"

"Her name is Beth and she's four years younger."

"And your parents?"

He went still. "What about them?"

"Well, what are they like? Where do they live? What do they do?"

"My father doesn't do anything, not anymore. He's dead. My mother . . . last I heard she lives somewhere in Florida."

"The last you heard?"

Something icy slid into his eyes. "Yes, the last I heard. Is the interrogation over now, or was there something else you wanted to know?"

Her spine stiffened at his tone. Hurt, she stirred her coffee in a circular motion, her eyes lowered. "No, I don't want to know anything, not if you don't want to tell me."

"Look, it's not that, not exactly." He sighed and set down his fork. "I don't much like talking about my past, that's all. It's nothing personal."

She pushed her dessert away, barely touched. "Fine. I won't ask again."

He picked up his glass of ice water and drank half, then set it down with a snap. "All of us didn't grow up in a nice house in the suburbs with a loving family and lots of money. Some of us lived in a cramped, run-down hovel where you sweltered in the summer and froze in the winter 'cause the heat only worked half the time. The months your dad was sober enough to remember to pay the bill, that is.

"You didn't have to listen to him after he'd crawled down deep into a bottle of cheap brew," he went on, jabbing his fork into the remaining piece of medium-rare steak on his plate.

"Blubbering on hour after hour," he continued, "about how he would have made it to the Show, played big-league ball if he hadn't gotten robbed after only a year in the minors. How his coach was a narrow-minded son of a bitch who didn't understand the pressures a family man was under. And you didn't have to listen to him sob about how he'd given up his dream for a wife and kid he didn't want. For a mistake he'd made one night as a teenager in the backseat of a car."

She reached out a hand. "Zack—"

He ignored her and went on. "You didn't breathe a sigh of relief every time you left for school, savoring the calm, the peace of knowing you didn't have to listen to your parents argue and fight and scream at each other, for a few hours anyway. You didn't have to watch your mother take off with some out-of-town insurance salesman, then have to explain to your six-year-old sister why she wouldn't be coming back again—ever. You didn't get the hell out of some backwater town you hated, the second you could. Swearing never to return, never to look back. Did you ever have to do any of those things, Madelyn, in your perfect little world?"

She jerked back her head as if he'd slapped her, then pulled in a breath. Visibily, she composed herself. "No, I didn't, but that doesn't mean my world was perfect. And it doesn't give you the right to criticize or condemn me."

A tense silence fell between them.

"I'm sorry your childhood was so unhappy," she offered in a stiff voice.

"Don't be." He shrugged. "My sister and I did all right. It could have been worse. Our folks didn't beat or molest us or anything like that. And somehow Dad always managed to hang on to his factory job, keep a roof over our heads, such as it was."

Until bitterness and alcohol had worn him into an old man long before his time, Zack thought. Put him into an early grave.

He looked across the table at Madelyn, so fresh and pretty.

And yes, so innocent in her way.

What was he doing? Where had all that meanness come from? Erupting like a monster from somewhere deep inside. Why had he told her so much? Revealed parts of himself, secrets he'd never revealed to anyone else before?

Suddenly tired, he rubbed a pair of fingers over the bridge of his nose. "I'm sorry. I don't know why I decided to take this out on you. It doesn't usually bother me."

She folded her napkin and put it carefully back on the table. "I guess I pushed a button. It . . . it's getting late. Maybe I should go."

"You don't need to go. We've got the room for the whole night."

She climbed to her feet. "We've also got work tomorrow. It'll be easier for me to get dressed and ready in the morning if I'm at home."

As she started past, he caught her by the wrist. "Stay," he said.

"I think it would be better if we both had some time apart. A chance to sort through our thoughts."

He didn't like the sound of that. "No."

He tugged her across his lap, wrapped an immovable arm around her waist. "You're not walking away from me, not tonight."

He pushed the robe off one shoulder and buried his face in the curve of her neck, possessively taking her naked breast in his hand. "I'm not done yet. Not nearly done wanting you."

Then his mouth was on hers, demanding a response, demanding her surrender.

*   *   *

For the space of a few endless seconds she struggled, trying not to give in to the fire already starting to burn inside her body.

Then she yielded, meeting him, matching him touch for touch, kiss for kiss, taking him with the same raw power with which he was taking her. Anger and hurt faded beneath the force of her desire.

He took her there, on the chair, without gentleness or mercy, forcing her to accept everything he had and more. No longer quite himself. No longer entirely rational.

And she let him, urging him on, letting him spread her, fill her, pushing her senses high, then higher still, until she felt as if she were soaring, flying free without need of wings or a net.

When the passion was over, when they'd both come back down to earth, hearts no longer threatening to hammer from their chests, lungs filling normally with air, he carried her to the bed and lay beside her on the sheets.

In a move of blatant possession, he looped an arm and leg around her body as if still worried she might try to leave.

A brief while later, Madelyn stroked her hand down the warm, supple skin of his naked back and listened to his breathing.

Gentle.

Even.

Asleep.

She thought about their conversation, about everything he'd told her, and his demands afterward. She thought again about the way she'd given in to him and the strength of their mutual passion.

No, whether she liked it or not, she realized, she wasn't done yet with wanting him either.

And it worried her—the knowledge that she might never be again.

CHAPTER SEVEN

She found the movie ticket in her coat pocket the next day. It was for a show scheduled to play that evening at an older theater in Brooklyn.

The ticket must have come from Zack. She knew of no one else who might have left her such a thing. But when had he had the time to buy it? she wondered. More important, how had he managed to slip it into her coat without her knowledge? She'd barely been out of her office all day.

A yawn caught her and she raised a hand to cover her gaping mouth. Today had been tough. Made tougher by the scant hours of sleep she'd gotten last night.

Just after five this morning she'd slipped from the bed, needing to return home and change into something suitable for work.

Zack had been awake.

She'd sensed him watching her as she'd dressed in the sliver of light shining around the bathroom door. He'd said nothing. Neither had she. Then she'd let herself out of the room.

At work, responsibility had set in with all the subtlety of a brick crashing through a plate glass window. One demand after another, calls and meetings and impossible deadlines piling up until she'd been about ready to scream.

Desperate for a break around eleven, she'd escaped outside for a breath of fresh air. Or at least what passed for fresh air in the city.

That's when she'd found it, a stiff rectangle of paper, a one-by-four-inch featherweight intruder hiding in the pocket of her coat. For a long moment she'd considered its meaning and the man who'd left it for her. Then she'd tucked it away and returned to the office.

The film's previews were rolling, the theater dark, when she walked inside at half past six. The wide set of wooden double doors, with their long, thin slits of window, swung shut at her back.

Momentarily blinded, she stood in the aisle to give her eyes a chance to adjust. A handful of people sat scattered in the hundred-seat-capacity room, making it an easy task to pick out the back of Zack's head and his broad shoulders a few rows down.

She moved forward and, with barely a sound, eased into the seat next to his.

He didn't speak right away. "I wasn't sure you were coming," he whispered.

"Traffic was heavy," she whispered back.

He'd bought a giant tub of popcorn. He nudged it toward her, balancing it on the armrest between them. Madelyn took a handful and began to eat, one kernel at a time. The movie opened with a sweeping flourish of music, credits forming and re-forming over rugged hills of green and miles of cloudless indigo sky.

Zack angled his head toward hers. "Your day okay?"

"Long. Busy. The usual. How was yours?"

"About the same," he said. "Too many meetings."

She paused. "The movie ticket surprised me. How'd you manage to slip it into my pocket with no one seeing, including me?"

"Handy skill I acquired in my youth."

She decided it wisest not to probe further, knowing what she now did of his past. Instead she ate a few more kernels of popcorn.

Silence settled between them, filled by the voices of the actors on the screen. "So are you going to tell me why we're here?" she asked.

"To watch the movie."

She studied him in the screen glare for a long moment. He seemed tense, uneasy, troubled. "That's not why we're here."

"No, I suppose it isn't." He sighed and rubbed a hand across one thigh. "I wanted to talk and not on the phone. Since the office was obviously out of the question, I chose this."

A woman two rows ahead turned and shushed them.

Madelyn waited a minute, then lowered her voice as much as she could. "What was it you wanted to talk about?"

"Last night." He paused as if he were trying to find the right words. "I wanted to say ... well ... to tell you ... that I'm sorry."

"Sorry for what?"

"For being too rough. I didn't hurt you, did I? Is that why you left so quickly this morning?"

She turned to him, reaching for his hand. "No. How could you think that? I left because I needed to go home and change clothes for work. You didn't hurt me. You couldn't."

But he could. Very easily, he thought. Didn't she realize? She was a strong woman. Yet even strong women had fragile bones.

Soft bodies.

Tender hearts.

"I was angry," he said. "I didn't give you much choice."

"We were both angry. If I'd really wanted you to stop, you would have stopped."

"You're so certain?"

"I am. Besides, I'm not a doormat. If you'd hurt me, Zack, I wouldn't be here with you now. I'd never accept something like that from a man. Not any man."

He considered her statement and recognized the truth of it. Madelyn wasn't a woman who backed down or kept silent about things she believed needed to be said.

She laid a hand against his cheek, already grown rough with evening whiskers. "Making love is always good with you. Each time, it only gets better."

He wrapped a hand around her wrist to press a kiss into her palm. "You told me you needed time apart. Do you still?"

"And if I said yes?"

He looked into her eyes. "I wouldn't like it, but I'd give it to you anyway. If it's what you really want."

Something warm and waxen seemed to pool inside her, spreading through her body all the way to her heart.

And in that instant she knew. She just knew. He was the man for her.

Improbable as it might seem, she was in love.

With Zack Douglas.

She met his eyes in the flickering light from the screen, shook her head. "No. I only want to be with you."

He set the popcorn aside to draw her close—as close as he could manage with the armrest in the way—then pressed his mouth to her own, gently, tenderly.

"Do you want to stay for the movie?" he asked.

"What movie?" she whispered.

He laughed.

Other patrons joined the first woman in another round of shushing.

"I don't think we're very popular tonight," Madelyn said sotto voce.

"I don't think so either. Maybe we should leave." He linked his fingers with hers. "I'm not ready to say good night yet."

"Me either." Madelyn considered their options, the possible consequences. "We could go to my place."

"That's against the rules. Under no circumstances," he quoted, "are we to meet at either of our apartments."

"And we won't, not after tonight. But it's dark and cold and if you don't mind parking a few blocks away, you can come around to the back entrance. No one will see you. Do you have a hat?"

"A hat?"

"You know, the thing that fits over your head to protect it from the weather. A few people wear them as fashion statements."

"I would not be one of those people. No, I don't have a hat."

"Then keep your head down and walk fast. I'll buzz you in."

"No doorman?"

"Just electronic security."

"All right. You ready?"

"Yes, but I don't think we should leave together. You stay here, then follow me out in a few minutes."

"No one's going to see us here in Brooklyn."

"You never know."

"Unlikely, but all right. Let's switch our departure schedule around, though. What do you say I go out first and wait? Then you leave a few minutes later. That way I can make sure you get to your car safely."

"You'll wait at a distance?"

"Of course."

He kissed her again, then slid past into the aisle.

Alone in the dark, she watched the movie, or tried to. But she'd missed too much of the story to understand what was happening up on the screen.

Her own life felt a little like that right now, she realized.

Confusing.

Out of control.

She wondered what in the hell she was going to do about it.

"Did anyone see you?"

Zack shrugged out of his coat. "No. No one saw me."

"You're sure?"

"As sure as I can be without running a police sweep of the neighborhood."

"Sorry, I just—"

"Don't want anyone to know," he finished. "After all, it might sully your pristine reputation."

"Pristine? Is that how people think of me?"

"In certain circles, you're considered quite . . . wholesome."

She turned away to hang up his coat. "And do you share that opinion?"

He came up behind and wrapped her in his arms, feathering kisses over her cheek before nuzzling a particularly sensitive spot behind her ear. "How could I? The past few weeks have taught me what a wicked woman you really are. So, do you want to be wicked out here or in your bedroom?"

Madelyn chuckled softly. "Why don't we let a little anticipation build and decide after we've eaten dinner?" She stepped out of his arms. "All I ate for lunch was a quick salad and I'm starving."

He sighed and trailed her into the small, square kitchen. "If you insist. What's on the menu?"

"I don't know." She pulled open the refrigerator door to peer inside. "I usually fix something simple during the week. A sandwich or soup, maybe some leftovers from a meal I cooked on the weekend. For some odd reason, though," she added tongue in cheek, "I haven't had much time lately for cooking on the weekends."

Or for going to the grocery store either, she realized, casting a doleful eye over the meager contents on the shelves in front of her. She didn't need to open the freezer to know it had even fewer items inside. Inspiration struck when she saw the bottle of maple syrup. "How about pancakes?"

"For dinner?"

"Yes. Or are you one of those people who believes breakfast should only be eaten in the morning?"

"Not at all. I practically lived on pizza during college. Cold for breakfast, hot for dinner, and whichever I had time for at noon. Pancakes sound great. Want some help?"

"Thanks, but I think I've got it covered." Madelyn stocked the counter with eggs and milk and pancake mix.

Zack relaxed in a straight-backed kitchen chair to watch her work. That was when he noticed the pair of walnut-shaped green eyes observing him from beneath the table. He stretched down a hand, letting it hang unthreateningly at his hip.

A full minute later the inquisitive feline approached and gave his fingers a cautious sniff. Deciding she approved of the stranger in her house, the cat inched closer, allowing him to run his hand over the velvety length of her gray-and-white-striped fur. Then with a high, whisper-soft meow, she leapt onto his lap and began to purr, kneading her paws like tiny pistons against his thigh.

He petted her in leisurely strokes from head to tail. She lowered her eyes to pleasured half slits and increased the volume of her purrs.

"Who's this little motorboat?" he asked.

Madelyn turned from the counter where she was beating eggs and milk together in a large bowl. The fork in her hand fell still as she took in the scene. "Would you look at that. Millie never makes up to strangers. She usually hides until they're gone."

Zack rubbed a finger beneath the cat's grateful chin. "Sounds like a smart cat. She must know I'm not really a stranger. Don't you, sweetheart? You know I'm not a stranger," he murmured to the adoring animal.

Millie head butted his hand, then moved closer and leaned her body against his chest.

"That's incredible. Even my cat can't resist you."

He looked up and grinned. "Women adore me; what can I say?"

Madelyn snorted and turned her back on him. She picked up the mixing bowl and began whisking the egg and milk mixture into the pancake mix.

Of course he was right, she thought. And she was the worst one of all, in love with a man who drew women to him like bees to clover. But she'd known that going in, hadn't she? It was just that she hadn't counted on the game turning so serious—at least for her.

She set a skillet on the stove burner with a tad too much force. The bang startled Millie, who jumped off Zack's lap and disappeared into the other room.

He raised an eyebrow as he dusted a few cat hairs off his pants. "Something wrong?"

"No, not at all." She turned on the heat under the pan. "Just thinking about—"

Yes, what could she say she'd been thinking about other than him?

"Work and the account I've gotten saddled with."

"Which one is that?"

She slanted him a look, grateful he hadn't seemed to

notice her earlier hesitation. "The neon-colored chips from hell."

"Oh, *that* account."

"Yes. And don't you dare grin. It isn't funny."

Zack sobered. "You're right; it isn't. Is the product really as awful as rumor would have it?"

"Worse. Far, far worse." Pancake batter sizzled gently as she poured two circles of it into the buttered skillet. "Which means there's no easy road out."

"It won't be pretty, I agree. Have you decided on your strategy?"

"Something other than quitting or fleeing the country?" He looked amused.

Madelyn sighed. "Not really, and Peg's no help. She's been joking that we should suggest a new marketing campaign aimed at dogs. Apparently her current love interest has a beagle and Fido thinks they're fantastic."

"It's Carmichael Foods, right? Who's the account exec on that? Have you talked it over with him?"

She flipped the pancakes over to brown on the other side. "Yeah, I've talked it over. It's Phil Novena, and you know what he's like. He told me in that officious voice of his to remember that taste is a subjective thing. Just because I don't like the product doesn't mean other people won't love it. So I'm supposed to keep my mouth shut and be creative. But how can I, Zack? No matter how great a job my team does, when these chips hit the shelves they're going to tank."

"Phil Novena's a horse's ass and everybody at F and S knows it. Of course, he's a devious horse's ass. Most likely the reason he's risen as far as he has. Do you want me to see if there's anything I can do?"

"No," she told him firmly. "Thanks, but no thanks. I have to deal with this on my own, however unpleasant it might be." She opened the oven door and slid the finished pancakes onto a plate warming inside. She straightened to pour another round of batter into the skillet.

"Whichever way you go," Zack told her, "I'm sure you'll make the right decision."

If only she had his confidence, his determination, how much easier things would be. Almost as easy as flipping pancakes. With a wry smile, she slid her spatula under one and sent it winging into the air.

Zack awakened her with a kiss just before daybreak. "I'd better get going. I set the alarm clock for you, so go back to sleep."

She forced her eyes open, her body warm and drowsy. "*Hmm*, okay."

He chuckled and brushed his lips over her cheek. "Looks like I wore you out. We'll sleep in late tomorrow. Do you have the directions to the B and B?"

"*Umm-hmm.*" She looped her arms around his neck and pressed her cheek against his. His beard was scratchy. "You need a shave."

"I didn't think I should risk my face on your ladies' razor."

She leaned back and smiled sleepily into his eyes. "No. It's much too pretty to cut."

"Pretty, huh?"

"Yeah, you're a real-life Prince Charming."

"Well, Sleeping Beauty, get some more rest and I'll see you at work."

"I'll make sure to give you the evil eye if we pass each other in the hall."

"I'm looking forward to it. Oh, and thanks again for the pancakes. They were delicious."

"My pleasure. Thanks again for the sex. It was delicious too."

He laughed. "You're right, it was." He joined his lips to hers for a warm, penetrating kiss that left both of them aching and hungry. "Too bad," he murmured, "that we don't have time to indulge in one more helping."

"We could," she invited.

He shook his head and moved away. "Nine o'clock meeting and I can't afford to be late."

"All right, party pooper." She rolled away from him onto her side.

He smiled and gave her bottom a harmless smack through the thick comforter.

She listened with half an ear as he let himself out of the apartment. When silence descended once more, she snuggled deeper under the covers and breathed in the scent of him lingering on the sheets.

Sex. That's what she'd called it, no more than a basic physical instinct. The coupling of two bodies, one male, one female. But last night, she'd sensed a change in those long, dark hours together, as if some invisible barrier between them had come crashing down.

An accomplished lover, Zack made sure her needs were well met, her pleasure reached. But last night he'd taken special care, tender in a way she'd never known him to be. Unhurried, almost reverent, lingering over her with an unexpected measure of gentleness. One that had made her tremble and tumble for him even harder than she already had.

As she huddled now beneath the bedclothes, knowing she ought to sleep, she couldn't keep her heart from filling with a foolish, fragile hope. A wish she dared not allow herself to have.

He was a hardened playboy. A man who would never commit himself to just one woman. Who would never appreciate the quiet domesticity of home and hearth. Yet in the weeks they'd been together, she knew there had been no other woman in his life except her. His passion for her seemed only to have increased. Ripening with the intensity that familiarity could sometimes bring, as they learned more about each other, took more from each other, and shared more with each other as well.

She hadn't loved him when this whirlwind affair had begun; she hadn't believed such an emotion was even possible given their relationship. Yet here she was, filled to bursting with love. And if she felt that way, was it possible he might someday feel the same for her?

Clutching her hands to her chest, she closed her eyes and let herself dream.

CHAPTER EIGHT

Winter clung to the naked branches of the trees and to the ground, broad patches of white from an early March snow spread along both sides of the highway like peaks of cold, creamy icing.

Inside her car, Madelyn was warm and comfortable; her trip was an easy one. Yet it felt odd knowing Zack would not be waiting for her at the end of today's journey. For only the second time in nearly two months, they would be spending their weekend apart. But it was her sister Ivy's fifteenth birthday, and she wasn't going to miss it, not even for him.

When she arrived at her parents' home, she found the long, tree-lined driveway that led up to their impressive Tudor-style house lined with cars. On the front lawn a pair of dogs played tug-o'-war with a thick length of rope.

One of them spotted her as she exited her car, his great golden head arching up in excitement. Dropping the rope, he bounded forward, tail waving like a flag while his equally golden companion followed only a split second behind. The two of them skidded to an exuberant halt, rubbing dog hairs on the skirt of her emerald green woolen coat as they weaved around her with canine glee.

She reached down to greet them both with pats and hugs, receiving a warm, wet hand washing in return.

"I see you've been met by our resident welcoming committee."

Madelyn smiled at her father as he came down the front steps. "Kit and Caboodle are always glad to see me," she said.

"Not to burst your bubble, but those two are glad to see anyone. Your mother told me to let them out to run off some of their excess doggie energy. They were barking at the caterers." He lowered his voice as he exposed their crime.

"And where's Chipper?"

As spoiled as any true descendant of royalty might expect to be, Chipper was her mother's pedigreed King Charles spaniel.

"Inside the house, of course, hiding under one of the buffet tables hoping for a handout, or at least a convenient spill." He arched a ginger eyebrow. "So, have you got a hug for your old man?"

"You know I do." She turned and wrapped her arms around him, bussing him on the cheek.

She received a kiss in return, plus a squeeze that lifted her straight off the ground. Once she was back on her feet, she smiled into his mischievous eyes. He still looked boyishly young, his hair as red as hers with only a few scattered threads of white hinting at his age.

"You're not old, Dad."

"You won't be saying that when the youngest of your four children turns fifteen."

She laid a hand on her chest and rolled her eyes. "That'll be the day."

She opened her car trunk to take out her overnight bag.

Her father shouldered her gently out of the way and lifted the luggage out for her. "How are you doing, Peanut? The world treating you okay?"

"Depends on what section of the world you're talking about, but yeah, in general, I'm great."

"Good. Everybody's inside. Before we go in I wanted to mention . . . James is here. You all right with that?"

"I'm fine with that. I'd already figured he might be here. After all, Ivy would be crushed if he didn't come to her party. He's always been her favorite, and she shouldn't have to miss out just because things have been tense between him and me lately." She caught the look in her father's eyes. "Really, don't worry. It's not a problem."

Reassured, Philip Grayson relaxed. "Then prepare to meet the ravenous hordes. I swear, I think Laura let Ivy invite her entire high school class. Half of them teenage boys." He said it with such disdain, Madelyn laughed.

"They've already gone through a whole roast beef and an entire ham," he continued, "and the party's barely started. They've taken over the indoor pool and the billiards room too. I'm praying none of them get sick."

"You mean like Bobby Metzger did at my party when I turned sixteen?"

He shut his eyes. "Please, don't remind me."

"Philip, what are you doing with that girl? I've been waiting ten minutes already for you to bring her inside. You two will surely catch your death of cold if you stay out there much longer."

"We've been talking, dear," he indulgently told his wife.

"Well, you can talk inside where it's warm." She scolded with a gentle smile before turning toward her daughter. "How was your drive, sweetheart?"

Madelyn walked up the steps to exchange hugs and kisses with her mother, who'd come out onto the front stoop without a coat, trim and pretty in a peach-colored cotton-knit sweater set. "My drive was fine."

"The roads all clear? I wasn't sure they would be after that last storm."

"Perfectly scraped and salted. So where's the birthday girl?"

"Chatting with some of her friends the last time I saw her."

Philip whistled for the dogs, who came bounding across the snowy yard.

Inside the house, the party was indeed in full swing, with plenty of adult company—a smattering of family and friends who'd been invited as a defense against the unruly teenage horde.

Madelyn spent a few minutes visiting with her mother, until the older woman was drawn away to deal with some minor crisis brewing in the kitchen. Momentarily alone, Madelyn crossed to pour herself a soft drink from the beverage table.

"Hey, sis, how's it going?" A long male arm snaked around her waist and hauled her into an embrace.

"Hi, P.G." She returned his hug, then stepped back to look up at her brother.

"Where were you last night? We missed you. Even Brie, our frequently too-busy-to-make-it sister, made it down," he said.

"Long week, you know how it is."

In spite of a bit of guilt, she decided to keep the truth to herself—that she'd spent the night in bed with Zack after he'd sneaked over to her apartment. Somehow she didn't think her brother really wanted to hear about her love life.

P.G. poured a few ounces of ginger ale into a glass.

"Since when do you drink soda?" she asked him.

"It's not for me. It's for Caroline."

"Since when does Caroline drink soda?" Her sister-in-law usually preferred a simple glass of wine at get-togethers like this one.

A huge grin spread over his face. "Since we found out she's pregnant again."

"Oh, P.G., that's wonderful!" She set down her glass and gave him a second hug. "How long have you known?"

"A few weeks, but we wanted to wait until she was into her second trimester before we told anybody. Go over and talk to her. She'll be thrilled to fill you in on all the details."

"And I'm dying to hear them. I'll be there in a couple of minutes. First I need to track down Ivy to wish her a happy birthday. Have you seen her?"

"Not for the past few minutes. She's been drifting in and out, mingling with her friends like a good little hostess. Mom's taught her well."

Too well, Madelyn sometimes thought. As a late last child, Ivy had always been mature for her years and took her responsibilities seriously, like Madelyn herself. It wasn't something anyone had pushed on Ivy; it was just the way she was. But Madelyn knew her little sister had only a few more years of her childhood left and believed she should make the most of them by being as carefree and frivolous as she possibly could.

"I'm going to look for her; then I'll be back to hear all the exciting news."

P.G. poured himself a beer and raised the glass in agreement.

Madelyn made her way through the house, stopping several times to exchange greetings with clusters of her parents' neighbors and friends as well as an assortment of relatives. With relief, she finally reached the quiet, book-lined interior of the study and discovered the person she'd been looking for, plus the one she'd been dreading to see.

James and Ivy were standing in front of the row of windows, their two blond heads bent close in conversation.

Ivy was the first to notice Madelyn's entrance, breaking off whatever she'd been saying to rush across the room. "Malynn, you're here. You came." She threw a pair of scrawny arms around her sister's neck and hugged her.

"Malynn" was Ivy's special name for Madelyn. As a toddler, she hadn't been able to pronounce Madelyn's name correctly. By the time she could, the nickname had been used so long it never went away.

Madelyn gave her a hard hug in return. "Of course I came. I wouldn't miss your birthday."

"I know. I'm just glad to see you."

Ivy stepped back. She looked splendid in a pink-and-green-striped retro-style skirt and blouse—a combination no one past the age of eighteen could carry off.

Tall and willowy, Ivy had a figure others would one day come to envy. Right now she was still growing into her looks, caught in her gangly, awkward teens, unaware how lovely she was with her straight, pale hair and soft blue eyes.

"Look what James gave me," Ivy exclaimed. She squared her shoulders and lifted her chin to show off the lustrous strand of pale pink pearls around her neck. "Aren't they gorgeous?"

Madelyn leaned in for a closer look. First quality, rare, and extremely expensive. "Magnificent."

Ivy beamed, reaching up to caress the necklace with a reverent touch.

"I thought you were opening your presents later," Madelyn said.

James stepped forward. "It's my fault. I asked her to open my gift now."

"James has to leave in a little while." Ivy sighed. "He has an important business meeting overseas."

"Ah, well, that explains it, then." Madelyn gave him a pointed look.

Picking up on the tension between them, Ivy said, "I think I'll go show these to Sarah Witherspoon. She'll just die when she sees them."

Madelyn smiled. "And turn three shades of green."

They shared a laugh at the image.

Ivy spun back toward James. "Thank you again for the pearls. They're so incredibly beautiful. I know I'll love them forever."

"I'm glad you like them, Pumpkin. Happy birthday."

Ivy stretched up on her tippy-toes to give him a kiss on the cheek.

James leaned down to receive it.

"Come and say good-bye to me before you leave," she warned him in a soft, serious voice.

His blue eyes sparkled with affection. "Don't worry, I will."

Madelyn waited until her sister left the room before she spoke. "That was an awfully extravagant gift to give a fifteen-year-old girl."

He brushed it off. "You know I don't have a sister; I like spoiling her. Besides, the necklace wasn't all that expensive, and it makes me happy seeing her happy. So I figure it was worth every penny."

Maybe it wasn't that expensive to him, Madelyn thought. But then, James had been born to wealth, able to afford the best and most expensive of whatever the world had to offer.

"And next year when she turns sixteen," she asked. "How are you going to top it?"

"With a pair of matching earrings, of course."

She couldn't help smiling. Knowing James, he'd probably already purchased the jewels and had them safely tucked away in his wall safe at home.

He slipped his hands into his pants pockets, something he did only when he felt tense. "How have you been, Madelyn?"

"Fine. And you?"

"Not bad. Traveling a lot, working hard."

He always worked hard, she knew, often too hard.

Her mother had let it slip that he'd been pushing himself even harder over the last few months.

"And you've been healthy?" she questioned.

Last year he'd come down with a terrible bout of the flu that had left all of them worried over him for weeks.

"Yes, very healthy. I got my flu shot this year. And you?"

"Not even a sniffle."

This is terrible, she thought. They'd been friends for nearly sixteen years—best friends, and for a time much more than that—yet now they barely knew what to say to each other.

"You don't need to leave early on my account, you know," she said. "Ivy would be thrilled if you were suddenly able to take a later flight."

"Ivy has a whole contingent of friends her own age here to keep her entertained. And just what makes you think I don't need to catch a flight right away?"

"Maybe because it's Saturday and you own your own jet."

His lips curled derisively. "How do you know my meeting isn't in Papua New Guinea, over the international date line? It's Sunday there, you know."

"Do you have business holdings in Papua New Guinea?"

"No," he admitted with a guilty half laugh. "But I'll be sure I do before I see you again."

She chuckled and shook her head.

"Why haven't you called, Madelyn?"

His question sobered her instantly. She searched for

the right way to answer him. "I thought it might be best to give things time to settle, let some of the hurt mend."

"And it takes four months to do that?" he said on a bitter note. "Wounds usually heal in a few weeks; after that they have a nasty habit of turning septic."

She met his eyes, nearly as blue as her own. "I didn't know what to say and I wasn't sure if you'd want to hear from me. I'm sorry, James."

The starch came out of his indignation. He expelled a heavy sigh. "I've missed you, Meg."

"I've missed you too," she said, heartened by his use of her old nickname. Not long after they'd first met as teenagers, he'd decided she needed a moniker and had settled on Meg—the initials for Madelyn Elizabeth Grayson. "I've missed our talks. It's hard to lose your best friend."

"Isn't it, though? I can't tell you the number of times I almost picked up the phone to share something with you, to ask your advice or laugh over some ridiculous thing I'd seen or heard during the day," he confided.

"But you didn't because you're too stubborn."

"Don't talk to me about being stubborn. You could win a prize in that category."

"Are you trying to make me angry?"

"No, and I don't want to be either, not anymore. Friends?" He offered a hand.

Relieved, she took it. "Yes, friends."

For a long moment they grinned at each other like a pair of idiots.

James held on, pulling her hand against his chest. His expression turned serious. "Just one more thing, to clear the air. Obviously you weren't receptive to my proposal of marriage—"

Her eyes clouded and she tried to pull away.

He wouldn't let her. "No, let me say this. I don't entirely understand your reasons. I think we're great together. But I want you to be happy, and if you can't be happy as my wife, then I hope you will be as my friend. I want you in my life, Meg. It's as simple as that."

"James—"

"*Shh.* Let me finish. I love you, Madelyn. My feelings haven't changed, and after today, I promise I'll never speak of it again, if that's what you want. But should you ever change your mind, know that my proposal still stands. You have only to say the word."

"Don't waste your life waiting for me."

"It's my life. I'll waste it, or not, as I choose."

"And if there's someone else?"

His jaw tightened. "Is this someone else serious?"

"It is for me. I think I'm in love with him."

"Does he think he's in love with you?"

"I don't know. Probably not."

"Then that still gives me a chance. If it doesn't work out, I'll be here."

"James, you deserve better."

"There is no one better, only you." He forced a smile. "Now, why don't we talk about something else. What shall it be? Politics? No, too infuriating. The weather? Too unpredictable. How about work? What's new there? Have they had the sense to make you head of the creative department yet?"

"Not even close." Her shoulders sank in glum dejection. "In fact, I may not have a job when I go back on Monday."

"Why? What's happened?" He pulled her over to sit in one of the sun-filled window seats.

"I told a client the truth."

She went on to tell him the story of the terrible chips, her dilemma, and her ultimate decision to go against the edict of the account exec and inform her client there was a problem.

She flipped her hands over. "And after I told them, in as polite a way as I could, that the product was a disaster, I suggested they reformulate it and come back to us for the advertising when they're ready. Carmichael's people went up like an inferno. Yelling about test marketing this and lawsuit that and how they were going to pull their account and bad-mouth Fielding and Simmons to everyone in the business. It wasn't my finest Friday afternoon."

"What a bunch of idiots. They should be glad you're trying to keep them from making a huge mistake. If they go ahead with it as is, they'll be the ones with egg on their faces."

"Maybe, but that doesn't offer me much consolation in the short run. It's a major account, and if they yank it, I'll be reprimanded at best, fired at worst. I can't believe I might be fired."

He patted her hand. "You won't be fired. But even if you are, you can come to work for me. I'll give your drawing pencils and that sharp brain of yours free rein. You can advertise to your heart's content."

"Advertise what? You're an international financier. You don't exactly go around begging businesses to let you invest your money in their companies. It's kind of the other way around."

"True enough, but as an investor in a wide range of business enterprises, I am, in essence, part owner of said companies. Should I happen to suggest a brilliant and highly qualified new advertising firm, say, Grayson Designs? I'm sure they'd be enthusiastic about making a switch."

"I'm sure they would, but I wouldn't feel enthusiastic about accepting their business."

"Why not? How is what I'm proposing any different from if you quit and went out on your own, taking your F and S clients with you?"

"Because it is different and you know it. They'd be clients you procured for me, not clients I earned for myself. I'd never know if they were really happy with the product I'd be giving them or happy that they're pleasing you. Thanks, but I wouldn't feel right accepting such an offer."

"As I said earlier, you're a stubborn woman, Madelyn Grayson."

"And you, James Jordan, are an impossibly sweet man."

He snorted. "That's not what an Italian watchmaker told me last week when I cut off his credit line."

"Hey, you two, are you going to sit in here talking all afternoon? Mom's ready to bring out the cake and sent me to round up the stragglers." Brie hung in the doorway.

Madelyn tossed her a smile. "It's about time I bumped into you! Where have you been hiding?"

"Here and there. You know me, always on the go."

"Save us a spot on the couch and tell everybody we'll be there in a minute."

"Will do. And may I say, it's nice to see you guys

speaking to each other again. Now maybe the family can get back to normal." Brie snapped her fingers then pointed one of them at James. "Didn't you need to leave early? Some business trip or other?"

He and Madelyn exchanged a look.

"Oh, unexpected change of plans," he said. "I've decided to delay my departure."

Brie raised a blond brow. "Really? How convenient. Well, don't dawdle. I want my cake."

Madelyn settled back against her pillow and pulled the bedcovers high to ward off the slight chill in the room. Determined to sleep, she closed her eyes and willed herself to relax.

Falling asleep on Sunday nights was never easy for her. She was always too charged full of leftover weekend energy. But tonight was especially hard, as her mind was crowded with thoughts about the workday ahead.

The telephone rang, startling her. She picked up the receiver and listened to the dark velvet of Zack's voice wash over her, warm and soothing. "Am I calling too late?" he asked.

"No. I couldn't sleep anyway."

"Worrying about tomorrow?"

"Wouldn't you?"

"You did the right thing, Madelyn. It'll be okay."

"Will it? I'll be sure to note that on my résumé under the word 'fired' when I'm out looking for a new job next week."

"They aren't going to fire you."

"Demote me, then. I'll probably be doing layout illustrations for laxative and suppository ads. Boy, will those be fun."

"Well, somebody has to do them."

"Don't you dare laugh at me, Zachary Douglas. It isn't funny."

"You're right, it isn't, but you are. You want me to put on my trench coat and fedora and sneak over to cheer you up?"

"No, since I know your cheering-up method will guarantee I don't get any sleep tonight."

"Ah, but think how much you will have enjoyed your sleepless night."

"I am *not* going to let you tempt me," she told him firmly.

"Not even a little?"

"Not even a smidgen."

"We could talk dirty instead."

"Zack!"

"Hey, it was worth a shot. Did you enjoy your visit with your family?"

After that non sequitur, it took her a moment to regroup. "I did, very much. Birthdays are always fun."

Are they? Zack thought. *Maybe for Madelyn.*

His he remembered differently. Such as the year his mom had flown into a rage and thrown his birthday cake across the room at his dad, smashing it against the kitchen wall. And afterward how he and his little sister crouched on the floor to eat a few forkfuls from where the cake had shattered in upside-down chunks on the aged linoleum.

Or the birthday he'd turned sixteen, split a keg of beer

with a quartet of rowdy friends, and wrapped his dad's beaten-up Buick around a sixty-foot oak tree on the outskirts of town. He still had the scar just up under his hairline from the gash he'd received, along with the memory of the night he'd spent in jail.

Yeah, birthdays were always fun.

"Your sister enjoyed herself?" he asked.

"Yes. It was a wonderful party and she received so many lovely gifts."

"What was her favorite?"

The pearl necklace from James, she thought, but she couldn't tell Zack about that. Somehow she didn't think he'd be happy to hear she'd seen her ex-lover at the party. He'd be even less pleased to know she'd patched up her friendship with him and that James had asked her to marry him again.

On the other hand, maybe Zack wouldn't care, as long as he knew she would still make herself available to him for sex on an exclusive basis, for as long as it suited them both. The idea that one day it might not suit him anymore started a funny little ache in the center of her chest.

She rubbed the heel of her hand over the spot and drew a silent, calming breath. "It was the easel and set of oil paints my parents bought her. Ivy's a very talented artist."

"As are you. So will you be okay?"

His question started a fresh rush of nerves. Did he know what she'd been thinking, feeling? How could he?

"What do you mean?"

"About tomorrow and work," he said. "What else did you think I meant?"

"Oh, that. Yeah, I guess I'll have to be."

"You're going to be fine, Red. Now, quit worrying about it and get that sleep you won't let me disturb."

"I thought I told you not to call me Red."

"That's right, you did. Sleep tight, Red." He hung up the phone.

"Sleep tight, Zack," she replied to the sound of the dial tone.

She fluffed her pillow and prepared to deal with a long bout of insomnia, then, with a sigh, rolled over and fell asleep.

CHAPTER NINE

The fine hairs on the back of Madelyn's neck stood up when she received the midmorning summons.

She'd expected her supervisor, Larry Roland, to be the chosen bearer of bad tidings. She'd also expected him to put off the actual delivery of said tidings until the end of the day, since he was a master of avoiding confrontations for as long as he possibly could.

So when she received word that she was wanted in one hour, not in Larry's office, but in the executive suite on the top floor, her heart plunged straight to her stomach. It had to mean she'd been selected for a special dressing-down. Perhaps worse, she was going to be made an example of within the company before she was told to pack her things and go. Why, oh why, hadn't she just kept her big honest mouth shut?

She'd seen Zack first thing this morning in the otherwise unoccupied break room. On the pretext of reaching for the sugar, he'd squeezed her hand and whispered a few words of encouragement into her ear, then given her one of his warmest smiles, the kind that could turn an entire polar ice cap into slush, instantly.

At least it turned her to slush.

Luckily, she'd made it back to her office alone and unobserved, since her heart must surely have been shining in her eyes.

Fortunately, Zack had gone into a meeting shortly before she'd received her summons—otherwise she would have given up the game by running straight into his office to have a good cry on his shoulder.

Instead she'd headed for the ladies' room to indulge in a solitary cry inside one of the stalls.

Now, only a few minutes before the inquisition was scheduled to begin, she made a return visit to the ladies' room to freshen up her makeup one final time. She took a hard, considering look in the mirror, confronting the fear that showed in her eyes.

Graysons are not cowards.

She repeated the phrase in her head. No matter what happens, she told herself, no matter how dreadful things might seem, she would be fine. Stiffening her spine, she smoothed the skirt of her green wool dress, straightened the cuffs of her half-length jacket, and took a deep breath.

Graysons are not cowards.

It was her mantra as she rode the elevator to the top floor, and as she perched on a plush leather armchair in the executive reception area, notebook teetering on her knees.

"Ms. Grayson? Mr. Fielding will see you now." Tall, beautiful, and brunette, the executive assistant walked to a set of massive oak double doors. She opened the one on the right.

Mr. Fielding?

Lord, it was worse than Madelyn had imagined. She'd assumed she would be meeting with one of the vice presidents, not the CEO himself. The orange juice she'd drunk earlier that morning suddenly turned to lava in her stomach.

Her misery only increased when she entered the room and saw all of the men seated around a large table in the center of the room.

She recognized three of the four men present. Besides Harold Fielding, there was Stan Lindley, senior vice president and creative director for her department. He frowned through the pair of thick-lensed, wire-rimmed glasses perched on the end of his long, thin nose.

Next to him, looking as if he were in danger of being strangled by his own tie, sat her boss, Larry.

She didn't know the fourth man, but she had her suspicions. In his fifties, he was thick chested, with wavy iron gray hair and broad, hard-looking hands. His chin was as pugnacious as a mastiff's, his metallic gray eyes every bit as fierce.

Fielding rose and stepped forward. "Won't you please have a seat?"

Madelyn sat down at the table, folding her hands in her lap.

Fielding took his seat. "Ms. Grayson . . . Madelyn . . . you're probably wondering why we've asked you to join us here this morning."

Graysons are not cowards.

"Yes, sir, I am," she said.

"It's come to my attention—well, to our attention"— he signaled toward the assembled men—"that there's been a bit of a dustup concerning the latest product offering from Carmichael Foods. Your account, I believe?"

"For this one product, yes, sir, it is."

"Why only this one product?"

"Mark Stinson usually handles the art direction for Carmichael. This portion of it was recently assigned to me."

Fielding tossed a questioning look toward Stan, who in turn looked at Larry for the answer.

Larry squirmed in his chair. "Overloaded, too much work. We passed it on to Madelyn here. Didn't want Carmichael Foods getting short shrift."

"Um, yes." Fielding tapped a single finger on the polished wood-grain conference table. "Apparently there was a meeting last week between you and representatives from Carmichael?"

"There was, yes."

"And in this meeting you were supposed to outline proposed design concepts, packaging, media coverage, that sort of thing. Is that correct?"

"Yes, that's correct."

"Instead you arrived empty-handed and proceeded to tell the client that you would not be able to execute an advertising campaign for the product."

"No, sir, I told the client that although I could produce a design concept for their product, it would not be advisable for me to do so, not at this time."

Fielding scowled. "And why is that?"

Madelyn wanted badly to shift in her chair, much as

Larry had done a short while ago. She resisted the impulse, stiffening her back and lifting her chin. "Because I believe the product to be flawed."

"Flawed?"

"Yes, sir, flawed."

"On what basis?"

"On the basis of palatability."

"Palatability?"

"Yes, the um . . . the product . . . a potato chip . . . is not exactly, well, it doesn't . . ."

"Yes," he drawled.

"The product doesn't taste good."

"Really? The reports I have don't concur with that opinion. In fact, product testing shows a marked liking for the new chip. Focus group research also shows a high consumer preference for the new product when matched against the leading competitor's brand."

"I'm aware of that, sir. However, I've personally tried the product, as have trusted members of my team, and I can't agree. Not to offend anyone, but frankly, it's inedible. Which is the reason I felt it necessary to urge Carmichael to rethink their decision to put it on the market. Proceeding at this point would be a huge waste of resources, time, and money, for both of our firms. In my opinion, until the product is redesigned, any ad campaign, no matter how brilliant, would be doomed to failure."

"In your opinion. And is your opinion always so accurate?"

"Not always, sir, but in this case it is."

"Oh, so all the reports, the other people who've promoted this product, even the consumers, they are all wrong and you're right? Is that the way of it, Ms. Grayson?"

"I wouldn't put it quite like that. . . ."

"Wouldn't you?" he barked. "Are you wrong or are you right?"

Realizing they'd obviously decided to hang her, Madelyn decided she might as well keep her pride and step off the gallows herself. "I am right."

A look of satisfaction, even admiration, sparkled in Harold Fielding's eyes as he leaned back in his chair. He steepled his fingers, his words quiet. "Yes, Ms. Grayson, you are."

Her mouth dropped open. "Excuse me?"

"We know all about it and we have you to thank. I apologize for not introducing you earlier and for putting you through such an intense line of questioning, but, well, Patrick and I had our reasons." He gestured toward the gray-haired stranger who'd been stoically silent up to now. "Madelyn, this is Patrick Carmichael, owner and president of Carmichael Foods."

Madelyn nodded, not entirely certain what was going on. "Mr. Carmichael."

Carmichael nodded in return, a small smile lightening the severe angles of his face.

Fielding continued. "Patrick here heard about your meeting and the ensuing fireworks. He decided to do some investigating of his own. Well, perhaps I should let him explain the rest."

"Thank you, Harry," Carmichael continued. "Ms. Grayson, it's a great pleasure to meet you. It's not often I encounter someone with your sort of honesty and integrity. Refreshing these days, especially in light of recent events. When I heard about your refusal to proceed with the advertising design, I was astonished, and then perplexed.

Why would a woman in your position do such a thing? You must be either a lunatic determined to ruin your own career . . . or a person who believes she's right."

Carmichael drew a breath, then continued. "I'd let my lieutenants handle this product. Usually I keep my fingers in all the new pies, if you know what I mean, but in the last couple years I've been cutting back, taking more time for myself and my family. Wife's been complaining I spend too much time at the office."

He circled a hand in the air. "Anyway, I decided to look into the matter and actually taste the product myself. It wasn't easy to get hold of an actual sample, but once I did . . . Well, let me say that your description of it is kind. Those chips are crap. I've never tasted anything so awful in all my days. And to think we were about to unleash them on the American public. It took a little more digging, but it led me to uncover a deception that's been taking place in my own company."

Her eyebrows rose. "A deception?"

"Yes, I am sad to say, a cover-up perpetrated by several key people in my organization. I won't go into exact amounts, but suffice it to say a significant portion of the R and D budget was spent on the development of this product. When it became clear the formulation was less than the unqualified success hoped for, a decision was made, without my knowledge, to launch the product anyway. Steps were taken to falsify documentation, testing, and so forth."

He leaned forward, smiling. "If it weren't for you and your integrity, Madelyn, my company would have wasted millions of additional dollars on a product that was a guaranteed disaster. There's going to be a big shake-up at Carmichael Foods, I'll tell you that. Several upper-level executive positions will be opening up soon, I guarantee. If you'd like one of them, just say the word. We could use more people like you."

Before she could respond, Fielding interrupted.

"Oh no! You're not stealing her away from us, Pat Carmichael. We can't have our best and brightest employees jumping over to your side of the game. Besides, she'd be bored inside of two months. A brilliant creative mind such as hers trapped inside a world of snack cakes and cheese zoodles. No, the best we can do is let her take charge of all your advertising. What do you say, Madelyn? Think you can stand to take on Carmichael here?"

Stunned and elated, she said, "Yes, sir, of course, I'd be delighted to. But what about Mark Stinson? He—"

"Stinson's busy; Larry said so. This will help reduce his burden," he finished meaningfully.

Madelyn hoped she hadn't just made a lifelong enemy of Stinson, but she didn't have time to worry about it now.

Fielding continued. "And not to let you think hard work only gets you more hard work—which of course it does—you'll find a nice bonus in your next paycheck. Stan? Larry? You'll see to it."

In unison, perched next to each other like a pair of myna birds, they squawked, "Yes, sir."

Fielding glanced at his watch, then rose from his chair.

"Gentlemen. Madelyn. It's lunchtime and I'm famished. What do you say we continue this over a meal?" He turned to her with a warm smile. "I have a very tolerable chef. French. Other than an occasional heavy sauce, Jacques's dishes are quite delightful. Pat, you can stay, can't you?"

"If Jacques made chocolate éclairs like the last time, I can."

Fielding laughed. "I'm sure he has something to tempt even your discriminating palate." He turned to await Madelyn's answer.

"Lunch sounds wonderful," she said.

She fought the urge to pinch herself, just to see if she was dreaming. Not only had she *not* lost her job; she was slated to receive a bonus, an important new account, and to top it all off, an invitation to enter the career-affirming inner sanctum of the executive dining room.

In her imagination, she did a jig worthy of a *Riverdance* troupe and let out an earsplitting whoop. She couldn't wait to tell Zack; she wished she could hurry back to their floor now and share her fantastic news.

Instead, she reined in her excitement and joined the men as they all walked sedately down the hallway.

Fielding drew her slightly aside. "Madelyn, there's one other matter, and if I'm stacking your plate too high, just let me know. We've got a new luxury auto deal coming in—full-spread television and print ads with a major budget. Normally I'd be letting Zack Douglas steer that particular ship. He's a good man, Zack, don't get me wrong, and I still maintain every confidence in him. He's no suck-up and I can always trust him not to put on a dog and pony show with me. He's got spine and integrity, same as you. However, I'd like you to take on this car deal."

She blinked, not sure she'd heard him right.

Then Fielding continued. "I'm interested in seeing

how you run with a new ball, and whether this one will suit your interests. We need more women on the automotive side of the playing field. It's much too male dominated, and you just might be the perfect match. What do you say?"

What do I say? What other answer is there but yes?

Still, as great as this new opportunity undoubtedly was, she found herself hesitating. The news wasn't going to sit well with Zack. Not only would he be angry, but there was a very real possibility he might feel betrayed. The last thing she wanted to do was hurt him. She loved Zack. But she'd be a fool to turn down this chance; she'd worked too long and too hard to let sentiment stand in her way. Hadn't she? If the situation were reversed and Zack were in her shoes, she knew what his answer would be. Surely he would understand. After all, wasn't he the one who always said that business was business?

Madelyn hesitated only a moment longer, then stuck out her hand to shake Fielding's. "What I say is yes."

"*Oh-my-God, oh-my-God, oh-my-God*, is it true?" Peg skidded into Madelyn's office so fast it was a wonder she didn't gouge permanent grooves into the carpet with her heels.

"Is what true?" Madelyn leaned back in her chair, amazed how fast news traveled. She hadn't been back in her office more than five minutes, tops.

"You know what, and don't toy with me. This is Peg knows-all-and-sees-all Truman you're talking to, remember? Did you, or did you not, just have lunch upstairs in the executive dining room?"

Madelyn couldn't contain her grin. "I did." She swept

a clean protective tissue off the top of a dessert-laden paper plate on the corner of her desk. "Napoleon, cream puff, or baba au rhum? I took what I could, but any more would have been gauche."

"*Ooh*, the rum one definitely." Peg reached out, picked it up, and took a bite. "My God," she sighed. "It tastes just like sin. Yum-yum." She licked syrup off her lips, eyeing the plate. "Would you mind if I took one of the napoleons for Todd?"

"Todd March? Since when do you bring dessert to Todd March?" Since when did Peg even know he existed? Madelyn wanted to know.

Peg flushed slightly. "I lost a bet. I'm hoping this will square us."

"What kind of bet?"

"The kind I'd rather not talk about."

"Oh, you'll talk," Madelyn promised. "But I'll wait and torture the details out of you later." She motioned a hand toward the pastries. "Go ahead. Knock yourself out."

Peg placed the confection on a paper napkin. "Thanks. Speaking of details, let's hear the dish on *you*. When you went up there this morning, you were all but ready to ask for your last rites."

"I know." Madelyn leaned forward and told her everything that had happened.

"That's incredible," Peg said once Madelyn finished. "All because of a rank chip. Who'd have thought? And boy, is Zack Douglas going to be steamed when he hears about Giatta Motors. I'm surprised we haven't heard the explosion down the hall already."

Determined to keep Peg from knowing absolutely

everything that went on in the office, and out of it as well, Madelyn planted a smug little smile on her lips. "You know what they say: payback's a bitch."

"Yeah, and that's exactly what he's gonna think you are—a bitch. Giatta's his baby, besides being his favorite account. Those ads always feature a herd of sexy long-legged Italian models, and as all of us know, Zack's not above fraternizing with the help. The last time they shot ad footage here, I heard he did the town, plus a whole lot more, with a pair of very well-endowed twins."

"Somehow he'll have to learn to live with the loss."

Madelyn fought off the irrational spark of jealousy that burned through her, channeling the emotion into a mask of disdain. "New car, new campaign, and I'm in charge. The Italian models may just have to go, or may have to change gender. Nothing wrong with sexy male models, now, is there?"

Peg's eyes lit up at the idea. "Still, I'd watch my back."

Madelyn caught the movement of a very familiar shape out of the corner of her eye. "I don't think it's my back I'm going to have to watch," she murmured to herself.

Zack loomed large in her doorway. One look at his face showed her he was in a serious temper. Uninvited, he walked into her office. "How's it going, Peg?" he asked, teeth clenched.

Madelyn couldn't recall ever having seen him talk through his teeth before.

Peg swiveled around in her seat. "Great. How about you?"

"Wonderful. Now, if you wouldn't mind, Madelyn and I have some business to discuss."

"Oh, I don't mind. You two go right ahead." She settled back in her chair, obviously prepared to enjoy the show.

Zack pinned her with a dangerous look.

"On second thought," she amended hastily, "I really should be returning to my cube. So much to do, so little time."

Madelyn stood, glad that the desk was between her and Zack. "You don't have to leave, Peg. I'm sure we all have a pretty good idea why Mr. Douglas has so rudely barged into my office. He can say whatever it is he has to say in front of us both."

"What I have to say might shock Peg, and I wouldn't want to offend her. She should leave."

He was really angry, Madelyn realized, even more so than she'd expected.

Madelyn lifted her chin. "She's staying."

Zack had had enough. "Fine. You want an audience? Why don't we invite the entire office?"

"The way you're carrying on, they're already starting to gather. I've seen three people conveniently drift by already."

"You're the one who started this." He took three giant steps forward. "What in the hell do you think you're doing stealing one of my accounts?"

He banged his fist against her desk. Pens and paper bounced, a cream puff jumping up and down on its plate.

"I did *not* steal it," she said, hurt and not a little offended. "It was given to me."

"Like hell it was," Zack bellowed.

"Like hell it wasn't," she shouted back. "Fielding gave it to me himself."

"You know, I really should be going," Peg whispered.

"I'll just take Todd's dessert." She ducked under the line of fire to get the pastry, gathering up the abused cream puff while she was at it. Quietly she slipped out the door.

Zack moved to slam it shut behind her, taking a second before he did to glare at a cluster of onlookers loitering in the hallway. Seeing his expression, they scattered like geese.

"Now that the cavalry has abandoned you," he said, facing her again, "we're going to have this out."

"No, we are not. Not here, not after the scene you've started."

"*I* started?"

"Yes, *you*. Charging in here like a bull after a red cape. Why, they're probably lined up ten deep out there to listen to every word we say."

"And your buddy Peg is probably in the lead."

"Yes, she probably is."

They glared at each other for a long, tense moment.

Madelyn lowered her voice to a bare whisper. "I am not going to discuss this with you right now."

Zack approached, planting his palms flat on her desk. "Yes, you are," he growled. "How in the hell did you do it anyway? That's what I want to know. You go upstairs with your head on the chopping block and come back wearing a crown. That's an awfully neat trick, Madelyn. You'll have to teach it to me sometime."

"It's a long story, but apparently my actions uncovered some graft going on at Carmichael Foods and they decided to reward me."

"By giving you *my* best account!"

"They gave me the Carmichael account too. And you

aren't completely out of Giatta Motors. I'll only be working on their brand-new sports line."

"Yes, I know. Harry Fielding called me himself to give me the good news."

"Well, that's more than I ever got. It's about time the tables were turned. Gives you a taste of exactly how it feels to have all your hard work snatched out from under you and handed to someone else. You've done it to me since the day you arrived."

"I have not. At least not intentionally."

"This wasn't intentional either."

"You could have turned it down."

"This is an opportunity that could make or break my entire career. If you were me, would you have turned it down?"

Their eyes locked. They both knew the answer.

Madelyn laid her hand over his. "Your pride is wounded right now. Believe me, I know how that feels and I'm not even male. Somehow, though, you'll find a way to heal."

A glint of grudging humor slipped into his eyes. "Is that right? Well, since this is your fault, what are you going to do as recompense to ease my pain?"

"I may be able to think of something. Actually, though, if one of us is to blame, it's you."

"Me?"

"You're the one who told me to follow my own instincts, to do the right thing. See what my honesty got you?"

"Next time remind me to be a bad influence on you."

"Now, unless we want to give everyone congregated outside that door the idea that we don't hate each other nearly as much as they think we do, we'd better break this up."

"We'll continue it later, in private," he murmured. "I'll stop by tonight."

"You shouldn't. I'm letting you stop by far too often these days."

He reached out to trace his thumb over the delicate crest of her cheekbone.

Her lashes fluttered; her lips parted.

"But you'll let me in anyway, won't you?"

They both knew her answer.

He took a step back, then raised his voice. "Oh, yeah?"

He winked at her.

"Yeah!" she yelled, stomping across the room to fling open the door.

In the corridor, heads ducked and bodies scurried with the speed of kitchen cockroaches fleeing a midnight light.

"Now, get out of my office!" she ordered.

"With pleasure." Zack stalked away.

Madelyn slammed her door. With a little smile playing on her lips, she went back to work.

In bed, Madelyn sat up, sheets pooling around her waist, her arms folded over her up-drawn knees. "Are you still mad?" she murmured.

Lying next to her, Zack slid a hand along the satiny length of her bare back, his fingers tracing the small bones that formed her spine. "About what?"

She dropped her cheek onto her forearm and slanted a look back at him. "About work. About your account."

His hand slowed for a long moment, lying warm against her skin. Then he resumed his stroking. "No. Not much anyway. And not at you, not anymore."

He leaned forward and pressed his lips to the sensitive flesh at the very base of her spine. "Besides, how could I be angry when you put such a spectacular effort into making it up to me?" He snaked an arm around her waist to hold her still for another kiss, this time on the fleshy curve of her bottom.

She squirmed and laughed, twisting away from him. "I'll have to remember that, to use as strategy the next time they give me one of your accounts."

"There isn't going to be a next time." He lunged across the bed and wrestled her beneath him.

"Don't be too sure," she teased. "Besides, you're just annoyed about Giatta because you won't have a chance to cast a whole new bevy of big-breasted Italian models."

Surprised by her remark, he lifted an eyebrow. "You know perfectly well I don't do the casting. I only get to enjoy the big-breasted results."

She cuffed him on the shoulder. "It's a good thing I'm doing this ad campaign, then, so you won't have any new results to enjoy."

He rolled them over so she lay atop him. "And why would I want to, when I can have a fiery, redheaded American beauty like you in my bed?"

"Even a small-breasted one who takes your best accounts?"

"Yeah, even one like that. And you're not small." He cupped her breasts in his hands, letting their soft weight settle against his palms. "See? Just right."

She met his shining green gaze, her heart skipping a beat.

Just right. The words repeated themselves in her head. *That's what he is for me. Just right.*

Fearing he might see more than she wanted to reveal, she buried her face in his neck.

He wrapped his arms around her. They lay quietly for a time.

Recovered, Madelyn leaned up. "So we're definitely square, right?"

"Definitely. I may even give you a few helpful hints every now and then if you'd like."

"I'd like." She brushed a strand of hair off his forehead.

Serious, Zack said, "You know they're pitting us against each other. We're both in line for the same promotions all the way up the ladder."

"I know." She sighed. "We always have been. Or didn't you think I was real competition before?"

"Oh, I've always known enough to recognize you as the enemy. And you know what they say about enemies?"

"No, what do they say?"

"That you should keep them close, even closer than you keep your friends." He locked their mouths together for a scorching kiss, his hands roaming everywhere.

And when he had her trembling on the brink, he fit them together close, as close as two people could possibly be.

CHAPTER TEN

Madelyn propped the heavy bag of groceries she carried against her left hip and struggled to fit her front-door key in the lock.

Her neighbor's door down the hall opened a crack, a gray-haired head peeking out. "You're home. I thought I heard you."

Madelyn glanced up. "Oh, hi, Mrs. Strickland. How are you this evening?"

The old woman, sparrow thin in a peach cable-knit wool sweater, bold persimmon sweatpants, and yellow Keds, took a measured step out into the hallway. Gay colors, as she called them, colors that cheered her spirit even on the days she'd rather forget it all and just stay in bed.

"Oh, my knee's paining me some," Betsy Strickland said. "But then it usually does come spring, especially when it's due to rain anytime like it is today. Otherwise I can't complain. I keep busy with my knitting and my

TV programs. I'm addicted to that cable cooking channel; keeps me hungry half the day. Then there are my books. I just started a very juicy romance novel." She flashed a naughty grin.

Madelyn shifted the groceries to her other hip. "If it stays good, you'll have to let me borrow it."

"Well, sure I will, but with that new young man of yours coming and going at all hours I don't suppose you have much time for reading these days. And so handsome, why, he could be a hero from one of my stories."

Madelyn frowned. "You've seen Zack?"

"And spoken to him a time or two. Such a charming devil. He brought me cheesecake from that heavenly shop over on Ninety-third last week just because I happened to mention how partial I am to the stuff. Nearly made myself sick on it, I ate so much. But it was worth every bit of the misery."

Zack and Mrs. Strickland had been having discussions? He'd been plying her with cheesecake? "He didn't tell me you two had met."

"Didn't he? Well, it must have slipped his mind. He explained how you two want to keep things quiet for now. I know the way it is when you're first in love. All you want to do is be alone together and shut the rest of the world right out." Mrs. Strickland placed a finger across her lips. "Rest assured, no one will hear so much as boo from me until you say otherwise."

For a moment, Madelyn's tongue felt limp. She cleared her throat. "Yes, well, thanks, Mrs. Strickland. We appreciate your discretion."

"Think nothing of it. You're a sweet girl, Madelyn. I'm glad to see you happy."

Was she happy? Madelyn mused. She supposed she was, come to think of it. A warm glow spread through her veins, her lips softening into a smile.

"Will I be watching Millie for you again this weekend?"

"Yes, if you're sure you don't mind. I hate to be an imposition."

"It's no imposition. That cat's the best kind of company. Friendly, affectionate, and she doesn't talk back. Well, not too often anyway; only if I'm late with the cat food," she amended. "Oh, I almost forgot—"

Madelyn's front door opened from the inside with a smooth click of the lock.

"Your sister's here. Hello again, Brie."

Brie peered down the hall. "Hi, Mrs. S. I heard voices and finally decided to investigate. Thanks again for taking pity on me earlier and letting me in."

"Glad to, dearie. Good thing I had that spare key Madelyn loaned me. Now, you girls have a good visit." She glanced at the time on her watch. "I've got to get inside. They're making Chateaubriand today and it's the closest I'll be getting to any." She waved and went into her apartment.

Madelyn turned toward her sister. The bag of groceries she kept wrestling with got in the way of a proper hug. She did her best to compensate and pressed cheeks with Brie. "Hey, what are you doing here? Why didn't you call? If I'd known you were coming, I'd have met you at the station."

"It was a spur-of-the-moment impulse," Brie said. "Here, let me take those." She hoisted the weighty grocery sack into her arms and turned toward the kitchen.

Madelyn raised an eyebrow but remained silent, grateful

to have been relieved of her burden. *Something is up,* she thought. Brie never did anything on impulse, especially on a Thursday during a regular workweek. Quietly, she closed and locked the door, set her purse on the sofa, and trailed into the kitchen.

Busy unloading groceries, Brie had the sleeves of her gray Washington Wizards sweatshirt pushed to her elbows, her short blond curls held away from her narrow high-boned face by a slender pink hair band.

Brie set a loaf of bread and carton of strawberries on the counter. "It's a good thing you went to the market. Your cupboards are practically bare and your refrigerator's a disgrace. Half a quart of milk, one raspberry yogurt, and a single leftover pork chop."

"Yes, Mother. That's why I went shopping."

Brie made a face and laid a pound of raw shrimp, wrapped in butcher's paper, on the counter. "I ate the pork chop, by the way, and drank the last of that bottle of wine you had sitting around."

"My cooking wine. There won't be any for the scampi now." Madelyn crossed to her sister's side and reached into the sack, lifting out a box of dry pasta and two cans of organic whole tomatoes. "That's what I was planning to cook for dinner, unless you'd rather go out."

"No, scampi sounds good even without the wine."

"Good thing I always buy extra shrimp to freeze, or we'd be eating light tonight," Madelyn said. "So, when did you get here?"

"This afternoon. Around three."

"Then you really should have called me instead of waiting around half the day." It was now well past seven o'clock. "I'd have left work early."

"Exactly the reason I didn't. I knew you'd feel compelled to rearrange your entire afternoon because of me. I figured springing myself on you without a word was enough of an imposition."

Madelyn shot her a stern look. "You're never an imposition."

"You didn't say that the time Mom made you take me to the movies and I ruined your plan to meet Stephanie and Jill so you three could sneak over to Craig Tidewater's senior siesta party."

"That's because you were a thirteen-year-old pest who squealed louder than a Nazi informant."

"Only because you refused to take me with you."

"You didn't have any business going to a party with all those upperclassmen."

"Neither did an innocent little underaged sophomore like you."

"*Hmmph.* Well, that's all water under the bridge now, even if I still haven't completely forgiven you."

They exchanged mock sisterly glares, then broke into grins.

Brie continued to unpack the groceries, pulling a small white bag of high-end coffee beans out of the sack. She perused the small gold label. "Since when do you drink Jamaican Blue Mountain? I thought you liked tea at home."

The beans were for Zack. He enjoyed a cup in the evenings or for breakfast when he stayed over, and Madelyn didn't mind paying a little more for the good stuff. "I do. The coffee is for . . . um . . . friends."

Not a total lie, she assured herself. Zack qualified as a friend these days, didn't he? And their relationship was supposed to be a secret, although she guessed telling Brie wouldn't do any irreparable harm. She wasn't eager to discuss him, though. She trusted Brie; that wasn't the issue. Pride was.

With her sharply honed lawyer's memory, Brie was sure to dig Zack's name out of her mental Rolodex. Once she did, every nasty remark Madelyn had ever made about him would come flooding back; that's when Brie's fun would begin. Serious as she could be, Brie was also a merciless tease when the mood suited her. And there was no doubt the mood would suit once Madelyn confessed she was embroiled in a red-hot love affair with a man she'd once referred to as Lucifer's spawn.

"Lucky friends," Brie murmured about the coffee. "You won't mind if I indulge in a cup later on?"

"Hey, it's your sleepless night."

Casually, Madelyn emptied the last few items from the brown paper bag. Folding it into thirds, she tucked it away with a stack of other paper sacks stored in a rack next to the refrigerator.

Brie waved a hand toward a pair of bakery bags filled with cookies and a bottle of extra-virgin olive oil. "Tell me where these go and I'll put them away for you."

"Cookies in the cupboard, there." Madelyn pointed a finger. "Just leave the oil out. I'll use it to cook dinner." She turned to wash her hands at the sink. "Let me change out of these work clothes; then we'll talk."

Brie's expression sobered. "Yeah, all right."

After Madelyn walked from the room, Brie placed the strawberries and a wedge of cheese into the refrigerator. A short search through the cupboards unearthed a stainless steel colander. She'd set it in the sink and prepared to clean the shrimp; then the buzzer rang.

Someone was downstairs.

"Madelyn!" she called, moving into the living area. She heard the sound of water flowing through the pipes and caught a glimpse of the closed bathroom door on the opposite side of her sister's bedroom.

Millie lounged in a sprawl of gray-and-white splendor across the lilac-colored quilt on the queen-size bed.

The buzzer rang again.

Brie moved toward the front door, pressed a button on the wall. "Yes?"

"Hi, it's me. Let me up."

It was a man's voice, low, provocative, and obviously well acquainted with whomever he thought he was talking to. Maybe he had the wrong apartment.

"Who's this?"

He hesitated. "Madelyn?"

"No. It's Brie, her sister."

Silence.

Curious reaction.

Who do we have here? Brie wondered, intrigued. *Does Madelyn have a man she hasn't told anyone about?*

Unaware of the drama, Madelyn strolled from her bedroom dressed in an ancient pair of blue jeans and a well-washed sweatshirt, long since faded to dusty plum. She saw the look in Brie's expressive aqua eyes, the small quirk curving her lips.

She stopped. "What?"

"You have a visitor. Downstairs."

"Who?"

"He didn't say." Brie stepped away from the intercom. "Great voice, though. Very sexy."

Oh, hell, Madelyn thought as she moved to take her sister's place. Why did Zack have to pick tonight to drop by? They usually spent Thursday apart, to catch a full night's rest before the weekend. She pressed the button. "Hello?"

"Red? Is that you?"

"Red?" Brie mouthed, her eyes dancing.

Madelyn turned, leaned against the wall as if that might make her conversation more private. "Yes, it's me," she said in a low voice. "I wasn't expecting you tonight. My sister's here, visiting."

"So I heard. I didn't know you were planning on company."

"I didn't either. This evening's been one surprise after another."

He paused. "Perhaps I should go."

Yes, perhaps he should. But what was the point now? As far as Brie was concerned, the cat was not only out of the bag; it was sitting on the front stoop, flicking its tail, and meowing to come in. She might as well give in gracefully and open the door.

But Brie didn't give her the chance to decide one way or the other as she moved forward and mashed her finger against the door release. It buzzed like a hive of angry bees.

"What'd you do that for?" Madelyn demanded.

"I couldn't let you send him away. I've got to meet this mystery man. Why haven't you told any of us about him? What's the matter? Is he ugly?"

"No, he isn't ugly."

"Fat, then?"

"No, he's not fat either."

Brie's sense of humor revved into high gear. "A cross-dresser? An excommunicated priest? A dangerous felon on the run?"

Madelyn crossed her arms, shook her head in exasperation. "No. No. And no!"

Brie's playfulness faded. "He isn't married, is he?"

"No, of course he's not married. Why would you even think such a thing?"

Brie shrugged. "If he's gorgeous and single, then how come you're hiding him?"

A fist rapped twice on the other side of the door.

"Because he's Zack Douglas."

Madelyn left Brie to puzzle out the name and went to let him in.

Dressed all in black, Zack could have passed for the felon Brie had mentioned, a handsome thief on the run, the sort that populated major motion pictures and graced fashionable magazine covers. He was a man of dangerous magnetism and power. Was that why she'd fallen so easily? Taken to the low habit of lying? Even to her sister.

He walked in, a few drops of rain clinging to his leather jacket. Without thinking, Madelyn reached up and brushed them away from his shoulders in a gesture of telling intimacy.

He smiled and leaned close to whisper in her ear. "Sorry about this."

She met his look. "It's okay. I didn't realize it had started to rain."

He slipped out of his jacket and hung it on the coat rack. "Just a drizzle." He turned to greet her sister.

"You must be Brie," he said. "I feel like we've already met. I'm Zack." He held out his hand and gave her a friendly glimpse of his straight white teeth.

Brie wasn't any more immune to Zack than any other woman, Madelyn noticed, watching the way her sister had to shake herself clear of his spell after a lengthy pause.

A light of recognition flashed to life in Brie's eyes. "Lucifer's spawn, I presume." She accepted his hand for a quick shake.

This time, he was the one who looked like he needed a moment to recover. He gazed at Madelyn, then back to Brie. "I haven't heard that one before. I'll have to add it to my collection."

"The family was a bit surprised when Madelyn chose art over writing," Brie commented. "She's got a tongue that can shave steel."

"She is gifted with language, I agree," he said.

Madelyn sighed. "You two stay here and continue your insults in private. I'm going to make dinner." She stalked off to the kitchen.

"So what's on the menu?" Zack inquired.

"Shrimp scampi over fettuccini. Have you eaten?" Brie asked.

"No, and I'm starved."

"Then we'd better get in there and help. Otherwise she's liable to botch the meal just to spite us."

But they needn't have worried. Madelyn relaxed as she cooked, listening to the two of them tease and bicker like a pair of kids trying to one-up each other. They were arguing sports by the time she set the meal on the table.

Brie's sweatshirt had sparked a basketball debate. Town loyal, Zack favored the Knicks and was doing a fine job talking trash about the Wizards. He tossed in some choice put-downs for the Celtics too, who were Brie's old home team, adopted after she'd moved to Cambridge, Massachusetts, for college and law school. Then it had been on to Manhattan until six months ago, when she'd taken a new job in Washington, D.C.

"They're doing fine this season," Brie defended.

Zack scoffed. "If you call four straight losses fine." He shifted his chair forward, careful not to dislodge Millie, who'd sought him out earlier and curled into his lap to sleep. The cat opened her eyes, tensed, then settled again after Zack rewarded her with a few reassuring strokes.

"There've been some injuries, and that's slowed them down," Brie continued.

Zack pointed a fork across the table. "What's slowed them down is they can't play for shit—"

"Now, now, children," Madelyn interrupted. "Time to eat. If you keep this up, I'm the only one who'll be having any dessert."

They both fell silent.

Zack spoke first. "Is she always like this?"

"Sometimes she's worse," Brie told him.

They let Madelyn steer the conversation onto a few less contentious topics, ones in which she took some actual interest, and the meal progressed pleasantly.

They were nearly finished when Brie set down her

fork, leaned back in her chair, and took a bead on Zack. "So how long have you been doing my sister?"

Madelyn's eyes rounded. "Brie, my God."

Zack stopped chewing, met the marble-hard expression in Brie's eyes. He swallowed, then calmly wiped his mouth on his napkin. "I've been seeing your sister since the New Year."

"Strange she hasn't mentioned you to the family."

"Mentioning me or not is Madelyn's choice."

"Then you aren't coercing her in some way? She never used to have anything good to say about you."

It was Zack's turn to relax into his chair. "We've been business rivals. We still are. But business isn't personal, and what I have with her is personal. Very personal. As for your other question, Madelyn's a strong-willed woman, independent, resourceful. I don't believe I could coerce her into doing anything she didn't want to do."

"No, but even strong-willed, independent, resourceful women can be manipulated now and then by the right individual. Anyone can be used given a certain set of circumstances."

The legs of Madelyn chair screeched as she pushed away from the table. "End the cross-examination, counselor. I'm involved with Zack because I want to be. No one's being used."

"Then why the secrecy?" Brie persisted, eyeballing Zack.

He opened his mouth to answer.

Madelyn responded first. "Because that's the way we want it." She tapped a finger to her chest. "The way *I* want it. Zack and I work for the same company, in the same department, and we've agreed it's best, particularly for me, if our relationship is kept quiet. He's been considerate enough to respect my wishes on this count. I hope you will be as well."

"Of course, Malynn," Brie said, using the family nickname. "If that's how you wish it."

"It is."

"I only want to see you happy."

Madelyn softened. "I know, and I love you for it." After a pause, she motioned toward Brie's dinner plate. "You done with that?"

"Um, yes. It was wonderful."

Madelyn took her sister's plate, stacked it on top of her own. She turned her head to the left. "Zack?"

He twined up a last forkful of shrimp and pasta and popped it into his mouth. Chewing, he set his empty plate onto the stack, then reached out for Madelyn's wrist before she could turn away. Food swallowed, he drew her toward him for a quick kiss, ignoring her reluctance in front of company. "Delicious," he murmured, smiling as he released her.

Pink cheeked, Madelyn gathered the dishes and headed toward the sink.

For a long, silent moment, Zack and Brie assessed each other across the table.

"You seem like a straight-up guy despite things I've heard," she told him in a voice meant for his ears only. "Nothing against you. I just don't want her hurt."

"I don't either. It's never been my intention to hurt Madelyn."

Brie studied him another minute, then nodded. The tension between them dissipated.

From across the room, Madelyn turned, her back to

the counter. "I put coffee on for you two caffeine fiends."
She lifted a pair of thin white bakery sacks into the air,
one in each hand. "Cookies are for dessert. Your choice—
chocolate chip or white chocolate macadamia nut."

An hour later, Zack said his good-byes. Madelyn
didn't feel comfortable letting him stay over, not since
Brie would be sleeping only a door away, tucked in for
the night on the sofa bed. Without discussion, Zack understood Madelyn's wishes and went to retrieve his coat.

To give them a moment's privacy, Brie slipped into
the bedroom and closed the door behind her.

"Sorry about this weekend," Madelyn said, joining
him at the front door. "You could come by tomorrow or
Saturday. I'll make dinner again."

"You make great dinners, but family comes first. You
need to spend the time with your sister. She didn't come
all the way up here to see me."

She rubbed a palm over the supple leather of his
jacket. "Sorry about the grilling. Brie's not one to hold
back, even if it means being rude."

He wrapped his arms around her. "I've faced tougher.
And I can understand her concern. I've got a sister. If
she brought a guy like me home, I'd be rude and overly
protective too."

She smiled at the notion.

Their eyes met, lingered, a caress of blue to green.

She laid her palm against his cheek, traced the smooth
skin she found there; he'd shaved his usual evening beard
off especially for her. "Maybe you could come by on
Sunday," she invited. "After Brie heads home."

His eyelids drooped heavy, his gaze lambent. "Maybe
I could at that." He tightened his hold, hard enough to

flatten her breasts to his chest. "I'll need a kiss though, a thorough one, to tide me over."

She looped her arms up around his neck. "Then come down here and take it."

Late Saturday evening, Madelyn and Brie returned to Madelyn's apartment, exhausted, footsore, but satisfied, a pair of valiant warriors returning home, booty-laden after a day of glorious battle. At its most intense, Madelyn considered shopping to be an act of war, and today the Grayson sisters had taken no prisoners.

Brie flopped onto the sofa, nearly disappearing beneath the rows of bulging shopping bags draped over her arms.

Madelyn dumped her load of packages just inside the front door, then staggered over to collapse beside her sister. "Lord, I'm beat." She kicked off her shoes and thought if she listened closely enough, she could hear the sound her toes made as they sighed in relief.

Heads back, the women luxuriated in a downy haven of plump sofa cushions and feather pillows.

"We must have walked fifty blocks," Brie exclaimed.

"More like a hundred."

"And I think we visited every store in the city."

"Half of them at least."

"Found some great stuff, though."

"And some splendid bargains." Madelyn closed her eyes. "All in all an excellent day."

"Hmm." Paper rattled as Brie set an armful of shopping bags on the floor. "Where's the raspberry tart?"

"Who knows? Probably squished under that lamp you bought."

"Oh, I hope not."

Madelyn tossed her a quizzical look. "How on earth are you going to lug that thing home anyway?"

"What? The tart?"

"No, the lamp."

Brie shrugged. "I'll figure something out. I always do."

She was right, Madelyn thought. An organizational wizard, Brie had a way of working out solutions, even for seemingly impossible tasks. Still, that didn't mean she was infallible, especially when emotions were involved. Something was troubling her. It was the third day of her visit, yet the only reason she'd given so far for her unexpected trip north was the need to see a familiar face. New to Washington, D.C., Brie was still making friends, she said. Perhaps loneliness was the only explanation necessary. Then again, perhaps it wasn't.

"Do you honestly have room for sweets?" Madelyn laid a hand across her stomach. "I'm still recovering from dinner."

"Chinese never sticks no matter how much of it you eat. An hour from now, you'll be starving again. We'll split a slice." She surveyed the sea of shopping bags. "Assuming I can find it."

"All right. But make my piece small."

Madelyn got up and went to the kitchen to put the kettle on to boil. Millie wandered in, brushing her tail against the backs of Madelyn's legs before assuming a sphinxlike pose on the multihued rag rug at the base of the sink. A quiet cat, Millie had ways of making her wishes known with a minimum of fuss. She looked up at Madelyn, meowed silently, then resumed her wait. Madelyn knew the routine; Millie wanted to eat.

Brie strolled in with a white bakery box.

Madelyn crossed to a quiet corner on the far side of the room, set down the bowl of fresh cat food. Millie padded over to enjoy the offering.

Wisps of steam began to curl from the kettle. "Is tea all right?" Madelyn asked.

"So long as it isn't herbal." Brie rinsed her hands, then got out plates and a knife to cut the tart.

Madelyn measured loose tea leaves into a celery green ceramic pot. "You haven't really said all that much about your new job. Are you glad you took it?"

Brie paused, considered. "At first I wasn't sure. Lawyering for the government's a lot different from private practice. But now that I've settled in, yes, I do like it. I'm working on a really compelling fraud case. When it's over I'll give you the highlights. Lord knows, I don't miss staying up until four in the morning writing briefs or scrambling for every billable hour I can find. And it's nice to have more than Christmas day at home."

"Still, you seemed to love it at Mitchell, Brown, and Lovell. From all appearances you were on the fast track to making partner. You never would tell any of us in the family why you left the city so suddenly."

Brie went still, the knife poised over the delicate confection. A second later, she made her cut, careful and precise. "It was time to move on."

Madelyn snapped off the range burner and lifted the wailing kettle, a thick plume of steam billowing forth. She poured boiling water over the tea leaves, returned the kettle to the stove, and set the lid on the teapot with a tiny clink. "What happened, Brie?"

"I needed a change. Look, I'd rather not talk about

it." Brie carried their dessert to the table, planted herself on one of the chairs.

"If you didn't want to talk about it, you wouldn't be here. Enough now. Out with it."

A long hush fell.

"She had a baby," Brie murmured.

"Who had a baby?"

"Stephen Jeffries's wife. A boy, last Tuesday. Connie called to chat, to catch me up on things that have been going on at MB and L since I left, and she mentioned it in passing."

Madelyn took the chair across from her. "He's one of the other attorneys there, isn't he?"

"Yes. And the newest partner."

"And?" she prompted.

Brie looked up, eyes bright with unshed tears. "And I'm a fool, a stupid fool who let herself be used, manipulated, deceived. I knew it was wrong, what we were doing, but I loved him, and love justifies almost anything, or so it seemed."

She gave a hollow laugh. "I thought he'd come after me once I left. I figured if I took a job in a new city, it would finally push him to divorce her, the way he'd always promised me he would. I still have friends at the firm. I know I could talk my way back in, even now. Then I heard about . . . his son." She choked over the last word.

"I still thought he'd show up one day," Brie went on, "catch me as I was leaving for work or for home. When he did, he'd be a free man, divorce decree in one hand and an engagement ring in the other. That's when he'd propose, beg me to come back with him where I belong."

She paused, swallowing hard. "But he lied; until the

very last he lied. Hah, until I actually loaded the last box in my car and drove away, he was pleading with me to stay, to give him a little while longer. And she was already pregnant."

Brie mashed a fist against her forehead. "I fell for all the lines. How he hated his wife. How cold she was. How he couldn't bear to touch her. How they hadn't been intimate for years and kept separate bedrooms. He stayed with her, he said, for the children's sake, for appearances. When I heard about the baby, I nearly fell apart. I had to get away. I couldn't bear to be by myself, so I came to see you."

"I'm glad you did."

Brie met Madelyn's eyes. "I can see I've shocked you. Your little sister involved with a married man. How could it happen? How could I do such a stupid, immoral thing? I've asked myself the same things a hundred times and I still don't know. In the beginning, I believed he was divorced. Then after we'd become . . . involved, he told me he was only separated. He wanted a divorce, he said, but . . . well, you can figure out the rest."

"Brie." Madelyn didn't know what to say.

"He never loved me, Madelyn. Out of all of it, I think that's the worst. It was just a cheap thrill for him, nothing but a meaningless game."

"Maybe you're wrong. Maybe he did love you, does love you in his own small way, and he's just a coward."

"No. He's a liar and a cheat, a despicable bastard who hides behind a handsome smile and a clever tongue. Three years I gave him, three years. And now I know the truth, that he was sleeping with his wife when he told me I was the only one. I wonder who else he was with. I wonder if he cheated on me too. Oh God, how could I ever have done such a thing? How could I let myself love him?"

Madelyn reached out a hand. "Don't torture yourself. You don't choose love; it chooses you. You made a mistake, but you're out of it now. You left him, remember, on your own terms."

"And tossed aside my career, my reputation, my pride, in the process."

"You still have all those things; they're only a bit bruised. Oh, sweetie, I hate to see you hurting like this."

"It's my own fault. I'll get over it."

Eventually she would, Madelyn knew, but at what price? Would her sister ever truly trust any man again? Love another man again? Mustering the most cheerful smile she could, Madelyn suggested, "Why don't I pour us both a cup of tea and we'll try this tart? It looks delicious even if it's not chocolate."

"Malynn." Brie stopped her with a hand. "About your relationship with Zack. I think you should consider where it's going."

"It's going just fine. We're happy, both of us, the way things are."

"And you don't want more? You don't want permanent? I can tell your feelings for him run deep. How deep do his feelings run for you?"

"I'm not sure," she admitted. "He wants me, I know that. He cares for me."

"And love?"

Madelyn dropped her eyes.

"If it's not right," Brie said, "if your relationship with him isn't headed where you need it go, don't waste your time. Don't waste years like I did, waiting for him to change. He won't. And then all you'll be left with is your loneliness and your regrets. Don't let him hurt you, Malynn, while you still have a choice."

But Madelyn knew she didn't. It was already too late. Gently, she pulled away. "I'd better get the tea."

CHAPTER ELEVEN

Madelyn fanned the swizzle stick through her piña colada and decided that of all possible human emotions, guilt was the worst.

It was guilt that had led her to avoid a girls' night out on the town for months, making excuse after pitiful excuse. And it was guilt that had convinced her to let her three stalwart friends, Suzy, Linda, and Peg, drag her out for an evening of fun and celebration. It was guilt as well that was keeping her from relaxing and enjoying herself tonight, far too aware of the lies she'd told them and the ones she knew she would keep on telling them.

"Happy birthday, Madelyn!" The other women cheered, lifting their glasses high.

Madelyn raised hers and tapped it to theirs in a toast. She smiled. "Thank you guys for everything. Dinner and the drinks, and of course the presents. I love them all."

"You're very welcome. And there's cake still on the way," Peg volunteered.

Madelyn's shoulders slumped. "The waiters aren't going to sing to me, are they? You know I hate that."

"This place is way too classy for that. As birthday girl you get a complimentary dessert served with a side of pure silence. No singing allowed."

"Thank heavens."

Peg finished off her drink. "No, thank me. Suzy here wanted to take you to one of those Mexican places where they clap and sing so loudly you can hear it in the next state. Linda, on the other hand, suggested a strip club."

"One with male dancers," Linda added. "Considering the occasion, I thought it might be fun. It's not every day a woman turns thirty."

"Don't remind me." Madelyn groaned. "Besides, I still have three more days left until my actual birthday."

"Yes, I noticed you're taking Monday off from work," Peg said.

"I always take my birthday off. You know that."

"Are you doing something special? Is James whisking you away to a romantic locale?" Suzy rested her elbows on the table in anticipation of the answer.

Guilt, the ugly beast, rose inside her again. It had been months now and she still hadn't told them about her breakup with James. In fact, she'd even told them she'd seen him. Which wasn't totally untrue. She had seen him—two months ago at her mother's house, as a friend. And talked to him several times on the phone, as a friend.

Trouble was, if she told them she and James were no longer a couple, her friends would start trying to set her up. When she refused to be set up, they'd demand to know why, then worm it out of her that she was seeing someone else. Once they discovered she had a new man in her life, full disclosure was all but assured.

Relentless as hounds after a rabbit, they'd never leave off until they'd uncovered the identity of her mystery man. Better not to tempt fate, she'd decided. Better to continue shamelessly using James as cover.

"We are going out of town," she said. "I just don't know where yet. He's surprising me." There, she thought, that hadn't been much of a lie. Everything she'd said was true, except that the "he" in this case happened to be Zack.

"Oh, that sounds like fun," Suzy gushed. "May is such a beautiful time of year to travel."

"When your boyfriend's as rich as hers is, anytime's a beautiful time to travel." Linda rattled the ice cubes in her glass.

Suzy, ever the romantic, ignored the remark. "Maybe he's going to propose. We've all been dying to know when you two are finally going to tie the knot."

Peg and Linda hushed her.

"What?" Suzy protested. "You both said yourselves a woman who wants a family ought to quit fooling around and get on with it by the time she turns thirty. And then only if she's really into her career. I plan to be married and have two kids by the time I turn thirty."

"Linda, did you bring the noose with you? Or should I walk up the street and buy a handgun?" Peg asked as she glared at Suzy.

"What?" Suzy protested again. "It's not like she doesn't have somebody serious. They've just got to set the date. Right, Madelyn?"

Madelyn forced a smile. "Right."

Their waiter appeared, bearing a small white frosted cake. "At least someone has good timing," Peg said. "And the cake'll do double duty by giving Suzy something to stick into her mouth besides her foot."

"Really, everybody, it's fine," Madelyn said. "I'm not upset. It's nothing my mother doesn't bring up at least twice during every conversation."

"You'll get married when you feel the time is right." Linda reached over to pat her hand. "I was married, had three kids, and got a divorce all before I turned thirty. Rushing into a commitment can be a terrible mistake, even with someone you think you know. There's nothing wrong with making sure."

"Thank you, Linda."

"Just don't take too much time making sure. James is wonderful, a real catch. He's far too good to let slip away."

Wouldn't they all just die, Madelyn thought, if they knew she hadn't just let him slip away but had actually tossed him back? And afterward had allowed herself to become entangled with a charmer who was unlikely to ever get caught? She pasted a happy look on her face, reached for the knife, and drove it deep into the cake as if it needed killing.

The party broke up less than an hour later, after Madelyn turned down an offer to continue the fun with a round of barhopping. Linda needed to get home to her kids. Peg, known for her endless capacity to party, seemed oddly distracted, as if she had somewhere else to be. And Suzy—well, Suzy at twenty-three was on the hunt for a man and had the annoying habit of latching onto the cutest male available, then disappearing with him for the rest of the evening, abandoning her friends without a second thought.

The three of them tucked Suzy into a crosstown cab, then decided to walk a block up and over, where they figured they'd stand a better chance of finding rides home for themselves. Halfway to their destination, Peg slowed. "Hey, isn't that Zack Douglas? There in that restaurant?"

In a booth next to the window, he sat as visible as an actor spotlighted on center stage. No doubt at all, it was Zack.

And he was with a woman.

Even from a distance, his companion had the look of a siren, a dark-haired beauty, lush and steamy, with a touch of the exotic blended in. She laughed and twirled a swizzle stick through a tall, boldly shaped martini glass. She turned her head and for an instant the light caught her eyes, glinting as green as shards from a broken bottle, the lipstick on her mouth a hard slash of crimson.

Only Zack wasn't laughing with her, his body held in a posture of displeasure and, if Madelyn wasn't mistaken, barely veiled contempt. She watched him toss back a finger's worth of liquor, then motion to the waiter to bring him another. He rarely drank, usually opting for club soda or black coffee. Knowing what she did of his past, she'd never questioned his reasons. But he wasn't abstaining tonight. Who was the woman? Why was he with her? And what did she mean to him?

"I wonder who she is," Peg said. "You don't suppose she's the reason he's been such a good little boy at the office lately? Angie Lewis in media was actually complaining how he barely flirts anymore. Said he walked right by her a couple days ago and didn't do more than give her a smile and a quick hello."

Madelyn glanced away for a moment, even more uneasy than before. She didn't relish the idea of Zack making time with every female at work, but neither did she want a marked change in his behavior, one that would provoke people's curiosity—especially people like Peg. She'd have to mention it to him. *If* she decided to mention anything to him ever again. Who was that woman? She narrowed her eyes.

"Whoever she is," Peg mused, "the two of them certainly are striking together with all those dark, sultry good looks."

A cruel wave of jealousy rolled through Madelyn as she watched, tempered only by the conviction that he was not having a good time. At least she hoped he wasn't. The idea that he might be made her already low spirits sink even lower.

Linda made an impatient noise. "As riveting as Zack Douglas's love life is, the babysitter clock is ticking and if I don't get home soon I fear she may turn into a pumpkin. Or eat every last thing in my fridge. So let's get a move on, you two."

Taking one last penetrating look, Madelyn trudged along the concrete sidewalk after her friends.

They had agreed to meet at the house of one of Zack's friends, someone with no connection to work, who'd offered to let them store one of their cars in his garage over the weekend—so she and Zack could drive together. Zack still hadn't told her where they were headed, wanting to keep it a surprise as long as possible.

With last night's mystery woman fresh in her mind, Madelyn almost decided to stay home — almost. For just as fresh remained the memory of Zack, his unhappy demeanor and the uncharacteristic way he'd been tossing back drinks. The obvious answer — that he was seeing another woman — simply didn't add up.

Eyes bloodshot and tired, he looked a bit rough around the edges despite his neat casual clothes and close shave. Expecting a typical show of male pride, she was surprised when he asked if she'd drive. He had a headache. She agreed without commenting on his health, accepting his murmured directions as they left the city behind.

For late morning on a Friday, traffic was light, allowing her to settle easily in the center lane. After several minutes of silence, she switched on the radio and tuned it to a classical station. The car interior filled with the gentle, melodic strains of Bach.

Five minutes passed. "Do you actually like that highbrow stuff?" Zack shifted in his seat, unable to stretch his legs their full length even in her well-appointed automobile.

"Yes, actually. I like all sorts of music. I thought your head might appreciate this a bit more than hard rock or hip-hop, but if you'd rather I can—"

"No, leave it. It's fine. For now." He checked their progress, then closed his eyes again. "How was your birthday dinner last night?"

"Nice. The food was great and the girls gave me a very pretty scarf plus a stack of lottery tickets — thirty — one for each year. Who knows, maybe I'll get lucky and hit the jackpot."

"If you do, there's a gold Rolex I've had my eye on for a while." He rolled his head toward her, a grin on his lips.

Madelyn didn't return his smile.

"Hey, I'm joking, you know."

"I know." She locked both hands firmly on the steering wheel. "How was *your* night? Did you do anything in particular?"

He studied the passing scenery for a moment. "No, nothing special. Had dinner, read for a while; then I went to bed."

"Hmm." Her hands tightened involuntarily. "Quiet evening at home, then?"

A long silence ticked past. "For the most part."

Her heart sank. "That's odd. Peg and Linda and I saw you out, having dinner with a woman around ten o'clock. Who is she, Zack?"

"She's no one," he said, his words clipped.

"She didn't look like no one."

"She isn't important. She has nothing to do with you and me."

Anger settled as hard and cold as a stone inside her chest. "You told me once that you didn't like to share lovers. I don't either."

"Is that what you think?" He sounded amused.

"What else am I to think?"

"For one, that she's rather old for me. You obviously didn't get a good look."

Annoyed, furious, she shot him a glance as she shifted into the slow lane. "We were passing by in front of the restaurant."

"Were you ladies spying on me?"

"Don't flatter yourself. We were walking up a block

to flag down a cab when Peg spotted you. If you didn't care to be noticed, you shouldn't have chosen a window seat."

"Touché. But then, you see, I didn't care. Believe me, Madelyn, she's no one you need to concern yourself with."

She sighed. "If that's true, then why won't you tell me who she is? Why the lies?"

"I haven't lied to you. Omitted a few details, perhaps, but not lied."

"A few details?" she scoffed. "Maybe I should just turn the car around."

"You are not turning the car around. Jesus, you're the most obstinate female I've ever met. She's my mother, all right?"

Shocked, Madelyn looked him full in the face. "Your *mother*?"

"Yeah. Hey, watch where you're going before you run us off the road."

She returned her attention to the highway, taking a moment to digest what he'd revealed. "I thought your mother abandoned you when you were a boy."

"She did." He rubbed a hand over his jaw, bitterness leaching into his words. "She found me a few years ago, after I earned my degree, after I landed my first decent job. I still don't know how the hell she tracked me down."

"Because you're her son and she wanted to know you."

His lips curled cynically. "You're sweet, Red, you know that? Really sweet. No, what she wanted was my money."

"Surely not."

"She has a habit of running low on funds when she's between men," he explained. "Last night she gave me the heartbreaking news that she's split with her fourth husband.

"God, you'd think she'd learn her lesson and have enough taste to shack up with them for a while, instead of going to the bother of making it legal. With all the lawyer fees, she never comes out with anything more than a few new dresses and some jewelry that she eventually winds up pawning. When she's tapped out, she finds me."

"Why don't you tell her no?"

He laughed, but it was without humor. "Don't think I haven't wanted to. If it were just me, I'd have cut her off without a cent long ago. But she knows where Beth lives and she's threatened to drop in on her for a visit—to see her grandchildren. I'm not going to let her bother Beth. She's ruined her life enough as it is."

His sister, he was protecting his sister. Madelyn reached for his hand. "I'm sorry, Zack. Does she ask for a lot?"

"Enough. She's not bleeding me dry or anything. Most of the time she links up with a guy who has enough cash to bankroll her high-maintenance lifestyle. She likes feeling important. She'd be thrilled, by the way, to know you thought she was young enough to pass for my date, even if she was only seventeen when she had me. I guess the plastic surgery's been worth every penny."

A heavy silence hung between them.

He sighed. "I'm sorry I lied to you. I didn't want to bring her up, that's all. I didn't want to spoil your birthday."

"You haven't spoiled my birthday. We are going to Atlantic City, I assume," she said as they passed under a road sign that pointed them in that direction.

"We are. I thought you might enjoy the glitz."

"I've never been to a casino before," she admitted.

"Never? Not even in Vegas?"

"I've never been to Las Vegas. My family's not big on gambling, and I was ill the one time a bunch of my college friends decided to fly out there."

"Then it will be my distinct pleasure to corrupt you."

"*Hah, hah,* this is fun!" Madelyn gave the lever a solid pull and watched the dials spin in wild succession.

"Slots are for suckers. We should go back to the blackjack tables," Zack said as he leaned over her shoulder to watch.

"Everybody there's too serious, staring at their cards as if they expect to witness the Second Coming, mumbling, 'Hit me, hit me,' then cursing when they go bust. I like this." She patted the side of the machine. "Just me and the pretty box."

"Looks like the pretty box ate your money again."

"But if I keep playing, it's eventually bound to cough it back up."

"These machines are rigged, and at a dollar a pop you'll be broke before the hour's out."

She drew herself up, sitting straight on the padded stool beneath her. "It's my money and my birthday and I'll waste it however I choose, Zachary Douglas."

The machine ate another one of Madelyn's dollars.

He shook his head and wrapped a hand around her

ponytail, pulling gently on it to tip her head back for his kiss, a slow, easy slide of lips and tongue that warmed them both.

"Why don't I go get us a drink?" he suggested, releasing her.

"Um, sounds good. Something cold and wet and non-alcoholic for me. I need to keep my wits sharp for the game."

"The fleecing, don't you mean?"

"If you disapprove so much, you should never have brought me here. Now shoo. I've got work to do."

"Yes, ma'am."

Zack strode away from the casino area, his footsteps mute on the plush red and gold carpet beneath his feet. It was a pleasure to see Madelyn having so much fun. He congratulated himself on the decision to bring her here. The gaudy opulence of the hotel was exactly what she needed after weeks of intense pressure and hard work. The new ad campaign—the one that was supposed to have been his—was proceeding well, but at a punishing pace. Forgetting the work and the responsibility for a short while could only do her good, and him as well. In this palace of unabashed hedonism and shameless greed, one couldn't help but find enjoyment.

At first, he'd thought he might have to coax her into letting loose, but she'd surprised him by adapting almost immediately to the easygoing style of the place. Over the past two days, she'd been happier and more relaxed than he'd ever known her—the only exception the times they made love. When they were alone together, intimate, she seemed to glow, losing herself to him with an abandon that never failed to steal his breath. Just thinking about her now fired his blood with need. No matter how many times they came together, it was never enough.

He'd expected their affair to be over by now, or at least on the wane. Contrary to his reputation, he didn't invite every attractive woman he met into his bed. He was far more discriminating than most might imagine. Still, his relationships tended to be short-lived, ignited by passion, doused by disinterest when the flames burned low. But with Madelyn it was different. Yes, there was the sex, and yes, it was wonderful, but there was far more between them. The simple fact was he enjoyed her company, more than he could remember enjoying any woman's company, ever. And that, above all else, left him uneasy.

He wasn't looking for commitment. He didn't believe in love—not the hearts-and-flowers kind the poets wrote about, the sort people claimed would last forever. Love was impermanent and fleeting, a fickle bitch who led you on, then turned her back and left you to bleed. It had no place in his life.

Yet there was such a thing as want, desire, need. And with Madelyn he felt all three, craving far more than a weekend with her and a handful of hours stolen in between. Being here together, free of the subterfuge and secrecy, made him long for a more honest arrangement where they no longer had to hide what they were to each other. Where he could exist in the open as part of her life.

But he couldn't fault her motives, her caution. And when the day came and the passion between them died, he didn't want to see her hurt or shamed or damaged—especially at work—because of what they'd been to each other.

His mood pensive, Zack ordered their drinks.

On his return, bells were ringing, sirens clanking, electronic whistles hooting in celebration as he wove a path in among the rows of slot machines. From the sound of it, somebody was a winner.

A crowd of people had formed, preventing him from reaching Madelyn. Being tall came in handy on occasion, and he put that advantage to use now, peering over the sea of heads to scan for a familiar glint of red-gold hair. His eyes widened when he located her and realized she was not just part of the hoopla but the main attraction.

"*Zack!*" She flung an arm into the air and waved. "Zack, I won! Oh, let him through," she pleaded, motioning for people to step aside so he could reach her. Parting as if they were the Red Sea and he Moses, the crowd opened a path.

Bemused, Zack walked forward. "You won?"

Coins overflowed from a host of buckets scattered across the floor, gleaming and sparkling like booty spilled from a pirate's treasure chest, an occasional straggler coin tumbling now and then from the machine to clink onto the heaps below.

"Can you believe it? I won. I won." Laughing, exuberant, she launched herself toward him, leaping up to wrap her arms around his neck, her legs around his waist.

He staggered back a step or two, soda sloshing over the rims of the cups he still carried. Only he didn't care, too busy enjoying the sensation of Madelyn's lips moving with feverish excitement against his own. He kissed her back, abruptly hungry, losing himself in the scent and taste of her. The place and the people around him faded to nothing, the world spinning away.

Far too soon, Madelyn pulled away, returning once more to solid ground and her own two feet. "I won!" she squealed again.

"I know. How much is there?"

"A couple thousand at least. I was ready to quit, but since you weren't back, I thought, 'What the hell?' and plunked in one more buck. All of a sudden the machine went wild, like it was going to explode, and wow, I hit the jackpot."

He set their drinks aside, then hugged her hard, spinning her around twice. "Congratulations, baby, and happy birthday."

CHAPTER TWELVE

By evening, Madelyn was more than a little tipsy. High on wine, intoxicated by Zack.

Dinner at the hotel's elegant five-star restaurant had been divine. And despite her winnings, all $4,784 of them, Zack had refused to let her pay for a thing—part of his birthday gift to her. Afterward, they'd decided to take in the show of a well-known singer. Twenty minutes into a superb performance, Madelyn had begun nibbling on Zack's neck.

At first, he'd tipped his head to one side to allow her better access but soon found himself wishing he hadn't encouraged her, not in so public a place. She was unrelenting, reaching up to loosen his tie and unfasten his collar in order to give her lips and tongue a broader canvas on which to play. She began opening his shirt buttons, freeing a good half dozen before he realized he had to stop her. A shiver ran through him as she slid her hand inside to caress his bare chest in a most distracting way.

He'd whispered to her to quit, but it did no good. With people beginning to stare, he'd done the only thing he could do.

Leave.

Propelling them up and out of the theater with as little fuss as possible, he tried to keep her hands from wandering over portions of his anatomy not generally fondled in public.

He yanked off his half-knotted tie and stuffed it into his pocket as he hustled her down a carpeted hallway toward a bank of elevators. "You're like an octopus. If you don't stop, you're going to get us arrested."

She giggled, then confessed in a loud stage whisper, "I've never been arrested."

"Believe me, it's not an experience you'd enjoy."

"I know an experience I *would* enjoy." She snaked an arm down to grab his ass.

Zack sent her a disapproving look and walked them faster toward the elevators. He startled when she buried her face against his exposed chest, her lips and tongue roaming over his skin before pausing to suck on one of his nipples.

"Have I ever told you how good you taste?" She sighed, licking him. She gave his hard, flat nipple a gentle bite that turned other parts of him even harder.

"No." He moaned, giving the elevator's up button a savage punch with his fist. "Cut it out, Madelyn. I mean it." His words sounded weak, even to himself.

She wrapped both arms around his waist and pressed her body flush against his. "Oh, I hope you mean it." She rubbed herself sinuously against him. "I know I do."

"I should never have ordered that bottle of wine."

"But it was so sweet," she crooned, blinking up at him. "A thirty-year-old bottle for my thirtieth birthday. I'm going to have to find some way to thank you for making my day extra special."

She wrapped her arms around his neck and began tugging his head down for a kiss.

He evaded her, reaching up to unwind her arms. "You already have thanked me. Now, behave yourself. Someone's coming."

Madelyn snuggled closer and dropped her head onto his shoulder.

Zack held her upright with one arm and gave a polite nod to the elderly couple who'd stopped to wait for the elevator as well.

The older woman, her head crowned by a thick puff of snow white hair, sniffed disdainfully and raised her eyes to the lighted panel of numbers above. Her husband, on the other hand, perused the pair of them with open interest, his lips curved with prurient amusement.

The elevator dinged and after the passengers inside disembarked, the four of them walked on board. Zack pressed the button for the twenty-fifth floor.

The old man pressed the one for the twentieth. "Newlyweds?"

After a short pause, Zack said, "No."

The old woman sniffed again, lips pursed. Under her breath she muttered, "Shameful."

Before Zack could stop her, Madelyn spun around and flattened herself against him, caressing his thighs through the material of his pants. "There's nothing shameful about it," she declared. "It's my birthday and I'm here with my man to celebrate."

She thrust out her breasts, proudly displaying the expanse of cleavage revealed above the top of her evening gown along with the opal and diamond pendant nestled in between. "He gave this to me. Isn't it beautiful? I adore it."

The old man leaned in for a closer look.

His wife gave him a hard smack on the shoulder and yanked him around to face forward. "We're getting off," she said, pushing the button for the next floor—the sixteenth.

Zack angled his head and whispered into Madelyn's ear. "God knows I'm going to do the same if you don't quit with that rubbing of yours." He captured her hands to still them.

The other couple must have heard him, the woman's spine stiffening so much it was a wonder it didn't crack. Her husband choked out a laugh as the elevator doors opened and his wife hauled him out.

Zack wrapped his arms around Madelyn as the doors slid shut and the elevator glided upward. "What's gotten into you, Red?"

"I don't know. She made me mad, that's all. And I don't want to be mad, not tonight."

"Then don't be." He turned her around and took her mouth in a ravenous kiss that quickly had her purring against him.

Somehow they made it to their room without causing another scene.

Zack had left a small lamp burning; it cast the furniture in dim shades of amber, the bed a wide plain of inviting shadow. Between the elevator and their room, Madelyn had managed to unfasten the rest of the Zack's shirt buttons. He yanked the tails out of his pants and flung the garment behind him as he and Madelyn danced, lips locked, toward the bed. The mattress gave a squeak as they fell upon it, bouncing once.

Consumed by desire and the overpowering urge to feel the silk of her bare flesh beneath his hands, to sheath himself inside the hot, honeyed depths of her body, he yanked down the zipper of her dress with one hand as he thrust up the long formal skirt of her gown with the other. Slipping a grateful hand beneath her panties, he cupped her rounded bottom and fondled her flesh.

He was poised to move on to even more interesting territory when Madelyn stopped the wicked things she'd been doing to his neck and propped her elbows against his chest.

"I've gotta tinkle," she announced, levering herself out of his arms and off the bed.

Zack groaned in acute frustration and flung an arm over his face. He could wait, he assured himself. She wouldn't be long. He hoped she wouldn't be long. In a cruel way, this was nothing less than he deserved for making love with an inebriated woman. He should never have bought that wine.

Eventually, he heard the toilet flush. Renewed anticipation surged through him, intensifying the ache lodged in his groin. She'd be back any second.

One minute ticked past, then two; still no Madelyn.

"Zack?" she called from inside the bathroom.

Oh no. Please, he prayed, *please don't let her be sick.*

"Zack? Can you come in here?"

He doubted he could even walk. "What's wrong?"

"I need you."

Yeah, he needed her too.

Urgently.

But not in the bathroom. Although . . . ?

He shook his head, immediately banishing the idea. With an audible grunt and an abject groan, he pushed himself off the bed and delicately made his way across the room.

The door was wide open, and there in front of the sink stood Madelyn, a toothbrush in one hand, a tube of partly squeezed toothpaste in the other. A heavy frown of confusion wrinkled her brow. She looked a sight, half of her once tidy topknot hanging in a messy russet tangle over her shoulder. Her right dress strap dangled near her elbow, leaving one pert breast exposed. And she was lopsided, forced to take an occasional hop to keep herself steady on the single three-inch heel she still wore.

The sink basin was a sight as well, covered with several misdirected globs of white-green paste. She held out the tube and brush—his, he noted—her blue eyes pleading. "There's something wrong with this stuff. It won't stay on the brush."

"You can brush later. Come to bed," he told her, his body still throbbing for release.

"No, I won't be sexy for you unless I brush. Don't you want me sexy?"

Right now, he just wanted her. But considering the state she was in, he realized he'd have to tolerate another small delay. Sighing, he plucked the toothbrush out of her hand—pausing to exchange it for her own—then the toothpaste. He squeezed a short dab across the bristles and handed it to her.

She sent him a wide smile of gratitude. But when she

tried to move the brush over her teeth, her arm refused to lift high enough to do the job, her loose dress strap binding her elbow to her side.

Aware that she was currently incapable of figuring out a solution, Zack took pity. Pausing a moment to drop a kiss on her naked breast, he inserted a single finger beneath the pesky strap and pushed it up and over her shoulder, settling the loose bodice of her dress in place. He turned the tap on for her, then crossed his arms and leaned against the countertop. "Better?"

Madelyn scrubbed her teeth, delighted to find her movements no longer hampered. She spat into the sink, then gave him a big grin and a nod, her teeth and lips sticky with foamy flecks of toothpaste.

The ludicrous nature of the moment struck him and he tossed back his head laughing.

"What's so funny?" she mumbled around the brush.

"You." He skimmed a finger down the bridge of her nose. "You make a cute drunk. Annoying but cute."

"You're cute too. I've always thought so."

"Have you?"

"Oh, yes." She leaned over to rinse her mouth. "Even when I believed you were a womanizing creep who didn't deserve to lick my boots, I thought you were cute. More than cute; beautiful, actually. You're every bit as hot as any movie star, even Brad Pitt."

"Gee, thanks." He picked up a fluffy white washcloth and patted her face and hands dry. "So you just want me for my body, huh?"

"Well, it is an awfully nice body." She ran her hands over his muscled arms and shoulders.

He sucked in a sharp breath when her palms played

over his taut stomach, barely an inch from his fly; his erection stiffened full force once more. If only she would touch him there, he knew he could die in peace.

Unwilling to wait even a second longer, he bent his knees and lifted her over his shoulder, carrying her to the bed. He laid her against the sheets, then stripped her bare.

She raised her arms above her head. "I like your mind too," she said, continuing their conversation. "You're smart and interesting, superinventive and fun. You don't put up with crap from idiots, but you're generous and kind, much more than I would ever have suspected. You can be so incredibly sweet; sometimes it takes my breath away."

Sweet? he thought. Jesus, right now he was about as far from sweet as a man could get.

Naked, he spread himself over her and parted her legs to fit himself between them. He claimed her mouth with demanding heat, taking care to touch her body in all the ways he knew she liked best. He suckled her breasts, tonguing her nipples with firm strokes to make sure she was ready.

Madelyn shifted beneath him, moaning with clear need.

"I guess it's like my necklace," she panted, her hands roaming over the limber curve of his back to trace his buttocks and the lean hollows along the sides of his hips.

His shaft throbbed, warning him just how close he was.

"It's thoughtful and unique," she said. "A beautiful gift that will remind me of this day and you, forever."

Zack shuddered, his skin on fire, need driving him

crazy. He couldn't wait much longer. He brushed scorching kisses over her neck and took her hips in his hands.

She threaded her fingers into his hair. "You've done so much to make this weekend special. Because of you it's been the best birthday I've ever had. I've loved it and . . ."

He thrust himself inside her, burying himself satisfyingly deep.

She arched and gasped. "And I love you too," she cried. "Oh, God, Zack, I love you too. So much."

Shock rippled through him at her words, but the animal need pounding inside him was too intense for anything but action. Pushing her declaration aside for now, he thrust again, driving her hard, then harder still, until the only sounds she could make were frenzied moans.

He fought his body's urgings to climax as he took her higher and higher, determined to make her come spectacularly. Suddenly she shattered around him, calling out his name in wild gasps. Only then did he let himself follow her over the edge, his mind and body quaking from the overwhelming pleasure.

Madelyn wore a pair of sunglasses to breakfast.

Her head throbbed, despite the twenty-minute soaking she'd given it beneath a stream of near kettle-hot water and the trio of aspirins she'd swallowed afterward.

Zack was quiet this morning. She'd awakened to find him dressed and standing on the small balcony outside their room, contemplating the shoreline. The waves were a rough blue-gray chop, the cloud-laden sky the color of dull steel.

When he suggested they dine at one of the hotel

restaurants downstairs, she'd been surprised. Every morning since their arrival, they'd dined in their room, usually in bed. This was their last day in Atlantic City; she'd assumed they'd spend it alone. By afternoon they would need to be back on the road, traveling home. Perhaps he just wanted one last chance to soak up the carnival atmosphere of the place, to take advantage of a final few hours of casino games and shameless, decadent fun.

Whatever the reason, she'd had no energy to argue. Incapable of facing the noisy whine of her hair dryer, she'd fastened her hair into a damp ponytail and allowed Zack to guide her downstairs.

The smell of fried eggs and cinnamon buns at the restaurant's entrance was sickening this morning. White cheeked, she trailed the hostess and slid carefully into a back booth, lifting the menu up to shield her face. At least they were away from the kitchen, with only the faint aroma of coffee perfuming the air.

"Take off those glasses," Zack said. "You look like a Hollywood starlet trying to hide from her fans."

She lowered her menu an inch. "The light hurts my eyes."

"It wouldn't if you'd let them adjust. What you need is a good hot meal to clear your head."

"I can't eat. I'll just have a cup of tea."

Zack was definitely in a mood this morning, she thought. Silent and brooding one minute, bossy and argumentative the next. Was he miffed at her about last night? She didn't see why he should be. He'd certainly seemed to enjoy himself, and the wine had been his idea after all. She tended to be a cheap drunk, flying high after only one or two glasses—one of the reasons she didn't partake too often. Last night she'd stopped counting after three. Despite her undeniably forward and embarrassing public seduction of Zack, she couldn't believe he'd minded enough to be carrying a grudge this morning.

Still, there were parts of the evening that remained a mystery, a hazy mix of bits and pieces that seemed more akin to dreams than reality. Trouble was she wasn't certain which was which, and she wasn't particularly keen on questioning him to find out.

The waitress arrived to take their order.

Madelyn listened quietly while Zack asked for blueberry pancakes with a side of bacon, hash browns, a large orange juice, and hot black coffee. She ordered tea with milk instead of the usual wedge of lemon.

He stopped the waitress before she could tuck her pad away. "Add an order of scrambled eggs and dry wheat toast to that for the lady, and an apple juice. Do you have any fresh strawberries?"

"We do, as a matter of fact, nice local ones. They're early this year."

"Good. Bring her a serving of those as well." Zack flashed one of his patented heart-melting smiles and handed the menus over. He didn't notice the doe-eyed look the woman gave him.

Madelyn did.

She waited until they were in private to speak. "Why did you do that? I told you I didn't want any food."

"And I told *you* that you need to eat. Caffeine and aspirin aren't going to cure your hangover. Now, close your eyes."

"Why?"

"Because I'm tired of staring back at my own reflection." He reached out before she could prevent him and plucked the sunglasses off her face.

Madelyn screwed her eyes shut like a nervous child, sure the worst awaited her on the other side. A full minute passed before she decided to brave it. Cautiously, she lifted her lids.

"Okay?" he asked.

Grudgingly, she nodded.

"You forget. I've had more experience at this sort of thing than you." He leaned forward, putting his forearms on the table. "Madelyn, I've been thinking. About last—"

"Zack?"

Hearing his name, Zack turned his head toward the sound. "Billy?"

A wiry, brown-haired man approached their table. "Hell, man, I thought it was you."

"Billy." Zack erupted up out of his seat. "Billy Aikens."

The two of them flung their arms around each other, pummeling backs and shoulders with fists and the flats of their hands. Grinning like fools, they pulled apart.

"What are you doing here?" Zack demanded.

"Same as you: testing my luck, wasting my money. Lord, how long's it been?"

"Hell, I don't know—four, five years? I thought you were out west roughing it in the California hills. Vegas wasn't enough of a trip for you? You had to head all the way east to find some action?"

"Actually, these days, Vegas is the longer trip. I moved back to Virginia about a year ago. You still in New York?"

"I sure am, deep in the heart of the city." Zack caught a glimpse of red hair out of the corner of his eye. "Hey, where have my manners gone? Billy, this is Madelyn. Madelyn Grayson. Red, Billy Aikens, an old friend of mine from days long past."

"So I gathered. How do you do, Mr. Aikens?" Madelyn offered a smile and her hand.

Billy accepted both, taking her palm, his own rough with calluses. "I'm doing well—better now that I've met you. Zack here always did have excellent taste in women. And the devil's own luck too. Bet he's won a pile of loot at the tables."

"Actually, it's Madelyn who did that. She hit the jackpot yesterday. On slots, no less."

"Well, congratulations; that's great. Just like I said, either he gets lucky himself or he passes it along to someone else. I know he did for me. Saved my life on our first tour of duty in the service."

"He exaggerates," Zack said.

"Exaggerates, my eye. Tell that to the maniac who was about to whack my head open with a tire iron. If Zack hadn't stepped in when he did, my nineteen-year-old brains would have been splattered all over the floor of that bar in Munich. As it was, Zack took some pretty solid hits, but he got us both out alive before the MPs arrived. A man can always depend on Zack."

Uncomfortable, Zack changed the subject. "So are you here with Vivian? What about the kids? Did you leave them with your folks?"

"Nah, it's just me." Billy hunched his shoulders and studied a spot on the floor. "Viv and I, well, we made our split official a few months ago. The lawyers are licking their chops over the divorce right now. Bloodsucking vermin. A few more weeks and it'll all be over."

"Christ, Billy. I don't know what to say. I'm sorry, man." Zack laid a hand on his friend's shoulder.

Billy shrugged as if it was just one of those things, but a deep sadness shone in his eyes. "Me too. Twelve years, you know. You think it's gonna last forever. Then one day you wake up and everything's changed. You deny it at first, until you realize it's too late. Too much has passed and no matter what you do or say, it's not ever gonna be the same again."

"Your kids?"

"Viv's got 'em. They're young. Kids need their mother."

Their waitress approached, hips swinging as she wrestled with an oversize tray stacked high with food.

Billy stepped out of the way. "Breakfast's here. I'd better let you two get to it."

"No, stay," Zack pressed. "Have something with us."

"Yes, we'd be delighted," Madelyn agreed.

"Appreciate the offer, but I'd just finished my own meal when I looked up and recognized this one here." He jerked a thumb toward Zack.

"Coffee, then?"

"Thanks, but I'll have to take a rain check. It's my last day here and I've got some recouping to do if I want to leave a winner." He thrust out a hand. "Man, it was great to see you."

Zack took his friend's hand and they shook, grips as hard as steel. "Look me up. You're always welcome in New York."

"Same for Virginia. McLean's not so bad if you don't mind all the government spooks." He winked.

In parting, they beat each other on the back one more time in the way men do.

Billy turned to her. "A true pleasure, ma'am. You take care and don't let this one pull any wool over your eyes."

"The pleasure was mine. And I already know to be careful of that wool."

Billy laughed, waved good-bye, and strolled away.

Zack resumed his seat. "Your eggs are getting cold. Eat up."

Hearing the curtness in his voice, and still feeling less than one hundred percent herself, Madelyn decided to set the subject of Billy Aikens aside for the time being. She eyed the congealing yellow globs on her plate and picked up her fork with a sigh.

CHAPTER THIRTEEN

Zack was quiet, unusually so. She could tell his thoughts were elsewhere even as he watched the highway ahead.

Madelyn fingered her new necklace, the one he'd given her, tracing the plump warmth of the opal, the pointed coolness of the tiny diamonds that encircled it like stars around an orbiting moon, and pondered the possibilities.

He'd insisted on taking the wheel even though they were driving her car, and she'd been perfectly willing to let him. Physically she felt much improved. As annoying as it was to admit, he'd been right; breakfast had been just the thing to sweep away the worst of her symptoms. Still, a weary sort of malaise lingered on, and she knew she wouldn't complain tonight when it came time to crawl between the sheets. Her only regret was that Zack wouldn't be there to crawl in next to her.

Out of the corner of her eye she watched him as she reviewed the events of that morning. As pleasant a person as Billy Aikens had seemed—and she had no doubt he was—Madelyn wished he and Zack hadn't happened upon each other. Ever since the encounter, Zack had been remote, although truth be told, he'd awakened in an odd, unfathomable mood, one she'd never seen from him before.

"Thinking about your friend?" she questioned softly.

He tossed her a glance. "Which one?"

"Billy, of course. What other friend did you run into today?"

Instead of answering, he maneuvered around a slower-moving vehicle.

"I just wondered," she continued. "You've been quiet ever since. Did it upset you? Seeing him again?"

"No, why would it? I always like meeting up with old friends, and he was a good one even if we haven't kept up the way we should have."

"What is it then? What's wrong?"

"Why do you think something's wrong?" He snapped, his tone sharp enough to cut through metal. "I'm just trying to work a few things out, that's all."

"Okay, I didn't mean to intrude." She crossed stiff arms over her breasts and angled her body away from him. "I'm tired. I think I'll take a nap."

Madelyn closed her eyes and concentrated on the sound of the tires beating in rhythm against the dark asphalt, the gentle hum of the engine, anything to keep the tears from falling.

Zack sighed.

She sniffed and tucked a hand beneath her cheek, pressing a thumb to the corner of her eye to hide the dampness she couldn't quite control.

"*Aw, God*, Madelyn, are you crying?"

"No." She sniffed again, harder this time, and screwed her eyes closed as tightly as they would go—a mistake that forced a near flood to erupt. "I've got something in my eye, that's all."

"No doubt from where I've been grinding my heel," he murmured. "Please don't cry, okay? I'm just tired and moody today."

She dug a tissue out of her purse and blew her nose. "Everything was fine . . . at least I thought it was fine, until this morning. Did I . . . did I do something last night to upset you? Was it because I was drunk?"

"Your being drunk's more my fault than yours. I'm the one who kept refilling your glass, even after you told me to stop. I didn't realize you were really serious when you said two glasses was your limit."

"I'm not much of a drinker."

"It's okay. Having a weak head for liquor isn't a crime, you know."

"It is when you can't remember everything that happened," she confessed.

"What do you remember?" His voice held an odd note of curiosity.

"Dinner and the wine, obviously. Then we went someplace in the hotel; they were playing music and a woman was singing. Then I started . . ."

"Yes?"

"Kissing you, touching you." She flushed. "Did I unbutton your shirt?"

"Yes, and left some rather colorful marks as well."

"Really? Where?"

His lips quirked. "Where it makes me glad I'm required to wear a suit and tie to work and not an open-necked jersey."

"Let me see." She reached out a hand.

He held her off. "No. If I show you now, I might wreck the car. You can look later. So go on."

"With what? Oh. Well, I . . . I remember kissing you again and getting in the elevator to go to our room, and . . . well, this can't be right."

"What?"

"Some prune-faced woman and an old guy who was staring at my chest."

Zack laughed. "You're batting three for three so far. Do you remember rubbing my thighs?"

"Your thighs?"

"Yeah. Luckily you hadn't tried to take off my pants yet."

"Zack!"

"Just my shirt. Go on." He prompted.

"Then we went to our room and started making love and somewhere along the way I stopped to brush my teeth. Is that right?"

"Yes, that's right. And then what?"

"We made love and went to sleep. That's it. Is there something else?"

He paused. "No. Your memory seems fully intact."

"Then what's bothering you?"

"I told you, I'm just tired and we have to be at work tomorrow. Last day of vacation grumbles, that's all." He reached over and laid a hand over hers where it rested against her knee.

She clasped his hand and relaxed. Still, she couldn't

help but feel he was holding something back. She dropped the subject and the two of them talked of ordinary things until they reached the home of Zack's friend.

She climbed out, enjoying the buoyant lift of warmth that signaled the approach of summer, the skies clear now. Zack retrieved his bag from her trunk, then stowed it in the backseat of his car.

She waited for him to come and kiss her as he did each weekend before they parted ways. Lately, those kisses had been long and intensely passionate, stirring her blood in a way that left her nerve endings humming for hours after, her mind crowded and cluttered with thoughts of him.

But when he walked back to her and took her in his arms, she saw that the shadows had returned to his eyes. And the kiss he gave her—no more than a brief pressing of lips—sent a chill straight through her heart. He was about to step away when Madelyn drew him back down, compelling him to kiss her again, grinding her lips against his own with heated determination. Something snapped inside Zack and he forced her mouth wide, brutal and bruising, uncontrolled.

Abruptly, he set her aside. "I'll see you at work."

And in that moment she remembered everything, the words resounding in her ears as clearly as if she had just spoken them.

I love you too. Oh, God, Zack, I love you too. So much.

She climbed into her car and started the ignition, hands shaking. She knew he wouldn't leave until she did, so she made herself pull away from the curb, thankful for the sparse traffic and the residential side street.

When he finally made the turn that separated them—

the one that would take him to his own apartment—she drove for two, maybe three blocks, then pulled over. She double-parked, ignoring the horn that blared from behind and the irate driver who squeezed around and roared away, tires screeching. She leaned her forehead against the steering wheel and let the truth wash over her.

She'd told him she loved him.

And he hadn't said it back.

She made herself go to work the next day even though all she really wanted to do was huddle underneath the bedcovers and pretend none of it had ever happened. Instead she forced herself up and into the shower, letting the hot water bring her fully awake.

She dressed in one of her favorite outfits, a teal blue midi-length skirt and a saffron yellow–and–white-striped silk blouse. On her feet she wore a pair of white Mary Janes; the opal pendant that dangled around her neck added the perfect finishing touch. She nearly took the necklace off but refused since doing so seemed like too much of an admission that her and Zack's affair might be coming to an end.

Her day was a hectic game of catch-up that left her little time to think of anything but work. At first she worried about running into Zack and seeing in his eyes what she feared—indifference or, worse, an uncomfortable kind of pity. Then she heard he'd left the office for a daylong taping of a television commercial, news that should have been a relief but lowered her spirits instead. By lunchtime, though, she was so wrapped up in her own work she managed to forget about him—well, almost forget about him.

It was late, the office empty by the time she rode the

elevator down to the lobby. After trading good nights with the building security guard, she headed for her car. Halfway there she remembered the file she'd left on her desk—the one she was supposed to have sent down to production hours before. Grumbling under her breath, she did a sharp about-face.

The hallways on the ninth floor were illuminated by lights that dimmed but never slept, the vacant offices and cubicle areas draped in layers of gray shadow. Anxious to complete her task and head for home—again—she walked briskly into her office, grabbed the file, and turned to leave. That was when she heard the sounds coming from the supply room at the end of the hall, muffled bumps and a small scraping noise, the kind you might hear when someone was trying to move furniture.

Curious, she approached, listening to the low murmur of voices, the words hushed and indistinguishable. Perhaps a pair of the administrative assistants had stayed late to inventory supplies and straighten out the stock, which had a habit of snowballing into a disaster zone every few weeks. She hesitated at the closed door.

That's when she heard the moan, high and keening, as if someone were in pain. Immediately she opened the door.

Posed in profile, a couple was making love. Braced atop a four-box stack of unopened copy paper, the woman's bare arms twined around the naked torso of the dark-haired man who held her, her skirt hiked up way past indecent, her bare legs curved around his waist as he kissed and stroked her, their movements rocking the boxes of paper she was sitting on, banging them inelegantly into a nearby filing cabinet.

Madelyn let out a squeak and averted her eyes, starting to back out. Then she caught a glimpse of the woman's face. *"Peg?"*

The woman looked up. *"Madelyn?"*

Peg's lover turned to look at her. *"Todd?"*

"Madelyn!" he squeaked.

"Oh—my—God," Madelyn said, each word spaced in stunned disbelief.

The lovers sprang apart, hopping around like chickens who'd just lost their heads as they tried to cover bare body parts.

Madelyn knew her eyes must be the size of dinner plates. "Oh, wow. Oh, gee. Oh, just . . ." She flapped her hands. "Just forget I was ever here."

"Wait. It's not what you think." Peg fluttered a hand, her blouse hanging askew and misbuttoned. "Well, it is what you think, but—"

"For Christ's sake," Todd muttered, his face stained with embarrassment. "I thought you'd locked the door."

"I thought *you'd* locked it," Peg told him.

"What's all the commotion? Is somebody hurt?"

Madelyn looked over to find Zack standing in the doorway, surprised that he was still at the office. He lifted one dark eyebrow as he surveyed the scene, a ripe grin spreading over his mouth as understanding dawned.

"I didn't know you two had hooked up," he said to Peg and Todd. "Well, carry on, by all means. Madelyn, shall we go?"

Madelyn met his eyes and nodded.

"No, wait, both of you!" Peg exclaimed as she gave her short skirt a firm downward tug. "Todd and I have an announcement." She reached out and grabbed Todd's hand, pulling him close. "Coming in here—it was just . . . foolish spontaneity. We got carried away from the excitement." She grinned, beaming as widely as a model in a tooth-whitening ad. "Congratulate us. We're getting married!"

Madelyn's jaw dropped. "*What?* You and Todd? How? When? No offense, Todd, but I didn't think you even came up as a smudge on Peg's radar screen."

Todd draped an arm across Peg's shoulders. "You're right. She barely knew I existed, not until that wonderful night when I forgot my wallet and missed my train home. The guy she was going out with got all bent when she arrived with me in tow. He really bristled up when she told him she'd offered to let me share their cab."

"You wouldn't believe the big asshole Bruno turned into," Peg said, taking over the story. "He was just awful to Todd, bellyaching about how he wasn't going to pay for an extra ten-block cab ride just to give a lift to one of my coworkers. How if Todd was any sort of man he'd make it home on his own. It was freezing that night and beginning to sleet."

"I remember," Madelyn murmured.

Peg continued. "He made me so mad, I told him he could forget the date; Todd and I would share a ride on our own. Bruno grabbed me and tried to force me into the cab he'd flagged. That's when Todd came to my rescue and hit him."

"Hit him?" Madelyn and Zack repeated together.

"Yeah, a real roundhouse punch right in the nose. Dude, you should have seen the blood fly, gushed all over Bruno's white wool sweater. He whined like a baby." Peg looped an arm around Todd's waist and smiled at him with the dopiest expression Madelyn had ever seen. "My hero."

Todd smiled back, losing himself in his beloved's eyes. A few seconds later, they were kissing.

Madelyn allowed them a moment, then clapped her hands. "Hey, break it up you two, or we'll be back where this all started. I assure you, I don't need to see it again."

"I didn't see it." Zack leaned a shoulder against the doorjamb. "If they want to stage a reenactment, they should go ahead."

Madelyn ignored Zack and his suggestion. "So what's the rest of the story?"

Flushed and breathless, Todd and Peg forced themselves apart.

Todd recovered first. "Peg and I took another cab. I'd banged up my knuckles pretty good, so when we got to her place, she invited me up to put ice on my hand. We started talking and before either of us knew it, half the night was gone. We found out we have a lot in common. Did you know her brother was best friends with my cousin Jim in high school?"

"I had no idea." Madelyn remarked.

Peg shot her a look. "To cut to the chase, Todd and I started seeing each other. We decided to keep it quiet at first, in case things didn't work out. Then later, well, it just seemed simpler not to say anything, what with our working together and all.

"I'm sorry I didn't tell you, Madelyn. I've felt just awful keeping a secret like that from you. But I was going to break the news to you tomorrow. Todd only proposed tonight. Even our parents don't know yet. I guess you and Zack will be the first to wish us happy. You do wish us happy, don't you?"

"Of course I wish you happy. Oh, God, you're getting married!" Madelyn rushed across the space that separated her from her friend and the two women embraced like a pair of out-of-control teenagers. Twin squeals of high-pitched girlish glee filled the small room; then they put their heads together as Peg showed off her brand-new diamond engagement ring.

Zack stepped forward and offered a hand to Todd. "Congratulations, March. Can't say I envy you the marriage noose, but every luck. Peg's a great gal."

Todd didn't know Zack all that well and lived a bit in awe of him, but he accepted the hand and the good wishes with a firm shake. "Thanks." He turned his sights on his fiancée, devotion pouring from his eyes. "I've loved her from the first day we met, but I never dared hope she would one day feel the same about me. It's like a dream and I don't ever want to wake up."

As Todd spoke, Zack watched Madelyn, so exuberant and excited in her pleasure for her friend. A strange knot formed inside his chest as he remembered her words.

I love you.

When a woman tells you she loves you, it's well past time to get out. The kindest move he could make would be to end their affair and spare her further involvement, further pain. But every time he thought of it, imagined himself saying the words, some part of him rebelled.

He just wasn't ready for it to be over.

And as selfish as it might be—and no doubt it was—part of him reveled in knowing she loved him. There was something profoundly satisfying in realizing that a woman as sweet and giving and intelligent as Madelyn could find him worth loving. The real him, not the practiced face and easy charm he showed the rest of the world. She saw through him in ways no one else ever had or had ever wanted to. And admitting that scared the crap out of him.

She looked up as if she knew he was thinking about her. For an instant their eyes met; then he glanced away to keep her from seeing too much.

Breaking off her celebration with Peg, Madelyn turned to Todd. "I'm so happy for you." She moved to embrace him.

"Well, if we're hugging now," Zack said, slipping back into his usual urbane mode, "then I claim the right to kiss the bride."

Madelyn crossed her arms. "She's not a bride yet. Kiss her at the wedding."

"Am I invited to the wedding?"

"Of course you are. Both of you are. In fact, Madelyn's just agreed to be my maid of honor." Peg looked between the two of them. "Hey, I just realized. What are you both doing here? Todd and I started fooling around because we thought everybody had gone home."

Madelyn stepped into the breach. "I did leave but had to come back for that file that needs to go down to production. I'm glad you reminded me, or in all the excitement, I might have forgotten it again." She walked over to retrieve the file she'd set down.

"And I had a late meeting across town and stopped back to drop off a few things," Zack explained. "When I heard all the noise, I came to see what was up."

"Since we've kept both of you so late, let Todd and me treat you to dinner," Peg offered.

"Thank you, but I couldn't," Madelyn refused.

"And I need my beauty sleep." Zack wagged his eyebrows. "Big presentation tomorrow."

Peg accepted their refusals with grace. "I suppose forcing the two of you into such a close social situation would be asking too much anyway. To make it up to Madelyn at least, I'll be happy to take that file off your hands and drop it off so you can go home. Zack, Todd and I will have to be beholden to you."

"Don't be. The pair of you are better than a whole season's entertainment. And since I'm sure you have better plans in mind, I'll force myself to walk Grayson here to her car. If she's game."

"As an engagement present to Todd and Peg, I accept."

CHAPTER FOURTEEN

"Thanks for walking me out."

Madelyn pressed a button on her keyless remote. The doors unlocked with a brief flash of the headlights and a single electronic chirp that bounced gently off the walls of the deserted parking garage.

"Of course," Zack said. "How about a quick lift—one level up?"

"Okay." They climbed into her car and she started the engine. "I thought you parked in one of the other garages."

"I used to. When my fees came due a couple months ago, I decided to switch. This seemed more convenient."

She made no comment as she put her car in gear. Moments later, they stopped in front of his car, a glossy black Lexus she knew he'd bought at a steal from a guy who'd gotten in way over his head on the payments. It was one of only a few cars left on that level.

Madelyn traced a fingernail across one of the pleats in

her skirt. "You could follow me home and I'll fix us some dinner. It's a little late, but I'm sure I can toss something together fast, even if it's only spaghetti." She met his eyes and wished he'd kiss her, or at least give her one of his gorgeous smiles.

Briefly, he laid a hand over hers. "Spaghetti sounds great, but I wasn't lying when I said I have a major presentation scheduled tomorrow. I need to be in the office early to finish up a few final details. It would be better if I wasn't yawning my way through them. Can we do it another night?"

"Of course, if you'd rather," she said, trying not to be deflated.

She waited for him to kiss her.

He did, but it was with a quick, almost sexless brush of his lips that was over almost as soon as it had begun.

"Good night," he said. "Drive safely."

"You too," she whispered around the sudden lump in her throat. "Good night."

She barely remembered the trip home. Her nerves were stretched as tight as a bowstring by the time she let herself into her apartment. Only when the door was closed and locked behind her did she give in to the tears.

It was Friday night and she'd had a long, dreadful week and an even longer dreadful day. Zack had called the night before, asking if they could meet at her apartment this evening instead of the usual out-of-the-way spot. He wanted to talk, he'd said. She hadn't asked about what. She already knew—he wanted to break up.

Madelyn fastened the backing onto the second half of a pair of earrings and checked her image in the mirror.

She was wearing a silky green pantsuit that hugged each and every curve. If he wanted to end it between them, there was little she could do to stop him. But she figured he should have one last eye-popping look at exactly what it was he was about to give up.

She couldn't even blame him. From the start, Zack had been up front about what he wanted. Sex without strings. Pleasure and no regrets.

But she did have regrets.

How naive and stupid she'd been to think she wouldn't. Casual romantic involvements simply weren't in her nature. Her emotions ran too deep. She felt too much, and with him she felt far more than she'd ever dreamed she could, or would. Lately, she'd indulged in the fantasy that he'd fallen in love with her too. Then she'd had to go and ruin what they did have by saying those three condemning little words, the ones that had made him pull away like a scalded cat.

Well, she wasn't going to grovel. She'd put on her best face, smile her brightest smile, and pretend that losing him didn't hurt worse than having her heart ripped out of her chest. As for the "I love you" that had rolled out of her big, stupid mouth in the heat of the moment, she'd been drunk, hadn't known what she was saying. People said and did all sorts of things they didn't really mean, especially in moments of inebriated passion. At least she thought they did.

The buzzer sounded. He was here. Without waiting, she pressed the door-release button to let him inside the building. She pinched some color into her pale cheeks, forced her lips to curve into a happy shape, and went to answer the door.

"You should check to make sure who it is before you buzz people in," Zack scolded as he bent to press a warm kiss against her lips. "You could have been letting a homicidal maniac into the building."

"There are only so many homicidal maniacs around, even in New York. I figured chances were good one of them wouldn't show up at the same moment as you." She closed the door behind him.

"Here, these are for you." He held out a bouquet of flowers—a cheerful mixture of pink roses, yellow lilies, and white baby's breath.

Surprised, she accepted them and buried her nose against the petals of one cool, satiny rose. The scent was pure heaven. Why had he brought them? Was it was usual for a man to give presents to the woman he was leaving? A consolation gift of sorts?

She shook the notion aside. "They're lovely. Thank you. I . . . I should find a vase." She fled into the kitchen.

Zack followed.

She seemed nervous, no doubt wondering what he'd stopped by to say. He was a bit nervous too, he realized, although he shouldn't be.

He loitered in the kitchen doorway, watching as she reached upward for a vase, one that resided on the top shelf of a tall cabinet. The sight of her was one he couldn't help but enjoy, especially the way the material of her pantsuit molded itself to the rounded curves of her bottom and hips.

He stepped close. "Here, let me get that down for you." It was an easy stretch for him; he retrieved the vase and handed it to her. But he didn't move away. Instead he took hold of her hips to press her back against him, then bent his head to skim kisses over her cheek, the arch of her neck.

"I meant to wait for a few minutes at least, but it's hard not to touch." He leaned into her a fraction more. "Very hard."

Madelyn set the vase on the counter, fearing she might break it otherwise. "You said you wanted to talk."

He turned her slowly to face him. "I did, but it can wait, for now." His lips lowered toward hers.

She stopped him with scarcely a breath remaining between. "No, you've got me curious—well, more than curious. Tell me now." Did he think he could enjoy one last mattress dance with her, then say good-bye? She didn't think so.

He paused, catching the insistent gleam in her eyes. "All right." He straightened but kept his hands steady at her waist. "Last weekend started me thinking."

"About what?"

"Us. How little time we have together. The way we have to hide ourselves and sneak around, pretending we feel nothing for fear someone else might see. The secrecy was okay at first, exciting even, but it's gotten old. I think we need to reconsider our current arrangement."

Her heart slammed inside her chest. Was this it? Was he going to end it now?

He linked his hands with hers. "I know we made rules, agreed to keep this between us and us alone, a fling we could both enjoy until the thrill ran out, but we've gone beyond that now. Seeing you on the weekends and an occasional stolen evening in between simply isn't enough anymore. I want you with me openly, at work during the day and in my bed at night, together whenever and wherever we choose. I want to quit hiding. I'm hoping you want that too."

"You mean you aren't breaking up with me?" she blurted.

"Is that what you thought? That I'd come here tonight to end things between us?"

She nodded. "You've been so distant this week, ever since our last night in Atlantic City when I said . . . when I said . . ."

"When you said you loved me?" he murmured. "So you do remember."

"Yes. I remember your reaction as well."

"I've had a lot on my mind, a lot of things I needed to sort through. I didn't mean to upset you." He cradled her face in his palm, tracing his thumb across her cheek. "Did you mean it, Red? About loving me?"

As blue as a summer lake, her eyes reflected the devotion she felt. "Yes, I meant it. Do you feel the same about me?"

Discussing his feelings was never easy, but for her, for Madelyn, he'd try. "I need you; I know that. I want you more than I can ever remember wanting a woman, any woman. But love, that's not an emotion I'm very comfortable with. And I can't say I actually believe it exists, not in the romantic way I think you mean. Caring, protecting, those are feelings I can understand. I care about you Madelyn. I want to be with you and to see you happy. I want us to be happy together."

What exactly was he saying?

He wanted her. He needed her. He cared for her and wished for her happiness, their happiness. Far from wanting to break up, it sounded like Zack was looking to make a real commitment. . . . A small tendril of hope sprang to life inside her. "Are you asking me to marry you?" she asked hesitantly.

His eyes widened. "Marry you? No, that's not what I meant at all. . . ."

She shrank back, crushed as if she were a bug he'd stomped into the floorboards. She yanked her hands free. "Oh, then never mind."

"Obviously I haven't explained myself well."

"No, you obviously haven't."

She tried to squeeze around him, to flee, but he caught her, trapping her with an arm on either side. "Madelyn, don't."

"Don't what?"

"You're taking this all wrong, especially the last part, the marriage part."

"And how should I be taking it?"

"Not personally, that's how. I'm not against marrying *you* per se. It's marriage I'm against."

"Oh? So it's a philosophical matter, then?"

"Exactly."

"Well, fuck your philosophy."

He winced but refused to back down. "This isn't some excuse I've made up to give myself a convenient out whenever I want one. I've got an out right now, a free pass we both know I can use anytime I want. It's what you thought I'd come here tonight to do, isn't it? To get out. And if I'd told you I wanted out, you'd have let me go."

"Yes," she agreed in a low voice. "Of course I would have."

He clasped her arms, rubbing his hands slowly up and down from elbow to shoulder. "But that's not what either of us wants. Why does the issue of marriage have to matter now when it didn't only a few minutes ago?"

Why? she mused. Because his feelings, his attitudes, were out in the open, because the truth once spoken could never be taken back. Because she loved him and wanted him forever and he didn't feel the same. Still, she had to know. "Why are you so opposed to marriage? I don't understand."

He released her and began to pace the room. "Because it changes people, Madelyn, and not for the better. Relationships don't last. Look at Billy Aikens. If you'd known him when I did, known his wife, you'd have thought it impossible they'd ever split up. They were happy; I mean, really happy. Even when they fought you knew it was only temporary, a quick storm that would blow through and leave no lasting damage. But time passes, things change, feelings end. If they couldn't make it, hell, who can? And what do they have to show for their twelve years? Battered hearts and a pair of kids that can't be conveniently split down the middle."

He fisted his hands. "And the kids—they're the worst part. They don't understand why their parents despise each other, wondering what they've done to turn them that way, desperate to fix it somehow. Only it can't be fixed. And of course they haven't done anything wrong; they're just pawns caught up in somebody else's nightmare."

She thought of his childhood, the small pieces of it he'd shared. His own parents fighting and hating and tearing each other to shreds in ways that had left him and his sister with lifelong scars.

"But some people make it," she reasoned. "Some

marriages last. My parents have been married for over thirty years and they're still together, still in love. I know they're happy. I see it in their eyes, hear it in their voices, know it by the way they touch and act when they're together." She stepped near and placed a palm against his chest. "Marriage doesn't have to be bad."

"Maybe not, but usually it is and it's not worth the risk."

"How do you know? Until you've tried it, how do you know?"

His eyes were bleak. "I have tried it, and it was a miserable failure. I'm never putting myself through such hell again."

Shock and understanding arrived at the same instant, a sturdy piece of her world slipping from beneath her feet. "You were married?"

"Yes. A long time ago, years now. I was young and stupid, far too stupid to know what I was letting myself in for."

"Who was she? What was her name?"

"Angela, although I don't know why that matters. I haven't set eyes on her since the day we filed for divorce."

"It matters because she was part of your life, for a while at least. You must have loved her, or thought you did."

"I suppose I did at first. But it wore off quickly. She'd gotten what she wanted, a hand up, a way out of the boring drudgery of her life, and a free trip to Europe courtesy of the U.S. Army. I was stationed in Germany for most of my tour of duty—I later discovered it was one of the reasons she decided I'd suit as a husband. She'd always wanted to travel, you see. And she wanted social importance, the kind she'd been excluded from at home.

"But I wasn't nearly important enough, not in the long run, especially after she realized I didn't plan to make a career out of the service. Her rationale, I guess, for seeking greener pastures and a different bed. I heard she married a colonel a few days after our divorce was final. She had initiative—I'll give her that."

"She sounds like a perfect snake."

"An apt description and exactly the reason she's not worth discussing any longer. She's part of the past and has nothing to do with our lives."

"But she does, only she's not the one being punished here. I am."

"My not wanting to marry you is a punishment? I guess I should be flattered at the sentiment. You ought to be counting yourself lucky, though, since believe me, I'm saving you a lot of grief. Sparing us both years of lies and arguments and bitter regrets."

Sadness overwhelmed her. "Is that how you think it would be between us? Is that what you think of me? That I'm like her, like Angela? Loving you so little that I'd be willing to hurt and deceive you? Betray you?"

"No, you're nothing like her. If you tried, you couldn't be half the cold-blooded bitch she was."

"Then you must believe I'm like your mother, promising you love, then taking it away."

"Madelyn—," he warned.

"Because she's part of this too, isn't she?" Madelyn said insistently. "She taught you early that you can't count on people, especially women. She taught you not to trust."

He scowled but didn't disagree.

"You say you want me and need me, but for how long?" she asked. "A few months? A handful of years until you decide it isn't working and move on? And what about a family? Children?"

His expression grew darker. "What about them?"

"Do you want those things? Children and a family? Because I do."

"You can't always have what you want. Sometimes you have to make do with what seems best. Bringing children into this world doesn't seem best, not to me."

"Why?"

He raked his of fingers through his hair. "Because kids get hurt. Because they don't understand when their parents lives go to hell and they get caught in the crossfire. I swore long ago that I'd never do that to someone else, especially a child that I was responsible for bringing into this world."

Madelyn said nothing, stunned.

"But why are we having this big debate about marriage and kids?" Zack went on. "We're a long way from either of those things. Can't we just enjoy being together? Why do we have to worry about the rest right now?"

"Because if we don't worry now, then when will we?" Madelyn drew a quiet breath. "Look, we've both said a lot tonight, things that can't be taken back. What I have to know is whether you think time will change your mind about any of this. Can you give me any reason to hope?"

Lie, she thought. *That's all you have to do. Just lie and say yes.*

All he had to do was tell her that his feelings about

marriage might mellow in time. That he might come around and want children despite the risk. That he might love and trust her enough someday that the wounds of his past wouldn't matter anymore so long as they were together.

She waited, praying.

Then he sighed. "No. I'm sorry. I can't."

Her chest began to ache. "So you're offering me what we have now with no secrets, no strings, for as long as it lasts?"

"Yes, for as long as it lasts."

She wanted to cry, but the pain cut too deep. All he could give her was temporary pleasure and nothing more. There would be no home, no family, no children. Not with Zack. Yet knowing all that, she still wanted him. She still loved him. She thought about Brie, how unhappy she was because of loving the wrong man.

An unattainable man who was never going to change.

"Why don't you sleep on it," he suggested. "You don't need to decide tonight."

Moving near, he bent his head and pressed his lips to hers.

For an instant she responded, kissing him back with a wild, almost desperate intensity, breathing him in as if she were taking her last breath. Then she wrenched herself away. If she didn't do this now, she knew she'd never find the strength again. "I don't need the night. My answer is no."

He was silent for a moment. "All right. Then we'll leave things the way they are. We'll keep meeting on weekends and an evening here and there."

She straightened her shoulders. "No, you don't understand. When I say no, I mean no to everything. It's over, Zack."

Anger and disbelief flashed in his eyes. "So you're ending it?"

"Yes, I guess I am."

"That's not what you wanted earlier."

"A lot has changed since earlier."

"And that's it? Your final decision? End of discussion?"

"Yes. It's the end," she said dully.

Of her heart.

Of her hopes.

And most of all, her happiness.

His jaw hardened, his eyes fierce. "Fine. Have it your way. I wish you joy in finding the perfect life."

He stormed out, slamming the door behind him with enough force to shake the walls and the pictures hanging on them. The dishes rattled in the kitchen cupboards as well, along with the vase on the countertop, sitting empty—the flowers he'd brought lonely and abandoned nearby.

That's when it struck her—the incredible irony.

She'd been so sure, so worried, that he'd come here tonight to break up with her. Yet in the end she'd been the one to break up with him.

She dropped onto a hard kitchen chair for support and began to cry.

"Which do you like better? Ivory bisque or the royal pearl?" Peg tapped one well-manicured fingernail against the wedding stationery samples spread across the table between her and Madelyn. "There's also this one— classic white. Todd liked it, but I don't know. With men it's usually 'the plainer the better and don't bother me with all that shade stuff.'"

"The white's nice," Madelyn said, sipping from her glass of iced tea.

"Really? You think so?" Peg's face puckered as she reconsidered. "I've been leaning toward the ivory bisque."

"The bisque is nice too."

"Or the pearl. Oh, I can't decide." Peg threw up her hands. "How do people do this?"

"Planning a wedding's a lot of work. The person you really should be talking to is my mother."

Peg sighed. "I wish I could, but, well, without sounding gauche, we can't afford your mother. You know Todd and I are paying for the wedding ourselves. My parents had given up on me ever getting married and blew my wedding money on a Hawaiian cruise. You should have heard the guilt in their voices when I told them the good news. But it's okay. This way Todd and I can have the wedding *we* want. If only I could decide what that is."

"Mother doesn't have to plan your whole wedding, and I'm sure she wouldn't mind offering a little free advice here and there. Chances are she'd even be willing to order some things for you at a discount—once you make up your mind. I'll ask her about it when I go up to visit this weekend."

Peg's eyes brightened. "You're sure? I don't want to be a bother."

"It's no bother. Believe me, she lives for this stuff."

Madelyn waved away Peg's murmurs of thanks, grateful when the waiter arrived bearing their lunch seconds later. She let Peg rattle on, brimming with excitement about her plans, and stabbed a fork into her Cobb salad.

Madelyn was happy for her friend—she really was—and genuinely flattered to have been chosen as Peg's maid of honor. Yet lately, all this talk of weddings was wearing on her nerves. As if it weren't bad enough listening to a constant play-by-play account of the impending nuptials, seeing Peg and Todd together, overflowing with joyous anticipation and beaming love, well, it was enough to give an iron-stomached sailor the dry heaves. And more than enough to remind Madelyn of everything missing in her own life and precisely how unhappy she was.

Over the past six weeks, she'd tried hard not to think about Zack. It was nearly impossible, though, especially at work, where she might turn at any moment to find him there, unexpectedly striding into a conference room or passing her in the hall, sparing her nothing more than a polite nod. And sometimes not even that.

At least her friends and coworkers knew nothing about her liaison with him, so she was spared any pitying looks or hushed whispers. Right after their breakup, she'd worried Zack might say something, let slip some unthinking comment that would give them away. But true to his word, he'd kept their secret. Deceit was the one thing he'd never practiced with her; afterward she'd been ashamed for doubting him.

She missed him.

It was as simple as that. The nights were dark and empty and endlessly long. The weekends were pure torture.

For Zack, their parting didn't seem to have affected him at all. Obviously, she'd been just one more woman in a long line of women who'd shared his bed. If only she could get over him as easily.

"I didn't know he came in here," Peg murmured.

The comment drew Madelyn from her reverie. "*Hmm? Who?*"

"Zack. He just walked in."

Madelyn willed herself not to look around. She shrugged. "Probably a client he's taking to lunch."

"That's no client. Unless business attire has changed and professional women are wearing four-inch Italian heels and lavender slip dresses to their appointments now."

This time she couldn't help herself. She whipped her head around and watched as Zack and his date followed the maitre d' to a table. Stunning, the woman had flawless features, a slender, curvaceous figure, platinum blond hair, and prominent breasts. The result of a cunning dye job and implants, no doubt—she'd probably had plastic surgery on her nose and chin as well. No woman could be that beautiful naturally.

Zack looked wonderful, lean and smart in a dark blue suit that emphasized the green in his eyes and complemented his dark hair.

Madelyn's eyes turned to the blonde again, jealousy curdling in her stomach.

"My guess is she's a model," Peg mused.

"Or a hooker."

Peg choked out a laugh. "If she were with any man but Zack, I might agree. Of all the men on earth, though, he's the last one who'd ever have to pay for sex. Flash that smile and the women come running for free."

"I'm surprised you never made a play for him your-self with that attitude," Madelyn said, deliberately turn-ing her gaze away from Zack and his date.

"I have to admit I considered it a time or two, a long time ago, well before I met my sweet Todd. But as we've both noted, Zack's got 'heartbreaker' written all over him in big red letters. I knew better than to hold my fin-gers out and burn them in that fire."

Madelyn had known better too. Feeling faintly ill, she set down her fork.

"Something wrong with your salad?" Peg asked.

Madelyn had barely touched her meal. "No, I'm just not very hungry. I ... um ... ate a doughnut late this morning. I guess it's ruined my appetite," she lied.

"That'll teach you to snack," Peg admonished.

Peg finished her own meal while Madelyn sat, forcing herself not to look in Zack's direction, trying to pretend he wasn't there.

He missed her.

It was as simple as that. He didn't know why he'd decided to torture himself today, coming to this restau-rant. Some perverse little masochistic streak in him, he supposed.

Hours earlier he'd overheard Peg mention plans to meet Madelyn here for lunch. So when Vonda—a boda-cious Swedish stewardess who dropped into his life ev-ery once in a while to share a meal, some intelligent conversation, and a few hours of unbridled, free-spirited sex—called to say she had a brief layover in town and would he like to meet, he'd agreed, suggesting they start with lunch. Then he'd chosen this restaurant.

He'd spotted Madelyn the instant he walked through the door.

Her hair was ablaze with color, twisted up off her neck in the neat little bun she favored, the one that always made his fingers itch to pull out the pins.

He watched her from the corner of his eye as he and Vonda made their way through the restaurant to their table. His breath caught when Madelyn turned to look their way. But then she swung back and didn't look again, as if seeing him with another woman made no difference to her at all. Perhaps it didn't, not anymore.

Tension he didn't know he'd been feeling eased from his shoulders when Peg and Madelyn finally paid their bill and left.

"So are you going to tell me who she is?" Vonda demanded in her husky, accented voice.

"Who?"

"The Park Avenue redhead, of course. The one you've spent the past twenty minutes desperately trying to ignore."

"She's no one."

"Hmm. Then I guess I will have *no one* to thank for keeping you out of my bed tonight."

"Who says I won't be in your bed?"

Vonda gazed back with knowing eyes. "Actually, it is kind of fun, you know, to see you like this."

"See me like what?"

She reached out and patted his hand. "Why, in love, of course, sweetheart. In love."

CHAPTER FIFTEEN

Warm, thick sounds of summer hummed around her, the drone of honeybees dusting themselves gold with pollen gradually giving way to a symphony of chirps and cricks as night creatures prepared for the sun to fade and the moon to take its place in the sky. Flowers and new-cut grass added a soft perfume to the humid twilight air, mingling with the human scents of grilling hamburgers and citronella candles.

Clustered beneath rows of Chinese lanterns that glowed like fanciful jewels above the spacious redbrick patio, people ate and drank and chatted in anticipation of the fireworks to come, courtesy of the nearby municipal government.

Typical of her mother, Madelyn thought, to have her house built on the one lawn in the area that boasted an unobstructed view of the Fourth of July festivities, despite the stately oak and elm trees that ranged the length of the property.

Usually her parents' parties were a chance for Madelyn to relax and enjoy catching up with old friends and acquaintances. But this year she found herself struggling to have fun. It was different this year.

She was different.

A low stone wall bisected a portion of the rear grounds, creating a secluded, semicircular perennial garden crowded with masses of flowering plants and slender-limbed trees. Madelyn seated herself atop the wall, as she had so many times over the years, letting her feet dangle above the grass. Closing her eyes, she drank in the mingled richness of rose, peony, and honeysuckle, scents that turned the air candy sweet.

She liked this place, where the light didn't quite reach, where she could survey the dazzle of the party and the people spread before her as though it were all some grand play. She took a sip from her glass before balancing it carefully next to her hip, then ate a piece of the cookie she'd taken from the dessert table.

"I knew I'd find you here." James slung his legs over the wall from the garden side to seat himself next to her. "Cookies and lemonade—I thought by now you'd have outgrown that disgusting predilection."

Startled, Madelyn raised a hand to her chest. "You shouldn't sneak up on a person like that. You nearly scared me to death."

"Me? Never. I needed to run over to the house for a minute and decided it would be easier to cut through your parents' backyard on the way back. It used to be the only way I ever traveled."

As teenagers, the two of them had made a habit of slipping back and forth between their homes via the garden wall. They'd spent many a pleasant hour sitting together exactly as they were now.

"You could have made some sort of noise to warn me you were coming," she scolded. "Last time I looked, Sheila Wharton had you cornered near the guacamole dip."

"Yes, she did," he grumbled.

Sheila Wharton was a voluptuous forty-three-year-old blonde widow with an unapologetic appetite for younger men, especially those with money. "It wasn't very nice of you to abandon me."

"I knew you could hold your own. Besides, I couldn't endure more of her arm-twisting. She's always trying to con me into hawking some homemade perfume of hers, seeing as how I have an 'in' with advertisers. I've tried to tell her it doesn't work that way, but explaining something to Sheila is like trying to convince a salmon not to swim upstream."

"I've always thought of her more as an octopus—eight clinging tentacles that refuse to let go."

Madelyn smiled. "Here, as a consolation present, half of my cookie to ease your pain?"

"Chocolate chip?"

"Of course."

He reached out to accept the treat.

Quietly they ate, listening to the abundant night sounds, watching partygoers mill and mingle.

"So are you going to tell me about it?" he asked, dusting a leftover crumb from his finger.

"About what?"

"Whatever it is that's troubling you. You can't fool me, you know."

"It's nothing. I've just been thinking—about a lot of things."

"About him, you mean."

She'd told James of her breakup with Zack not long after it happened. Her involvement with Zack was still a sore point with him.

"No," she defended. "I've been thinking about me. Oh, look, the fireworks are starting."

A trio of pyrotechnic bursts lighted the sky in a patriotic shower of red, white, and blue. Another round followed, rockets whining as they streaked upward, exploding in thunderous volleys reminiscent of cannon fire. Additional starbursts brightened the night, tiny pinwheels that whizzed and whirled in a crazy dance of corkscrew spirals.

"Have you come to any conclusions?" James asked.

"Only one. I need to stop moping and get on with my life. Whatever I thought I had with him, it's done. I need to accept that and move on. I need to feel happy again."

"Are you so certain it's over? You're positive he won't change his mind?"

If Zack were inclined to change his mind, he'd have done it by now. He'd had weeks in which to regret his decision. The two of them were more distant than strangers now, even the old rivalry between them unable to rouse more than a lukewarm spark inside her chest. He'd told her once that all he wanted was sex, that liking and loving had no part in his needs. She should have taken him at his word and kept her heart whole.

Another series of explosives raced high into the night, bursting open in a blaze of color and light and noise before fizzling and fading into nothing.

Madelyn inhaled deeply and let a door close somewhere deep inside herself. "No, there's no chance. He and I don't want the same things."

Their hands rested side by side on the stone wall, which was still warm from the residual heat of the day. James covered the top of hers with his own. "You and I do. We've been friends too long not to understand each other. Let me give you what you want, Meg, what both of us want. When we aren't in the city, you'd have the house here, right next to your family."

"The mausoleum, you mean," she teased, using their old name for his place.

"It's mine, now that my parents have moved to Italy for good. With your touch, you could turn that lumbering old elephant into the home it's never been. I'd give you free rein inside and out—change anything you like. The same with the apartment in town."

"Your penthouse is lovely just as it is, and no one could complain about the magnificent view of Central Park. A definite step up from the brick building I see from my current apartment," she quipped.

"And as soon as you like, we can start a family. Think of the beautiful babies we'd make. A whole patch of little strawberry blondes to bring laughter and joy into our lives. They could play right here in this very garden."

Madelyn gave a wistful smile at the thought. "Mother and Dad would adore it. But a patch? That sounds like a few too many. Just two will do, thank you very much."

He gazed full in her face, the glow from the fireworks reflected in his eyes. "Then two it will be. I love you, Meg. Say you'll marry me. Give me the chance to make you as happy as I know you'll make me."

Traitorously, an image of Zack flashed into her mind,

along with a wish that he was the one saying these beautiful things to her. But he wasn't. And he never would be.

She looked at James, her friend. The man who'd always been there for her, who'd always been able to make her laugh, even when she wanted to cry. She loved him. Oh, not in the same way she loved Zack, but in the end, was one sort of love really better than another? Perhaps she never would share with James the passionate intensity, the breathless fire that raged out of control at Zack's simplest touch. But neither would she suffer the exquisite pain, the empty, aching gap his loss had left in her heart.

Maybe it was time to put away unrealistic dreams and romantic fairy tales, to learn to be content with the wonderful gift she was being offered. And the wonderful man who was offering it.

A final glitter of color saturated the sky, accompanied by booming claps that were as loud as thunder.

Amid the fanfare, alone in their own shadowy retreat, Madelyn turned her hand over and threaded her fingers with his. "Yes, James, I'll marry you."

His eyes glowed with relief and delight, then deepened in a blaze of desire. He drew her into his arms, pressing her tightly to the width of his chest before joining his mouth with hers.

She let him take what he wanted, needing to give him everything she could. It felt comfortable, familiar, being with him again this way, and not at all unpleasant.

Their marriage would be satisfying, she told herself, a true partnership of friends. Unwanted comparisons rose in her mind as his lips played over hers, haunting memories. Ruthlessly, she pushed them away. She would be a good wife, she promised herself. She would make him happy. And somehow, some way, she would be happy too.

James lifted his head, his voice husky. "I almost forgot." He reached into his pocket and brought out a small, square box. "I guess I should have given this to you when I was actually proposing."

He opened the velvet-covered jeweler's case and lifted out a ring. She recognized it instantly. Originally his great-great-grandmother's, the nineteenth-century heirloom was passed on each generation to the eldest son. He'd shown it to her once many years ago when they'd snuck into his father's study and opened the safe during a party.

Massive and intensely yellow, the flawless emerald-cut diamond was secured in an old-fashioned Victorian setting of twenty-four-karat gold. As remarkably beautiful as it was, the ring was not one she would ever have chosen for herself.

"Is that why you had to go over to your house?" she asked. "So sure I'd change my mind, were you?"

"Not for an instant. Only hopeful." He hesitated, and the stone winked in the dark. "I know this thing's a monstrous old antique, and if you don't want it, I won't be hurt. We can ride in to New York tomorrow so you can pick out something else."

She knew he would be hurt, despite his assurances to the contrary. She held out her left hand. "No, this is lovely."

Pleased, James slid the weighty gem onto her finger.

The ring slipped sideways, then on around to fit against her palm.

"Looks like we'll be taking that trip to the jeweler's after all," he remarked. "Fat-fingered women must run in my family."

They both chuckled.

"Hi, what are you guys doing? Am I interrupting?"

They looked up at the same moment and found Ivy, tall and reed slender, silhouetted in a backwash of light from the party.

"No, not at all," James declared. "Matter of fact, you can be the very first to wish us happy." He took Madelyn's hand in his. "Your sister has just agreed to be my wife."

"Your wife?" Ivy squeaked. "You mean you're getting married?"

"That's precisely what I mean."

"But I thought . . ."

"What did you think?"

There was a small pause. "Nothing. I didn't think anything. This is great, really great. Congratulations!" Ivy rushed forward to embrace them both. "Just wait until Mom hears. She's going to be over the moon."

"She'll probably drive *me* over the moon with wedding plans before this is through," Madelyn murmured. "Maybe we should think about eloping."

"And listen to the family whine and complain for the rest of our lives about how we cheated them out of their special day? I don't think so. Even my parents would have a fit, and you know they don't much care what I do as long as I don't embarrass them. They'll probably even fly in from Italy."

Imagining it, along with the hordes of relatives and friends that would descend for the wedding, made Madelyn long to back out.

James sensed her distress. "Don't worry, sweetheart. The trick is to let everyone else do all the work, while you and I just go along for the ride." He grinned. "Piece of cake. You'll see."

She owed him no explanations, but Madelyn decided that first thing Monday morning she would tell Zack about her engagement. Of course, he probably wouldn't care. He might even hug her the way everyone else had done all weekend long, give her a kiss on the cheek and wish her happy. Somehow, though, she had trouble imagining that from him.

She nearly phoned him late on Sunday evening, after she'd returned to the blessed peace and solitude of her apartment. But what would she say? *Hi, Zack, it's Madelyn. I know we're not seeing each other anymore and it's probably no big deal to you, but I thought you might want to know. I'm getting married.*

His feelings shouldn't matter to her anymore, she told herself. Still, she didn't want him hearing the news as grist for the daily mill of office chitchat. Zack could be as affable and charming as they came. He could also on occasion be as unpredictable as a lightning storm. There was no telling how he might react. So she decided she would go into the office early and leave a brief, impersonal note on his desk asking him to stop by and see her. Satisfied with her decision, she turned out the light and fell asleep.

At precisely six thirty a.m., her clock radio switched

on. Worn out from the eventful weekend, and with the radio volume inadvertently turned down to a soft hum, Madelyn snuggled deeper into her pillow and slumbered on. Thank God for her trusty alarm cat, Millie, who awakened her forty-five minutes later with a brush of her whiskers and a great deal of noisy purring.

Groggy, flustered, and out of sorts, Madelyn made it into the office thirty minutes late. Thirty minutes too late to prop a nice, discreet little note in the center of Zack's desk. By now, he was sure to have arrived, along with nearly everyone else. In desperate need of counsel and caffeine, she settled for the easier of the two and brewed a pot of strong Irish breakfast tea.

"What is that on your finger?" Peg demanded from the doorway.

Startled, Madelyn nearly spilled hot tea in her lap.

Oh God, the ring. Why hadn't she remembered to take it off this morning? She still couldn't believe the jeweler had been able to size the band so quickly.

She and James had visited the exclusive store late Saturday afternoon. By the same time Sunday, the ring was finished, messengered special delivery to her at James's penthouse apartment. That was the kind of service one received, she supposed, when one's fiancé came from very old establishment money.

Madelyn dropped her left hand into her lap, but it was too late.

"Oh, no, you don't." Peg advanced into the room. "Get that hand right back out here where I can see it."

Madelyn set her tea mug down on her desk, then reluctantly complied.

Peg grabbed Madelyn's hand and yanked her to her

feet, trotting her over to the window, where the ring could be viewed under natural light. "*Oh. My. God.* It's real, isn't it? And it's huge. I'm surprised it doesn't make your finger ache. You finally did it, didn't you? James proposed."

"Yes. On the Fourth." Madelyn smiled, catching some of her friend's enthusiasm.

"During the fireworks?"

Madelyn nodded.

"Somewhere secluded, I hope."

"My mother's garden."

"*Ooh*, it sounds so romantic. As much as I love Todd, he could have picked a better place than the office to pop the question. But he redeemed himself this weekend. He's taking me to the Bahamas for our honeymoon." She broke off, flapping a hand. "Oh, would you listen to me, yammering on about myself, when I haven't even congratulated you yet." She pulled Madelyn into a fierce hug. "Every happiness. You deserve the best."

"Thanks, so do you."

Peg released her and stepped back. "Have you set a date?"

"No, not yet. But I know not to pick the fifteenth of November. That's your day."

"Yes, it is." Peg paused to dream a moment. "It's so fabulous. Can you believe it? We're both getting married," she exclaimed on a high note, almost pirouetting with excitement.

Madelyn couldn't help but laugh.

"Oh, and I just thought, unless you get married before me . . ."

Madelyn shook her head in a definitive no.

"... I'll have to be your *matron* of honor, since I'll no longer be a maiden." She fluttered her eyelashes dramatically.

Madelyn frowned. How to tell her. "Peg, about that— I really want you for my matron of honor, but ..."

Peg stopped her jigging, the smile fading a bit on her face. "But what?"

"It's just ... years ago I promised my sister that she could be my maid of honor. I'll explain it to Brie. She'll understand if I don't ask her."

Peg considered for a moment, the smile settling back onto her face. "No, she's your sister. If I had any sisters, I'm sure I would have asked one of them too. It's okay."

"Are you sure? You're the last person in the world I'd want to hurt or offend—"

"*Psht*, don't worry about it. It's already forgotten."

"But you will be one of my bridesmaids?"

Peg put her hands on her hips in mock outrage. "I'd better be one of your bridesmaids. If I'm not, it'll mean war." They smiled at each other, completely at ease.

"Now," Peg declared, "before any more time elapses, we have to go tell Linda. She can call Suzy from her desk. Just wait until they get a look at that ring of yours."

"We should probably wait and do it on a break. I have that layout for—"

"Layout, shmayout, it'll be here when you get back. I'm not hearing one more word of protest out of you." Peg grabbed Madelyn around the wrist and dragged her out into the corridor.

"Peg, let go of me!"

Interested faces and curious eyes peered over and around drab cubicle walls.

"Hey, everybody!" Peg called. "Madelyn's tying the knot! Her boyfriend finally asked her to marry him and she said yes."

Somebody hooted. Another few clapped. And everyone smiled and wished her happy.

Peg stopped and pushed the button to call the elevator. "If anyone asks, Madelyn and I will be back in a few minutes." She paused, then added dramatically, "Or longer."

There was laughter.

The elevator dinged, the doors slid open, and the two women came face-to-face with Zack.

Madelyn's heart jumped, her mouth suddenly drier than desert sand.

"Ladies." Zack looked from one woman to the other. His eyes drifted to Madelyn, skimming slowly over her body before letting them rest for a long moment on her flushed face. She looked away. He turned his sights to Peg, putting out a hand to hold open the elevator door. "How are you both this fine morning?"

"We're simply dandy." Peg tossed him a cheeky smile as she pulled Madelyn into the car.

"And up to no good from the looks of you. What's going on?"

"Weddings, that's what's going on. Two of them."

"Two?" A puzzled frown wrinkled his brow.

"Yeah, Madelyn's engaged. She and I are both getting married."

For an instant, Zack's eyes seemed to shift from vivid green to darkest jade. Then he blinked and the look was gone.

Thankfully, Peg appeared not to have seen a thing, as she was distracted by punching the button for Linda's floor. And she seemed not to have noticed, after the elevator doors sliced shut, the lack of an answering smile on Zack's face and his failure to wish Madelyn well.

CHAPTER SIXTEEN

A compact disc of photos for Giatta Motors had been sent to him by mistake. Zack flipped through a few of the images on his computer screen, as warm evening light streamed in through his office window.

The days were long this time of year—the end of July—as though summer were slowly reaching its fingers out toward forever. At least that's how the days felt to him.

Endless.

And how he'd felt lately.

Restless.

He sat up and blew out a puff of air as he clicked the file closed and ejected the disk. He thrust it back into the mailer. No question, it belonged to Madelyn's section of the account. He tossed the package onto the corner of his desk and decided that tomorrow would be soon enough to have his assistant walk it over to her.

He had a date. Kyla, a long-legged stockbroker he'd

met a few days ago at his health club. From the sounds of the naughty message she'd left on his answering machine, she had a lot more in store for him tonight than sharing a few hot stock tips. And if he didn't hurry, he realized with a glance at his wristwatch, he would be late.

He powered down his computer, locked his desk, and picked up his briefcase. He was just about to switch off the overhead lights when the mailer containing the CD caught his eye.

He hesitated, then backtracked and grabbed the package.

By this late hour even Madelyn would have gone home. Lately she'd been leaving right on time, ever since her engagement three weeks ago. A quick detour past her office would barcly slow him down. He might as well drop the CD off now.

Her lights were out, the door open, so he strode into her office without hesitation, only to be brought up short at the sight of her. Seated behind her desk, Madelyn had turned to gaze out the window. He took one step backward to leave, but it was too late; she'd heard him.

She spun around in her chair. "Zack. I didn't know you were still here. I thought everyone had left."

He recovered quickly. "I thought so too." He lifted the mailer. "I'm just dropping this by. Photos for Giatta. The photographer addressed them to me instead of you."

Her heartbeat, which had accelerated for a short, hopeful second thinking he'd come to speak to her, slowed once more and resumed its normal speed. Masking her disappointment, she held out a hand for the package. "Thank you."

He stepped forward. As he did, the sunlight refracted through the stone on her ring and drew his attention. "That's some rock, isn't it? I haven't taken a good look at it before."

No, she thought, *how could he have?* Since the moment Zack had heard the news of her engagement, he'd done everything in his power to avoid her. Really, she should be grateful to him for staying away, she told herself.

"Real, I take it?" he continued.

"Yes, of course."

The nonchalance of her reply seemed to hit a nerve. "Oh, of course. For a moment I forgot exactly who it is you're marrying. Is it worth it?"

"What do you mean?"

"Selling yourself," he charged. "Why else would you be marrying him? It can't possibly be for love, since only a few weeks ago you said you loved *me*. Or were you mistaken about your feelings? Is it so easy for you to change your mind?"

Her cheeks reddened. "No."

"Then why, Madelyn? Why your sudden decision to marry him? Wouldn't he ask you the first time around? Was getting involved with me your way of making him jealous enough to take the plunge? Was that part of your plan the whole time?"

Amazed and appalled by his outrageous conclusions, her mouth fell open. "I didn't have a *plan.*"

"Then why were you seeing him the whole time? I didn't put it together at first, but I know now you must have been meeting him behind my back." The blush spread higher over her cheekbones. "Were you playing the pair of us against each other?"

"No. He's my friend. I saw him only as a friend."

"Some friend. If it was all so innocent, why didn't you ever mention him to me?"

"Because you'd warned me away, told me not to see him. Because I knew you'd act exactly as you are now, jealous and territorial."

Zack folded his arms over his chest. "I'm not jealous. I simply don't share what's mine. And at the time, that was you."

"Well, I'm not any longer." She straightened. "Just so you know how twisted and preposterous your thinking is, let's get a few things straight. First of all, James is more than my fiancé; he's my friend, like I said. He has been my friend since I was fourteen years old. Just because I was having an affair with *you*, a very temporary one as it turns out, didn't mean I was going to cut him out of my life. I did meet James, twice, for lunch, while we were still together. Otherwise, he and I only exchanged a few phone calls, very innocent phone calls."

"So I was right about that too." He poked a finger at her.

"Yes, about that, you were right. As to the other, your ridiculous idea that I was somehow using you to get him to propose to me? Well, news flash: James asked me to marry him a long time ago, long before I thought of you as anything more than an annoying thorn in my side. Long before you and I became lovers. Your past is catching up with you, Zack, looking for dark motivations where there aren't any to be had."

"That still doesn't explain why you're marrying him when you claim to love me."

"My reasons aren't important."

"Of course they're important!" he exploded.

"Why? Have you changed your mind about me? About us?"

He knew what she wanted—love, marriage, commitment.

He knew what he wanted—*her*.

In his bed.

In his life.

His body hardened with sudden desire. If she said the word, he'd take her right here, right now, on the desk, on the floor, anywhere. And afterward, what then?

She wanted it all. Everything. The house, the kids. Hell, she probably wanted the white picket fence too. But the thought of marriage, the idea of legally tying himself to another woman, turned his stomach, made a cold sweat break out all over his skin.

Never.

He would never let himself be trapped like that again.

He would never let himself be hurt like that again.

"No," he said in a guttural voice. "I haven't changed my mind."

"It seems we have nothing further to discuss, then." She glanced at her watch, dismissing him with the gesture. "I'm meeting James for supper. I'll be late if I don't leave soon."

"I'll walk you to your car."

"No. I can ask one of the guards for an escort."

"Madelyn—"

"Good night, Zack."

He hesitated; then he leaned down to retrieve his briefcase. "Good night, Madelyn."

He was halfway to his apartment before he remembered his date with Kyla. If he hurried, he might still be in time to catch her.

Only he didn't hurry, nor did he call her later after he arrived home.

"Oh, Madelyn, how positively beautiful you look," her mother sighed, her hands clasped together in delight.

Madelyn eyed herself appraisingly in the floor-to-ceiling mirror of the couturier's salon and tried to decide if the full-skirted organza bridal gown truly became her. Obviously her mother liked it. Madelyn wasn't entirely convinced. "I don't know. It seems a little heavy. Don't you think I'll be too warm?"

"Not a bit. You can't judge that now, during one of the hottest starts to September on record. We're all sweltering, even in the air-conditioning. Believe me, come December you'll be glad for a little extra warmth."

"Maybe I should try the sheath dress on again?"

"I thought we decided the waist on that one was too long for you."

Discouraged, Madelyn sagged. "You're right. I'm sorry, maybe we should do this another day."

"But, dear, you know we shouldn't wait on this any longer. These gowns are all hand-sewn. And the beadwork has to be sent to Italy. It takes at least three months to complete, and that's if it's rushed. As it is, you're barely allowing time for the final fitting."

"Then I'll do without the beads."

Laura stiffened at her daughter's tone. "If that's what you want. I only mentioned it because you remarked earlier how beautiful you thought the beadwork was on this gown. It's entirely your choice."

"I'm sorry, Mother." Madelyn gazed again at the dress and the row upon row of tiny seed pearls embroidered across the bodice and skirt in an exquisite design of trailing vines and flowers. "If I didn't think the dress was beautiful, I would never have tried it on. I'm just feeling a bit tired today."

Laura relented, patting Madelyn's shoulder. "Well, of course you are, dear. You work far too hard. James told me the two of you were out quite late the other night attending some business function of his."

"When were you talking to James?"

"I frequently talk to James. Especially since you came to your senses and decided to marry the poor boy. He and I were discussing the guest list."

Sheer determination kept Madelyn from rolling her eyes. "You *aren't* inviting more than two hundred people, are you?"

"We're trying not to, since that's what you want. But honestly, it's going to be difficult at any fewer than four hundred, what with the extended family on both sides, the friends, and of course important business connections. You know how sensitive people can be when they aren't invited and believe they should have been."

"James and I agreed; we're only inviting friends and family. The others will have to understand."

"I know, and that's what he and I are doing. But 'friends' can be a very squishy term sometimes."

"Squishy?"

Her mother's lips twitched, seeing the humor. "As a mud pie."

They shared a smile.

"So, ladies, have you reached a decision or shall I give you more time?" A tall, dark-haired sales assistant approached, her teeth white against her smooth café au lait skin.

Laura raised an eyebrow at Madelyn. "I think you look stunning in this gown, dear, but it's up to you. Do you want to keep looking?"

Madelyn faced the mirror once more, pivoting slowly to examine her image from all angles. Her mother was right. The dress was magnificent and she did look lovely in it. Any other woman would be thrilled. So why the hesitation? Why the uncharacteristic indecisiveness?

Nerves, she assured herself; it didn't amount to anything more serious than that. Natural bridal jitters. This wedding was bound to be a huge success and one of the premier society events of the year. She simply wanted to make certain she appeared to her best advantage. Letting James down—or her mother, who'd joyfully taken on the brunt of the planning—was the last thing she wanted to do.

They were all so happy for her. Her friends, her family, coworkers, even people she barely knew.

Why, just yesterday the man who ran the newsstand a block from her apartment had waved her over and offered his congratulations. He'd seen her wedding announcement in the paper; wasn't it wonderful?

And her hairstylist, Gregor, why, he'd nearly broken into tears when she'd asked if he'd be able to arrange her hair for the ceremony.

Doing what she could to make them all happy seemed like such a little thing.

And she did like the dress. She really did.

"I don't need to keep looking," Madelyn announced, smoothing a hand over the luxurious material. "This is the one."

The assistant gave a cordial nod, obviously pleased. "If you'll follow me, then, we'll begin the measurements."

"Lord, it's good to be home."

James handed Madelyn one of the after-dinner liqueurs he'd poured for the pair of them, then took a seat beside her on the comfortable hand-tooled Italian leather sofa that graced the living room of his penthouse apartment. "I like Tokyo, but I thought those negotiations were never going to end. One week was not supposed to turn into two. Even the seasons changed while I was gone."

"The weather has a habit of doing that in October. But I think there are still one or two leaves left on the trees for you to enjoy."

"You know fall's my favorite time of the year," he complained.

Madelyn took a sip of crème de cassis, letting the tang of black currant linger on her tongue. "They have fall in Japan, don't they?"

"*Hmm*, but it lacks a certain piquancy when viewed from the inside of a conference room." He lifted her hand and brushed a kiss across the top. "It wasn't the same as being here with you. I missed you. You should have come with me." He kept her hand in his, settling it on his knee.

"You know I couldn't. My supervisor's having a hard enough time dealing with the idea that I'll be away for a month at Christmas. A week in Japan would have given him a coronary."

"I trust you reminded him you'll be on your honeymoon after Christmas?"

"Yes, but Larry rarely lets little things like sentiment interfere with the job. If Stan, his boss, hadn't given the okay to my leave request, we'd probably be honeymooning right here in this very penthouse."

James slid lower in his seat and drank a swallow of brandy. He rolled his head her way. "No pressure, Meg, but you're welcome to leave that job anytime you like. I'll set you up with something better. Or you can do nothing at all for a while if you'd rather."

"Become a society matron?"

"No one would ever call you a matron. You're far too young and gorgeous. A lady of the arts perhaps."

"You know that sort of lifestyle's not for me. I like my job."

He lifted a single skeptical blond brow.

"All right, I like my work," she amended. "You know I'd never be happy just sitting around."

"I'm not suggesting you sit around. I'm only reminding you of your options. Once we're married, you can do anything you like."

"A very kind and tempting offer." She gave him a soft smile.

"That's what I'm here for, to be kind and tempting." He dropped a kiss onto the center of her palm, then moved on to her wrist. "Especially the tempting part."

He set his glass aside. "Shall I tempt you some more?"

He leaned over and pressed his lips to the smooth skin of her neck, skimming them across her jaw before fitting his mouth against her own. He tunneled his fingers into her hair and intensified the embrace, his breath quickening.

Madelyn relaxed into his arms, enjoying the firm warmth of his lips moving over hers, the solid width of his shoulder muscles as they flexed beneath her hands.

He was a skilled kisser. No sensible woman could complain about his technique.

Still, a vital part of her remained detached, her heart beating at its regular, steady speed. Acknowledging the lack within herself, along with the stinging nip of guilt that followed, Madelyn closed her eyes and poured herself into the kiss.

Almost immediately she regretted her action.

Taking her response as an invitation to deepen their level of intimacy, James slanted his mouth over hers in an act of uncompromising demand. His hand slid downward to find and cover one of her breasts, his earlier playful mood evaporating completely. He moaned and slipped open a pair of blouse buttons.

"James, we shouldn't." She turned her head away, reaching up to still his fingers. "Remember what we agreed?"

He buried his face against the fragrant curve of her neck and went to work on the spot with his tongue, his other hand delving up under her skirt.

She flattened her hand over his to stop him, shimmying sideways in an attempt to wedge some space between them. "*James, no.* You said we'd wait."

Reluctantly, he straightened and blinked at her through hooded eyes. "I don't want to wait." He reached for her again.

Madelyn evaded him. "But you agreed, remember? I . . . I know it's hard, but it'll make our wedding night better."

"Let's go to the bedroom and make *tonight* better."

"No, you promised." Madelyn scooted to the far end of the couch and began fastening the buttons he'd undone. "You said you'd wait."

He collapsed back against the couch, leaning his head along the top. "I must have been insane when I made that promise. It's not like we haven't been together before," he growled.

"I know, and that's why I want to wait. If we don't, our wedding night will seem like any other night, nothing special. I want it to be special."

Actually what she wanted was time. The full six months of their engagement to heal and forget, to purge a certain someone else from her mind for good. Given that time, she felt certain she could enter into her marriage with a whole heart and never look back, never regret. Once she became James's wife, being intimate with him again would feel right, feel good. She wouldn't have to pretend.

James peered at her out of narrowed eyes. "You're not having second thoughts, are you?"

"No, of course not," she evaded. "I love you and I want to be with you. But we're going to have the whole rest of our lives to make love. What's another two months?"

"An eternity, according to the lower half of my anatomy." He groaned and closed his eyes in a silent plea for strength. "But you're right. As stupid as it was, I did promise, and if it's what you want, we'll wait. Even if it kills me," he added under his breath.

"Thank you, James." She smiled and leaned toward him.

He held out a hand to ward her off. "No, don't touch me, not for a while, probably the rest of this evening."

"All right." She folded her hands primly into her lap.

"So . . . um . . . did you finish addressing all the wedding invitations?" he asked, deliberately steering them onto an innocuous topic.

"Yes, all three hundred of them, and another two hundred for the reception. My wrist is still sore, even though Mother and Ivy helped me out."

He began to relax. "Did the caterer call your mother back?"

"He did, but he couldn't find enough of that champagne you suggested. He thought we should substitute the 'fifty-seven."

"Not from that vineyard. Tell him to try . . ."

"You're needed in Phoenix next week for the Giatta XJL shoot. I already told Stephanie to book your reservations."

Madelyn regarded Larry from her seat on the opposite side of his desk. "You know this isn't a good time for me to travel. I have three other accounts finishing up next week. Accounts I need to be here to oversee."

"Peg can pick up the slack on those. This is more important. Giatta is filming on location. You're needed there."

"I know Giatta's filming on location. I'm the one who set it up. The director is very experienced, though. He'll be fine on his own. If there are any problems, he has my direct office line and my cell number."

"Look, I can't change it. The decision's already been made. Giatta's president, Giancarlo Leonelli, has decided to be at the shoot in person. He's using it as an opportunity to combine business with pleasure, as the saying goes. Apparently, he fell in love with golf on his last trip to America. Since he'll be visiting the U.S. again, he wants to golf and he wants to meet you. So you're going to meet him."

"Have him come to New York. I'll meet him here."

"He's not stopping in New York. You'll meet him there."

She wanted to tell him no, she couldn't possibly, not with all the wedding preparations to complete—for both her own and Peg's, whose ceremony was now less than three weeks away. But she knew better than to even whisper the word "wedding" in Larry's presence. And any other argument she offered would be turned aside, a useless waste of breath.

"Fine," she said. "I'll meet him there. If there isn't anything more, I have a meeting in fifteen minutes." She rose from her chair.

"Oh, just one other item. Douglas will be traveling with you."

"What!" She couldn't help the squeak in her voice. "Why?"

"Because in the big picture, Giatta's still his show. The company wants you both in attendance."

Madelyn bristled, genuine affront camouflaging the dread spreading like poison through her veins. "I'm perfectly capable of handling this account on my own. I don't need a babysitter."

"Then don't think of him as one. Mostly he'll be there to smooth your way with Leonelli. I guess the two of them get along like a house on fire. He asked expressly for Zack to tag along."

She stayed silent, too busy digesting the staggering news.

"Is it going to be a problem? Working with Zack?" Larry tapped his pen on the desktop as he waited for her answer.

With the exception of their one unplanned exchange that late summer evening so many weeks ago, she and Zack had barely crossed paths. In many ways, it was as if nothing had ever happened between them. And to her everlasting relief, as far as the office was concerned, nothing had. To others, she and Zack were the same odd mix of oil and water they'd always been.

She wanted to tell Larry that she would rather be coated with honey and staked out in the blistering noonday sun on top of a desert anthill than accompany Zack Douglas on an out-of-town business trip. But work was work, and if she planned to continue on at F and S, she supposed she would have to learn to deal amicably with Zack.

This trip would be a good test, she reasoned, a chance to prove to herself that she was finally and totally over him.

She rarely thought of him these days, as her mind was

filled to overflowing with wedding plans and James and the lovely future they would soon make together. It was time to put her past with Zack behind her, once and for all.

"No," she said. "It's not a problem."

And in that instant, it was the truth.

CHAPTER SEVENTEEN

Madelyn gave her order to the waitress, then leaned back against one of the comfortable white wicker chairs provided by the Scottsdale resort hotel where she was staying.

She looked out beyond the carefully landscaped grounds to the manicured plains of thirsty green that made up the adjoining golf course complex. Past that to the desert, with its hard-packed earth and rough, rocky slopes; cacti dotted the raw hills like soldiers, armed and at the ready.

Nearly iridescent, the sky was vivid with striations of peach and violet and magenta. She couldn't remember ever having seen a more beautiful sunrise, a more breathtaking day.

Yesterday morning, she'd left James behind in a cold, gray New York drizzle with a warm kiss and a promise to call. Her business trip was expected to last three days.

Three days juggling work, desert heat, and Zack Douglas.

She could handle it. A simple matter of keeping all the right balls in the air.

The waitress returned and slid breakfast in front of her: orange juice, hot tea, fresh fruit, and a basket of assorted breads and pastries. Madelyn didn't have time for anything more elaborate.

In forty-five minutes or less, she needed to be in her rental car, on the road, headed north to the private ranch where the commercial shoot was scheduled to take place. Already, the crew was there setting up cameras, reviewing last-minute script changes, working with the professional stunt driver hired to climb behind the wheel of the new Giatta XJL model.

She chose a blueberry muffin, poured tea into her cup, and was about to dig in when a shadow fell across the table.

"Morning, Madelyn." Without waiting for an invitation, Zack pulled out the chair opposite her and sat down. "Sleep well?"

He looked fresh and vital, his dark hair neatly brushed and still damp from his morning shower. His teeth gleamed white against his tan complexion, his eyes blazing with an enigmatic green light.

What does he want? she wondered.

Madelyn kept her features even and ignored the increased thud of her pulse. "Very well."

"All the quiet kept me on edge," he remarked. "Too used to the big city, I suppose."

He didn't look the least bit sleepy to her.

"Maybe some coffee will wake you up," she suggested. "Why don't you have some? *At one of the other tables.*" She swept a hand out to encompass the nearly empty dining room. It was too early yet for most of the hotel's guests to have ventured from their beds. "There are plenty of tables available."

"I told the hostess not to bother seating me. I said I'd share with you."

"Tell her you've changed your mind. I'd like to eat my breakfast."

"Go ahead. Eat."

"Alone," she drawled meaningfully.

He leaned back in his chair, making no effort to leave.

She sighed. "What do you want, Zack?"

"That coffee you mentioned for starters. Then some food. All I had time for last night was a quick burger on my way between airports. I skipped the cardboard they serve in flight. I've been starving since about three this morning."

"Poor baby," she cooed with false sympathy, slicing her muffin in half with a sharp thrust of her butter knife.

"Coffee?" The waitress appeared at Zack's elbow, her mood far more chipper than the last time she'd stopped by Madelyn's table.

He held out his cup and flashed her a smile. "Yes, thanks."

She batted her lashes and darted her eyes up to his several times while she poured. "What can I get you?"

You, perhaps? Madelyn thought on a sour note as she watched the exchange.

"Eggs over easy with a side of grits and a bagel, if you can scare one up. With cream cheese. And hey, I'm pressed for time this morning. Would it be a lot of trouble to have the kitchen rush my order?"

"Not at all. I'll make sure they zip it right through."

She pitched him another giddy smile, then hurried off to the kitchen.

"It's shameless the way you use that." Madelyn took a careful swallow of tea, returning her cup to its saucer with a sharp clink.

She watched him pretend not to understand her meaning, his face the picture of innocence. "Use what?"

She refused to be drawn by his bait and glanced down at the weave pattern on the tablecloth. "You wanted something, Zack? What is it?"

Zack gazed at her for a long moment, drinking in her beauty as she sat in the clear morning sunlight.

You, he thought in answer to her question. *I want you.*

He kept his expression bland and shifted sideways in his chair to hide his sudden arousal. He hadn't actually stopped by her table to seduce her. Although he couldn't seem to keep from thinking about doing just that whenever she was near him for more than five minutes.

But he'd had his chance with her. He'd made his decision. And she'd made hers by agreeing to marry another man.

He picked up his coffee cup. "I wanted a chance to talk to you in private. It occurred to me that you might have wondered if I had anything to do with the decision to accompany you on this trip. I didn't. It came as much of a surprise to me as I'm sure it was to you."

"And?"

"And seeing that we are here, I thought it would make both our jobs a great deal easier if we put aside our personal difficulties and worked together as professionals."

"I am always professional, and as far as personal difficulties, I know of none that will interfere with my work. Whatever former . . . arrangement we had with each other, that's in the past. It's no longer important, certainly not to me."

His jaw stiffened. He willed his muscles to relax before curving his lips into a relaxed, friendly smile. "Good. Then you won't mind if we drive out to the set together?"

She glared at him. "Don't you have a rental car of your own?"

"Yes, but it seems a waste for both of us to travel separately when we have the same destination. Why not share one car and save the company some money?"

"I had no idea you could be so frugal. I'll have to remember to put you in for one of those employee awards. You know, the kind they give out to the thrifty little Boy Scouts who salvage used paper clips and dig barely scratched binders out of the trash."

Zack tossed back his head and laughed. "You have a real gift with language, Red, you know that? One of the reasons you're so damned good."

"What are you up to, Zack?" she demanded again, eyes narrowed.

"Nothing. Honestly." He sighed. "I just thought it might be nice if we could get along while we're here. Three days. Two and a half, really, since I'm leaving late on Wednesday afternoon."

She studied him for another long, considering moment. "And that's all?"

"That's all. Really."

"Well, I guess it is only three days. Two and a half," she corrected. "I suppose I can be civil and friendly to anyone for two and a half days."

"Even me?"

"Yes, even you," she said with a smile.

They shared a moment of warmth and camaraderie, the kind they hadn't shared in a very long time. Then the waitress arrived with Zack's breakfast and shattered the mood.

"Better eat up," he suggested as he tucked into his eggs. "They start shooting in an hour."

She glanced at her watch. "Less than an hour." Pushing aside the last niggling threads of caution, she stabbed a fork into a piece of cantaloupe and began to eat.

The first day's shooting went well.

Giatta's president, Giancarlo Leonelli, arrived around eleven, roaring toward the set in a sleek black luxury sedan—his own company's design, of course—trailing a plume of dust in his wake, kicked up off the unpaved desert road.

A lean, dark man of medium height and middle years, he had a fondness for Cuban cigars and attractive women, emerging from the car with one of each in hand.

His companion, a leggy blonde with a voluptuous Sophia Loren figure, paused for a dramatic moment in the piercing Arizona sunlight to slip on a pair of sunglasses and a stylish wide-brimmed hat. Only then did she deign to join the others already assembled.

Introductions made, Leonelli monitored the proceedings for a time from the shade of a temporary awning. Puffing his cigar in silent consideration, he watched the shoot while the blonde lounged in a nearby chair.

By early afternoon, the heat became oppressive and

the director decided to shut down production. Work would conclude tomorrow.

Before he left, Leonelli conferred with Madelyn and Zack, suggesting they meet him and his blonde companion, Nathalie, later for dinner and drinks.

Located about ten minutes from the hotel, in a quiet section of Phoenix, the restaurant Leonelli chose was a small but elegant Greek establishment where he dined whenever he was in town. Done in white and blue with pretty little curtains, neat wooden tables, and authentic Grecian decor, it was rather like stepping into another country. Even the scents in the air were different, exotic, mysterious, delightful.

Madelyn liked it immediately.

She gave Zack an easy smile as they were shown to their table.

He'd been true to his word today. Both of them had, burying their past under a comfortable layer of professionalism. She didn't know when it had happened, but their agreement seemed to have smoothed away the worst of her nervous edges.

This trip might work out all right, she told herself. The trick was to keep the focus on business and steer any other conversational gambits into safe, neutral waters.

The talk moved along at an easygoing pace while they feasted on a delightful assortment of appetizers followed by crisp salads dressed with feta cheese, kalamata olives, and a tangy Greek vinaigrette.

They were finishing their main course—Madelyn had selected a succulent roast lamb with tender baby vegetables—when Nathalie turned and spoke to Leonelli in a quick rush of Italian.

He'd explained earlier that although Nathalie understood a bit of English, she had little facility for speaking the language. She was far more comfortable using him as an interpreter, an indulgence he was happy to grant.

Leonelli focused on Madelyn. "She wants to know if she might have a closer view of your ring?"

Madelyn placed her fork on her plate. "My ring? Oh, of course." She held her hand out to the other woman, who leaned forward to see.

"Do you play golf, Signorina Grayson?" Leonelli chewed a bite of moussaka.

"Madelyn, please." She smiled.

He swallowed politely. "Madelyn." He waited for her answer.

"No, I'm sorry, I don't. My father tried to teach me years ago, but I fear I wasn't the best of students. I concentrated my efforts on tennis instead."

"Tennis is too hot and exhausting, all that sweating and chasing, and for what? A fuzzy little ball." He gave a dismissive gesture. "Golf is much better, a refined sport. You will play a round tomorrow, no? With Zack and me. Four o'clock. Now that you are a woman grown, you will like it as you did not as a child."

"Quanto bello," Nathalie pronounced, beaming and nodding her appreciation for the close-up view of Madelyn's ring.

Madelyn returned the smile.

"So, you will golf?" Leonelli persisted.

"Of course she will, Giancarlo." Zack nudged Madelyn's foot under the table. "Won't you, Madelyn?"

Barely, she kept herself from growling at Zack. "Four,

is it? The filming should be concluded by then. I'd be delighted to join you. Just don't expect too much."

"We will spot you a few extra strokes, and Zack can help you with your swing."

"I can take care of my own swing, but thank you for the suggestion."

Leonelli looked back and forth between the pair of them for a long moment, then let out a hearty chuckle. "Independent American women."

Nathalie interrupted him with another spate of Italian.

"She wants to know when you marry?"

Madelyn addressed her reply to Nathalie. "The wedding is in December, the twenty-seventh, just after Christmas."

Leonelli relayed the answer and another question. "She says she loves weddings. You send her a picture."

"All right. Of course," Madelyn agreed with a smile.

"She says too that you make such a beautiful couple and she knows you will be very happy together. Whatever little spat you've had, you must forget tonight and make it up in bed."

Madelyn's eyes widened in shock. "You think that Zack and I . . . ? No, she misunderstands. He and I . . . we only work together. We aren't getting married. I'm engaged to another man."

Clearly surprised, Leonelli relayed the information to an equally surprised Nathalie. "She apologizes for the mistake. You seem like two people in love; that is all. Well, perhaps we should think about dessert."

Feet planted in the short, clipped grass, Madelyn focused her energy on the small white ball beneath her. *Concentrate,* she told herself.

Line up the shot.

Swing the club.

And on the downward pass imagine the ball is Zack's head, centered smack-dab, right there on the tee.

Madelyn drew in a deep breath and lifted her club.

Whap.

The ball sailed in a clean, fast arc out over the fairway. Long and high, traveling, traveling, until it lost momentum and dropped onto the turf. After a pair of bounces, it rolled, quick and true, straight into a sand trap.

Damn, she hated this game. And it was all Zack's fault. Him and his opinionated foot.

She should have kicked him a good one last night for nudging her into this—literally—and used her heel to mash a couple of his toes in the bargain. She should also have been independent enough to have refused Leonelli's offer with a firm, polite, *Thank you, but no, thank you. I don't play golf.*

Instead, here she was, trapped. Not only in this viciously numbing game, but with Zack as well.

Ever since that dreadful moment last night when she'd been forced to explain it wasn't Zack she was marrying, she'd been on edge again. Whatever control she believed she'd gained over the situation, whatever ease, had vanished completely in that instant. She still didn't know what that blonde, that Nathalie, thought she'd seen. Certainly nothing in her. There was nothing to see, not any longer.

Zack must be responsible, the one who'd sent out revealing signals. Except that made no sense.

Nathalie had mentioned love, and if there was one thing of which Madelyn felt sure, it was that Zack did not love her. He didn't believe in such a useless, fragile emotion. Love, after all, was for fools. Obviously, Nathalie was a romantic with an overactive imagination, seeing emotions where they did not exist.

Leonelli strolled across the fairway. "Good try, Madelyn. The ball traveled well and you improve with each shot. I think if you keep trying, we make a golfer out of you yet."

"It's going to take a lot of trying, Giancarlo, especially now that I'm trapped in the sand."

"I been in the sand lots of times, but that will be our secret. Lucky for you, I know just the right club to get you out. Come on, we all keep playing."

The three of them climbed into the golf cart, Zack and Leonelli in front, and drove on. Zack led off next, his form impressive as he set up for his shot. Unlike Madelyn, Zack had a natural affinity for the game, coupled with the wisdom to know how to play well, but not too well. Trouncing the client was not the objective here.

As she stood next to Leonelli to watch and wait, she couldn't help but notice how splendid Zack looked in golf attire. The way his leaf brown polo shirt displayed each curve and angle of his torso. And the fascinating play in his loose-legged cotton trousers, the beige material tightening and releasing like a lover around his hard thighs and taut buttocks every time he bent or stretched.

Hands on hips, he studied the course, then placed his golf club onto the turf next to the ball, letting it lie in a line between his legs as he squatted to visualize the shot.

Madelyn forced her eyes away. "What did you think of today's shoot? I thought the rushes looked good.

Once the editing is completed, the commercial should have a strong visual impact."

Leonelli folded his arms over his chest, his eyes on Zack as the other man stood and moved into place to make the play. "I liked it, yes. It should keep people's attention. And as you mention, once the editing is done and the pretty women are added, it will be, how do you say? *Bellissimo.*"

"Pretty women? I'm not sure what you mean, Giancarlo. The ads for the XJL aren't slated to have models in them. It's a completely new product with a totally new campaign, one that showcases the car. There are no women."

"The ad is good. I tell you I like it. But when a man thinks about a car, especially a Giatta car, he thinks also of a beautiful woman, one he admires and longs to possess. For a man, there are no two things more desirable than to have the car and the woman. That is why we must have women in our ads. It has always been so."

Seeing Madelyn's speechless expression, he continued, "Do not worry. All will be as you have planned except in this one matter."

Zack swung his club up, then down in a clean, powerful stroke, his body forming a line of fluid precision and control. With a loud *thwack*, the ball flew fast and straight, as though borne on wings. Yards distant, it fell to earth and slowed, rolling until it stopped a mere inch or two short of the hole.

"Great shot," Leonelli called to Zack.

"Giancarlo," she said, "this is a serious change, one we need to discuss."

"*Grazie* for your concern, but all of this, it has been taken care of."

"Taken care of how? I don't—"

"Zack, he is a man. He understands and has seen to the details. He said not to trouble you with this, so don't be troubled. All is well." He selected a three iron from his golf bag. "Now I must make my shot or those behind us will grow annoyed."

A red mist of rage enveloped her as Leonelli's words sank in. So Zack was taking care of it, was he? she fumed. Seeing to last-minute details she need know nothing about? Changing her ad campaign, her commercials, interfering with her work without so much as a whisper? Her hands balled into fists at her sides and her neck muscles drew tight.

"Madelyn. It's your turn." Zack halted near her elbow.

When had he moved so close? And how could she have failed to notice? As for the game, she'd seen nothing—certainly not Leonelli's last shot—blinded, apparently, by her anger.

"Are you all right?" he asked.

She couldn't look at him.

She couldn't speak to him.

If she did, heaven knows what sort of dreadful invective might spew from her mouth. She was tempted to take a swing at him, to plant a fist right in his face. Wouldn't he be surprised? It might be worth it just to see his shock.

But for now she needed to control herself. Creating a scene in the middle of a public golf course, in the middle of a game, in front of a client, well, that would be unprofessional and juvenile. No matter the provocation, she would not give in to her emotions. At least not here. Grim in her fury, she gave Zack a curt nod then yanked a club out of her bag.

How she made it through the remaining six holes, Madelyn would never know. It took everything she had to keep playing, and what had rated up to that point as a barely adequate performance quickly deteriorated to the level of miserable disaster.

By the final hole, humiliation came in a close second to the anger still churning through her system. Too proud to cry, she donned her best smile and shrugged with the self-deprecating acceptance of a good sport.

Leonelli won.

As well as he'd played, Zack had been forced to take an extra stroke or two on a couple of holes, giving the Italian the advantage, narrowly. Madelyn was sure Zack had been deliberately careless with his putting. Recognizing his skillful duplicity only added fuel to the fire smoldering within her.

Back at the hotel, she politely refused Leonelli's invitation to dinner. A headache, she told him, an excuse that was fast threatening to become reality as a knot of pain gathered at the base of her skull. Eager for a few moments to herself, she made her way across the tiled width of the lobby.

She punched the button for the elevator and pretended not to notice Zack when he walked up next to her.

She maintained her silence for a full thirty seconds. "Don't even speak to me," she hissed, her eyes fixed on the lighted number panel above.

He sighed and folded his arms over his chest.

One of the four available elevators announced its arrival with a tiny *ding*. The illuminated arrow showed it was headed downward to one of the hotel's lower levels. She and Zack were going up.

A pair of teenagers dressed in bathing suits and flip-flops raced on, elbowing each other in between uncontrollable fits of giggles. The doors closed.

"We'll discuss it later; don't think we won't," she bit out. "Right now, I just want some peace and quiet."

Zack leaned over and pressed his finger against the already lighted up button. He said nothing.

"I can't believe you'd do such a thing." Madelyn tapped a foot against the floor, still refusing to look at him.

He slipped his hands into his pockets. "Leonelli's got a big mouth. I should have known he couldn't keep it closed for more than two minutes straight."

"It's a good thing for me he couldn't. What were you going to do? Order the new ads behind my back, then spring them on me once it was too late to have them redone?"

"I thought you didn't want to discuss this now."

She crossed her arms. "I don't."

The elevator arrived. He stood aside and waited for her to enter.

Once inside he punched the number for his floor on a panel to the right. She punched the button for her own floor on an identical panel to the left. The doors closed, leaving them alone.

"I was going to talk to you about it, you know," he declared as soon as the elevator car began to rise.

"Oh, is that why you told Leonelli to keep your little meeting a secret? Because you wanted to surprise me with the changes and not . . . how did he put it . . . trouble me with the details?"

"No, I didn't want him to mention it I because I knew you wouldn't like making changes to the ads and—"

"You mean adding bimbos to the ads?" she shot back.

"They aren't bimbos; they're actresses."

"You can call them that if you want. I've seen the old Giatta ads. No doubt it takes a great deal of acting talent to get a set of D-cups to jiggle just the right way. In fact, it gives me a great idea for a Fourth of July campaign. We could attach little sparklers to their—"

"Madelyn," he cut her off with a warning growl.

She faced him, hands on her hips. "Don't 'Madelyn' me, not after this. Meeting behind my back with my client. Making a deal you had no right to make on one of my accounts. And then having the nerve to tell that client to keep it a secret from me. I knew you could be low, but not this low. Even snakes crawl higher."

The elevator reached her floor; the doors opened. "Normally, I'd wish you a pleasant evening," she said, "but under the circumstances even that seems too good for the likes of you."

He moved, blocking the doors with his shoulder. "We're not done with this, Madelyn."

"We are as far as I'm concerned," she declared, marching past him into the carpeted hallway. "I've heard more than enough of your lies and excuses. I don't need to hear any more."

His temper flared, and without stopping to think, he charged after her. "What lies? And what excuses? All

I've been trying to do is explain. If you'd calm down for two seconds and quit overreacting, maybe I could."

"Overreacting?" She rounded on him. "Me? Overreacting? You stick your big nose into my business and I'm overreacting? You wouldn't say that if I were a man."

"I wouldn't need to—if you were a man."

"No, because if I were, we'd be outside right now beating the living daylights out of each other. If I'd done to you what you did to me, you'd be furious. Admit it."

In another time and another place, he might have conceded her point. But right now, he wasn't in the mood to admit anything, most especially not to her. He opted instead for silence, giving her a steely-eyed glare and a pugnacious upward thrust of his chin.

She tossed him a disgusted look, flung up her arm and spun away.

He pounded after her. "Look, the XJL ads may have been assigned to you, but Giatta is still my account and Giancarlo is still my client, whether you like it or not. He came to me this morning with his concerns, not to you, and since he wanted them addressed, I addressed them."

"You had no right to address them. What you should have done was send him to me."

"And if I had, what would you have done differently? Once Giancarlo gets something in his head, not even a nuclear attack can dislodge it. He's as bullheaded as they come. He wanted the ads changed and he wasn't leaving my room until he got that change."

Madelyn arrived at the door to her room, turning to face him. "Whether I would ultimately have agreed to Leonelli's stipulation is not the point. The point—the one that you, Zachary Douglas, refuse to see—is that the

XJL account is *mine*, not yours. You had no business agreeing to anything concerning it. Not without consulting me. Not without my say-so. I might have expected that sort of cavalier treatment from one of the other men at work, Larry or Mark, but I didn't expect it from you. No matter what's passed between us, I thought you had a bit more respect for me as an equal, as a professional. It seems I was mistaken."

He didn't like the look of betrayal in her eyes. The hurt she couldn't entirely hide. More particularly, he didn't like the way that look, that hurt, made him feel.

Her hand trembled as she shoved the wafer-thin bit of plastic that passed for a key into the electronic lock on her door. She yanked it back out so hard, the key nearly snapped in half.

"Madelyn . . ."

She closed her ears to him and pushed into her room. When he came in after her, she spun around. "How dare you come in here uninvited. *Get out!*"

"I had no idea you'd be this upset. I didn't mean to hurt you—"

"Hurt me? *Please*," she scoffed, "you haven't *hurt* me. To do that, I'd have to feel something for you, and I don't, not anymore. It's only your actions that offend me. Including that ruse of yours, coming to me claiming you wanted us to get along. How did the line go? Civil and friendly. That's right, civil and friendly, when all you really wanted to do was soften me up enough to drop my guard and give you the advantage."

"And exactly what advantage would that be?" He moved forward, forcing her to take several steps backward.

Defiant, she held her ground, arms planted squarely on her hips. "You know exactly what. Your plan to make my work on this campaign seem unimpressive enough that Fielding will decide to hand the entire account back to you. From the beginning you've complained about how I stole Giatta from you. This is your way of getting even."

"You know, that's not a bad plan, *if I'd thought of it*. Which I didn't. You have the most incredibly convoluted mind, twisting motives and coaxing schemes out of thin air. You know what your problem is, Red? You think too much."

"No, my problem is *you*. You interfering in my life, finding ways to cause me trouble at every turn. I'm tired of it and I'm tired of you. I want you out. *Now.*" She thrust a finger toward the door.

"Or what?" He crowded close, forcing her back, pinning her against the wall. "What will you do? You know, for a woman who claims she feels nothing for me, you're awfully passionate." He met her eyes and held them, then stroked a finger over the flushed curve of her cheek.

She trembled, the heat inside her turning from anger to a fire of another sort. "Get out," she repeated.

"But then you always were passionate," he breathed. "It's one of the first things I noticed about you, back when you made it a profession not to notice me. All that pent-up fire, that carefully controlled need, that longing, battling to get free. When you were with me, there wasn't any need to keep it bottled up anymore, was there? When we were together, you stopped thinking about all the things you're supposed to want and need and simply existed. Simply felt. What is it you feel now? What is it you want? This?" He skimmed a knuckle over the fullness of her lower lip, his touch nearly a kiss. "Is it this?"

She could have escaped if she'd really tried. She knew he wouldn't have stopped her. She pressed her hands flat against the wall. Pressed her body backward as if she could sink into the wallpaper itself, and fought the storm of desire that raged within her.

Relentless, Zack went on. "Does he set you free, Madelyn? When he touches you, does your mind go numb? Does he make your spirit soar?"

She lost herself in his eyes.

"Does he make your body sing?" he whispered.

She trembled and knew she could not lie. "No."

CHAPTER EIGHTEEN

Without thinking, without wanting to think, she swept her arms around him and pulled his head down to hers. She kissed him, devouring his mouth, sucking at his tongue, urgent and greedy, showing him the way she longed to be taken.

Zack needed no urging, as hungry for her as she was for him.

The pins popped from her hair as he thrust his hands into it, combing through the fiery mass before wrapping it around one wrist to pull her head back so he could lay siege to her neck, her breasts.

She slipped her arms up inside his shirt, yanking the material out of her way to touch the hard heat of his back. Trace the breadth of his wide male shoulders, tunnel her fingers into the short curling hair covering his chest.

She bit at his lower lip.

He bit back, playful yet intense. Then suddenly he was

tearing at her clothes, too impatient to wait a single second longer than he had to.

She gasped as he ripped her shirt in two, then did the same to the lacy cups of her bra, letting her breasts spill out into his eager hands. He fondled them, drawing a ragged moan from the back of her throat as he touched and rubbed and tugged in exactly the right way, exactly as he knew she liked.

He ground his mouth against hers as he went to work on the fastenings of her pants. Shuddering, she did the same for him, taking him hot and ready into her hand.

She was naked except for the scraps of cloth dangling from her shoulders. He lifted her high, pinning her against the wall, spreading her legs apart to drive himself deep.

Madelyn bucked and cried out as his entrance pushed her over the edge, the massive climax roaring through her with the fury of a hurricane, sending her spinning and floating, to leave her clutching him as if he truly were her only lifeline.

He thrust into her, his movements a rhythm as ancient as time, reigniting the spark within her.

She stroked her hands over him and buried her face against his neck, drinking in his scent, his texture. The slick, heated feel of sex, raw and elemental. And the sounds. The words she couldn't control. Spurring him on, daring him to take both of them as high as they could possibly reach.

And as he promised, he sent her soaring. He set her free. Filling her to the brim with more than just his body. Completing her in a way no other man could, or ever would be able to, complete her.

Then she forgot everything, even how to think, as he

rocked them both to crisis, fitting his mouth over hers to swallow her cry of completion, to let her drink in his own hoarse shout of release.

Slowly, when enough air had returned to their lungs to breathe, he let her slide to the ground and helped her to stand on unsteady legs. He brushed the last remnants of her clothes from her shoulders, then took her face between his palms and kissed her—long and slow and sweet. They both were trembling by the time he led her to the bed, where they slipped between the sheets for more.

Night was the color of molasses when she awakened, her head pillowed on Zack's shoulder, his arm wrapped just below her throat.

She lay for a while, relaxed and quiet, listening to him sleep. Aware how right, how complete, she felt.

And how wrong.

Guilt chewed at the edges of her conscious mind. She did her best to push the feeling aside.

There would be plenty of time for regrets later on.

He roused not long after with a yawn and a shivery stretch, then turned to press a kiss to her temple, his evening beard rough against her skin.

She said nothing, wanting him to speak first, hoping she wouldn't be disappointed with his words.

She was.

"I'm starving." He ran a hand down the flat of his belly. "You suppose it's too late for room service?"

She sat up. "I think they serve until two a.m." She got out of bed, crossing to a low bureau to find the menu.

She tossed it to him on her return. "Order me something, nothing greasy. I'm going to take a shower."

She came out of the bath a long while later, bundled in a yellow terry-cloth robe and thick cotton socks. Her hair was dark with wet and combed neatly down her back. The food had arrived, set up on a small table near the window.

Zack sat in one of the two available chairs, dressed only in pants, his chest and feet bare. A late-night television talk show droned on the TV.

He turned the volume down low. "Did you run all the hot water out?"

"Every last drop, I think." She slipped into the chair across from him and lifted the lids from the plates on her side of the table. Spinach salad with strips of grilled chicken and a bowl of tomato soup.

"It was that, pasta Alfredo, or some sort of sandwich," he said.

"This is fine. Perfect, in fact." She dipped a spoon into the soup to sample it. "Still hot." She ate another spoonful, only then realizing how hungry she was. A basket of rolls sat in the center of the table. She chose one and broke it in half. "And what are you putting in your cast-iron stomach?"

"A Reuben. It came with French fries, but I ate them all while you were showering." He took a big bite of his sandwich and chewed.

The low buzz of the television filled the silence for a few minutes as they ate.

Finished with his meal, Zack wiped his fingers clean on a red cloth napkin, then poured himself a second cup of coffee. "When are you going to tell him?"

"Tell who what?" She speared up a forkful of spinach leaves.

"You know, your fiancé, about us. You'll have to give him that ring back when you break it off." He wanted to tug the damned thing off her finger right now but knew she'd ruffle up if he started making aggressive demands.

Madelyn paused and drank some ice water; then she set her fork aside. "What makes you think I'm going to break off my engagement?"

It took him a moment to register what she was saying. He scowled. "What happened between us tonight makes me think that."

"And what happened? We had sex. We've had sex before. Did it mean something more to you this time? If it did, you certainly haven't said so."

He scowled harder, emotion turning his eyes dark. "Of course it did. It always means something . . . when it's with you."

He rose from his chair and paced the floor like a caged animal. "I want you, Madelyn. I want things back the way they were before. It was good between us. It can be good again. Move in with me. Come live with me."

"Live with you?" she repeated weakly.

"Yes. I've missed you, missed us. I know you want something more permanent, but marriage . . . well, I just can't do marriage, not again."

She closed her eyes against the temptation to relent and give him what he wanted, tears collecting behind her lids. She forced them away, forced her eyes to dry. She'd promised herself she would not cry. Not again. Never again over him.

"Can't or won't?" she challenged, then sighed in resignation when she read his look. "We've had this argument before. We can't agree and nothing's changed."

Frustrated, he smacked a fist into his palm. "But you can't marry him."

"I can and I will," she assured him sadly, "unless you give me a good reason why I shouldn't."

"I've given you a reason, the best reason. Because you don't love him, that's why. If you did, you wouldn't have spent the last few hours in that bed with me." He pointed behind him to the evidence, the rumpled sheets, the flowered spread that had been kicked to the floor. "You don't belong with him."

"Then who do I belong with? You? For how long, Zack? How long until you decide it won't work between us and you leave? Because deep down you've already decided, haven't you? That's why you don't want to marry me, because forever to you is something that just doesn't exist, something that can't exist. You expect to fail before you even start. And what happens to me when you decide it's over? When you pick up and move on to some other woman? I'll be alone and I'll have given up other things I want. Precious things—a home and a family, a man I can grow old with, who'll someday see the wrinkles of age and love me despite them."

"You'd find someone else," he said. "You wouldn't have a problem."

But he would, he acknowledged, fire burning in his gut at the thought of her with another man.

Any other man.

"And I would have hurt James, my friend," she went

on. "A good man who really loves me. If I leave him now, he won't take me back."

"What about tonight? Don't you think he'd be hurt if he knew about us?"

She flinched, his words a knife in her heart. "He would be very hurt. Are you going to tell him?"

I could, he thought. There would be a certain satisfaction in it, showing his rival who truly held the upper hand. But it wouldn't change what was wrong between him and Madelyn; all he would gain was her hatred.

"No. I won't tell him."

"Thank you," she said on a quiet sigh of relief.

She worried her fingernail over a nubby spot on her robe. "Zack, what we did tonight. It was wrong and should never have happened. James loves me and I've paid him back with betrayal. I've made promises, not only to him, but to my family and friends, to people who want what's best for me."

He knelt down in front of her and took her hands. "They may want what's best, but you are the only one who can decide what that is. It's not too late to call off this wedding, you know."

She lifted a hand to thread her fingers into his hair, so soft and dark. She loved the feel of it against her skin.

Slowly, she leaned forward and kissed him tenderly on the lips, pulling away before he could turn it into more than a brief touch. She slid her hands free of his. "You broke my heart once. I can't let you break it again. If you don't love me enough to want to try for forever, then please go away. Please stay out of my life."

He hung his head, still kneeling before her. And for the first time since he'd been a boy of ten, he wanted to cry. Standing heartsick and mute as he'd watched his mother pack a suitcase in the middle of the day. While he'd stood helpless and lost as she hurried from the house without explanation, without so much as a good-bye, leaving only the echoing slam of the screen door and the screech of car tires behind her.

A few simple words and Madelyn would stay. All her warmth and sweetness would be his for the taking. He only had to say the words, tell her what she needed, what she wanted, to hear.

He swallowed, his voice raw with emotion. "I'm sorry, Red. I just can't do it. I can't marry you."

Slowly he stood, gathered his belongings, and left.

The last leaves of October drifted from the trees, leaving bare November branches to usher in cooler days and skies turned sullen and gray with clouds. Heavy clothes and warm coats were brought forth in place of lighter attire. The toasty insides of homes and offices and schools took on a more welcoming aspect, if for no other reason than the shelter such buildings provided.

And on the congested streets of New York City, life continued at its usual frenetic pace. The wide-open vistas of Arizona blue skies were a distant memory. Yet not distant enough for Madelyn as she tried her best to forget.

As the days ticked by, she buried herself deep inside a mountain of work and wedding preparations, diving into both tasks with an intense abandon that gratified some and concerned others.

Her efforts on behalf of Carmichael Foods and the remainder of her accounts continued to garner praise.

And although she compromised on the Giatta issue, she managed to do so in a way that satisfied the client while still preserving the integrity of her original ad campaign.

In spite of her best efforts, she and Zack crossed paths with alarming frequency. In meetings. On the elevator. In the hallways. And once during an office birthday celebration when too many people crowded into the break room and shuffled the pair of them together, their bodies all but touching.

Madelyn knew it was an untenable situation that could not continue indefinitely—at least for one of them.

"Take a deep breath and you'll be fine."

"Oh, Madelyn, I'm so glad you're here." Peg rested her palm across her silk-covered stomach and drew a shivery lungful of air. "How do I look?"

Madelyn angled back for a better view of Peg in her wedding attire—from the top of her carefully styled brunette curls and sheer veil to the bottom of her dainty, low-heeled white satin pumps. The dress itself was a triumph of unembellished elegance, a flowing white sheath with tiny spaghetti straps that displayed each line and curve of Peg's splendid figure to perfection.

"Radiant, that's how you look," Madelyn answered. "The most beautiful bride anyone has ever seen."

The bride gave her a needy smile. "Do you really think so?"

"Of course I think so. I wouldn't have said it otherwise. You're going to knock Todd's socks off."

Peg's smile widened. She fluttered a trembling hand in front of herself. "Look at me, I'm shaking. I don't know why I'm so anxious. I mean, I'm happy. I'm really happy, but I'm terrified too. I love Todd so much. I can't wait to be his wife. But what if I screw up my vows? What if I say my name wrong? Or his name wrong? What if I completely ruin the ceremony?"

"You're not going to ruin the ceremony. Everything will be fine. Just remember to breathe."

"Breathe," Peg repeated to herself. "Breathe. I can do that. I can breathe." She reached out suddenly and grabbed Madelyn's hands. "Oh, just think, in only a few weeks this is going to be you. I'll be an old married woman, tanned and gorgeous and still recovering my strength after three weeks of incredible honeymoon sex in the Bahamas, and it'll be your turn to be terrified and happy all at the same time. Oh God, how much time's left?"

Madelyn reached into the tiny teal blue handbag that matched her bridesmaid's dress and lifted out her watch. "Ten minutes. Your dad's supposed to come and give us the signal."

"Oh, what a time to develop a nervous bladder. Tell Dad he'll just have to wait. I'll be back."

"We can't start without you, so don't worry."

"Don't worry," Peg mumbled to herself as she rushed away, repeating the word "breathe" as she went.

Madelyn returned her watch to her purse and thought about everything Peg had said, especially the part about being terrified and happy.

She completely related to the terrified part. The closer her wedding date got, the more frantic she became. As for the happy, she kept telling herself she was, or at least that she would be. If only she didn't feel as though she were acting in an odd, surreal play, cast in the role of the tragic heroine.

Marrying James was the right thing to do, she assured herself. Once her actual wedding day was at hand, the second thoughts that jabbed at her like tiny needles would vanish. She would be content as his wife; she promised herself she would. And as for the guilt that seemed to continually eat away at her over her unfaithful night in Arizona, she vowed to find a way to make it up to him.

Right now, though, she had her friend's ceremony to see to; the rest she should put from her mind.

Peg's wedding went off without a hitch except for the flower girl—Todd's four-year-old niece, Cicely—who grew tired in the middle of her walk up the aisle and plopped down where she stopped.

After that bit of tension-breaking humor, the rest had been easy.

Peg recited her vows in a clear, steady voice, all her earlier worries for naught. There were few with dry eyes left in the church by the time Todd slipped the ring onto his new wife's finger, sealing his own vows with a kiss.

Afterward, everyone converged outside to toss rice and best wishes at the bride and groom as the pair ran laughing to their limousine. It was decorated with streamers and aluminum cans, the words "Just Married" painted across the rear window.

With the couple safely away, the guests disbanded to find their own path to the reception.

Once there, Madelyn relaxed, tapping her toe to the upbeat tune played by the live band. She took a careful sip of champagne and watched the reception festivities around her. A cool stream of bubbles fizzed in her glass. She'd already decided this would be her one and only drink of the evening. She had no interest in leaving inebriated.

One of Peg's cousins, a lanky sixteen-year-old with too many hormones and not enough brains, was stalking guests with a video camera, claiming he was there to capture perfect candid wedding moments on film. So far all Madelyn had noticed him capturing were shots of attractive female guests.

One pretty young bridesmaid in particular had been forced to seek temporary refuge in the ladies' lounge. Another woman took her revenge by smacking him over the head with her purse when she realized he'd zoomed in on her breasts.

With a signal to the band, the bridal couple—who'd arrived only a few minutes ago after a lengthy session with the wedding photographer—were urged to the dance floor.

Time for the first dance.

Madelyn set her wine on a nearby table as a slow ballad began. Lovely and romantic, the notes twined in the air like a bough of delicate wildflowers. A collective sigh of sentimental awes soughed from the onlookers as the couple circled slowly.

Everyone watched as Todd murmured to his new wife, words meant only for her ears. An intimate answering smile parted her lips as Peg whispered back, their eyes meeting, joining, as they became lost in each other. Their love was shining like a beacon, clear for all to see.

A swell of bittersweet happiness gripped Madelyn along with a fist of self-pity and envy. She stood for a long moment lost in despair. From behind, a pair of strong, familiar arms slipped around her waist.

James pulled her snug against him as he leaned down to brush a kiss across her cheek. Awash in guilt for her unworthy thoughts, she crossed her arms over his and reached for his hands, squeezing them hard in silent recompense.

She closed her eyes and tucked her head beneath his chin.

"Just think," he said quietly, "only six more weeks and that will be us, dancing at our own wedding."

"Yes, just think," she sighed, watching the bridal couple complete a last few steps.

Why? she thought. *Why can't I love him like that?*

The dance ended, guests clapped, then the band took up a new tune, inviting everyone to join in.

"Dance with me," she murmured, turning in his arms.

"With profound pleasure, darling." On nimble feet, James swept her across the ballroom floor.

They danced the next two dances. By the end of a third, he had her laughing as they moved to a bit of fast-paced swing that left the pair of them breathless.

"*Whew*, that was fun, but do you think our legs will forgive us tomorrow morning?" James led them off to the safety of the sidelines. "Especially after that last kick?"

"I thought we tackled that last kick rather well. And you should learn to speak for yourself; my legs are fine." She knew his legs were fine as well since they'd played two sets of doubles tennis last weekend with friends and he'd barely broken a sweat.

"I agree, your legs are very fine. But," he warned with

mock seriousness, "after that workout, your muscles might need relaxing. How about a massage? You're not eighteen anymore, you know."

"And neither are you. I'll remind you who's the older one here."

"Only by six months. And you know what they say."

She crossed her arms. "No, what do they say?"

"Well, that women grow old, while men grow distinguished."

"Is that a fact? Then might I suggest you take your distinguished butt over to the refreshment table and bring this old woman a drink, preferably something soft. I'm thirsty."

"Your wish, as always, is my command." He bowed and came up grinning. "What about food? Are you hungry?"

"I could eat. Nothing too filling, though; I want a piece of wedding cake later."

"I'll find something you like. I know all your favorites." He dropped a quick kiss on her lips. "I won't be long."

Madelyn drifted over to the table where she'd left her glass of champagne. Not surprisingly, it had vanished, cleared away by the top-notch catering staff Peg had hired on Laura Grayson's recommendation.

Madelyn's parents were here somewhere, though at the moment she didn't see them. After introducing Peg to her mother, Madelyn had been amusingly pleased to watch the two women bond like a pair of professional jewel thieves planning a master heist, no detail too small.

If Madelyn had half that much enthusiasm for her

own wedding arrangements, she knew her mother would have been ecstatic. Although lately she'd been trying hard to be involved, anything to keep her mind occupied, active. Even hand-addressing wedding invitations was preferable to dwelling on thoughts of the man who plagued her nights and haunted her dreams.

To keep her mind off him now, she surveyed the room with lazy interest, absorbing the noise, appreciating the crowd. Her lips turned up at the edges as she watched a group of children skip, one after the other, around a circular table while they sang some silly nonsense song. Then her sights turned to a tiny white-haired matron who boldly shooed a huge, linebacker-size man out of his chair before calmly stealing his seat.

Madelyn was debating the benefits of slipping into her own seat—the one reserved for her and other members of the wedding party and their dates—when she saw Zack. He was standing across the room looking as tall, dark, and devastating as ever.

She'd known that Peg had invited him to the wedding. But when he hadn't shown up at the church ceremony, she'd relaxed in the assumption that he wasn't coming.

Apparently, she'd relaxed too soon.

He turned his head then, as though he'd heard her speak his name, and looked directly into her eyes.

Madelyn tried to break the link and walk away, but her eyes refused to lower, her feet resisting as if locked in place. She sensed his own attempt to pull away and his own failure to succeed.

A peculiar hum pulsed between her ears, a quiet rushing sound like a calm summer sea finding its way to shore. Her hands tingled. Her heart thundered. And in that instant the room dissolved into a mist, leaving only the two of them behind.

Entranced, Madelyn took a single step toward him.

"Here's the food," James declared. "I thought I'd never make it through the buffet line, it was so long."

CHAPTER NINETEEN

James's return shattered the spell around her.

Startled, Madelyn jerked and turned, her elbow catching him in the side.

Unprepared for her move, James reacted instinctively, weaving in a desperate effort to keep from dropping the plates of food and the drinks he carried. He nearly managed the trick with no harm done until Madelyn reached out in her own instinctive attempt to help, and ruined his maneuver.

Fizzy pink punch arced into the air, landing in a very large, very cold splash across the skirt of her dress.

"Oh no. Meg, are you okay?" Carefully, James stepped to a nearby table to put down what was left of their meal, then quickly returned to her side.

"Of course I'm okay," she said, holding the sticky satin away from her skin. "It's this dress that may never be the same."

"I didn't mean to scare you. You're usually not so jumpy."

Remembering the reason for her jumpiness, Madelyn glanced at the spot where Zack had been standing, disappointed to see that he was gone.

Actually, the accident had been providential. Who knew what foolish things she might have done if James hadn't returned when he had. What glimpses of truth he might have witnessed in her eyes had he caught her staring at Zack. Heavens, she hoped no one else had noticed her moment of spellbound fascination.

She darted a quick look around the ballroom, but no one was watching her, the party atmosphere running strong.

"The music's loud," she explained, "and I didn't hear you come up behind me. Don't worry about it and don't wait for me. Eat while I go try to rinse out some of this punch before it sets completely."

She found her way to the ladies' lounge and armed herself with a handful of wet paper towels, her hands shaking slightly as she worked to blot out the stain. Diligent effort removed most of the punch, but her skirt ended up wetter than ever. Until it dried, there was no way she could return to the reception. Patiently, Madelyn held her skirt underneath the hand dryer. A few ladies passing through offered condolences and disaster stories of their own.

By the time she pushed the door open and walked into the quiet corridor that led back to the main ballroom, she felt almost composed.

Then she turned her head and saw Zack approaching from the direction of the cloakroom.

His step slowed, his fingers falling from the buttons he'd been fastening on his long brown wool coat. Obviously he was leaving.

For a long moment, neither of them spoke.

"I see you managed to repair the damage," he remarked, nodding toward her dress.

She looked down, noticing the massive water stain that hadn't seemed nearly as bad in the ladies' room. "The worst of it anyway."

"Good. Well, I'd better be going." He hesitated. "Listen, Madelyn, I only came tonight because I didn't want to offend Peg and Todd by not putting in an appearance. I had no intention of spoiling your evening."

"You haven't. And you're right—Peg especially would have been hurt if you'd stayed away. A lot of people from the office are here."

"Yeah. Linda Hernandez brought her kids. Did you see them?"

"I did. They're adorable."

She could barely breathe, she realized. He was too close. And his eyes, so beautiful, so green. She felt herself sink into them and knew she could gladly lose herself there forever.

Ask me again, she wished. *Ask me one more time and maybe my answer will be different. Tell me you want me to go with you now,* she pleaded silently, *and see if I don't say yes.*

For an instant his lips parted, then closed again.

He pulled on a pair of gloves. They smelled of leather and man. Of him.

Madelyn inhaled deeply to catch the scent.

"I've got to go," he said, looking away. "I made my excuses ages ago."

She stepped back. "I need to go too. I told Peg I'd be there to watch her cut the cake."

After a moment, he nodded good-bye, then strode away.

She watched until he disappeared around the far corner, then leaned against the wall for support.

I can't keep doing this.

Seeing him at work, meeting him at parties and events like today's wedding. Slowly, quietly, it was killing her, and it had to stop.

Zack had never known such a cold December, with a bite that cut clear through to the bone. It was the kind of chill he'd felt for weeks now, beginning that warm Arizona evening when he'd deliberately turned his back on his own happiness for the second time.

More tired than he could ever remember feeling, he made the decision to take a few long-overdue vacation days. He chose a balmy locale, certain that a good dose of fun and sun would set him on the road to recovery. He'd relax, he'd sleep, he'd enjoy the sunny clime, and when it was all finished he would be able to return home with a renewed spirit and a healing heart.

When he arrived, he found Sanibel Island, Florida, as gorgeous as it always was this time of year. White sand beaches, miles of blue sky piled atop miles of blue sea. Warm salt breezes, swaying palm trees, sun and sport, and enough bikini-clad eye candy to lure a Tibetan monk into the warm waters of temptation.

By rights, he should have been having the time of his life, checking out the beach, or better yet, checking out the inside of a hotel room with any one of a dozen willing females.

Instead he was miles away from Sanibel's beach, seated in a rented beige Ford in the parking lot of an Episcopal church just outside Fort Myers.

In his pocket, he fingered the invitation he'd received before leaving for vacation. Normally he would have pitched it in the trash the moment he slit open the envelope and saw what was inside. But for some odd reason, one he still didn't understand, he'd tossed it into his brief-case, where the stupid thing had stayed before being added to his carry-on at the last minute.

His mother, for the fifth unbelievable time, was getting married. And for some perverse purpose known only to her, she'd invited him to the ceremony and reception.

What was it these days, he thought, with all these weddings? People had the common sense of moles, living in the dark and running around in circles, deluding themselves that marriage would make them happy. He knew better.

Or at least he thought he did, until Madelyn.

He rubbed a hand over his jaw and sighed as he thought of her.

Madelyn.

She seemed to have taken root inside his mind, and he couldn't force her out no matter how he tried. And believe it, he'd tried and tried hard.

In less than a week she would be another man's wife. He couldn't get that out of his mind either.

A familiar ache swelled in the vicinity of his heart. He

ignored it as he watched another cluster of guests, decked out in suits and ties and dresses, enter the church—every one of them a stranger.

He wasn't surprised. He'd never known his mother's family, respectable, middle-class citizens that they were. Uptight prigs, his father had called them.

As the story went, they'd cut their daughter off completely the day she'd announced at sixteen that she was pregnant and planned to marry the baby's father, Luke Douglas, a common boy of whom her parents did not approve. To Zack's knowledge, it was a breach that had never been healed.

As for the Douglas side, she'd had even less cause to keep up with them, not after running out on her husband and kids the way she had.

His lips curled into a cynical half smile and he shook his head at his own folly. He'd spent the better part of his adult life trying to avoid the woman. So what on earth was he doing here today at her wedding?

He sat in the car for another fifteen minutes before he climbed out into the humid midday winter heat, slamming the door behind him.

The service was already under way as he slid into a pew in the rear of the church.

At least she'd had the taste not to wear white, Zack thought. The light blue, knee-length dress she wore was an attractive choice for a bride of her years and dubious marital history.

The groom, from what Zack could tell, seemed a harmless sort, balding, with a slight middle-age paunch and thick glasses that made his eyes look too large for his face. No doubt the poor schmuck had a fat bank account and the promise of more to come, meeting his mother's number one requirement in a mate.

Zack had always assumed that particular shortcoming was one of the chief reasons why his own father had never measured up. What he'd never been able to reconcile was why she'd stayed as long as she had. Eleven years in one place was a long time for a woman of Georgia Douglas's habits and tastes. Correction: Georgia Steadman, now that the vows had been said—assuming he remembered the name on the invitation correctly.

The church, located near the shore, boasted an extensive flower garden and its own private stretch of beach. Arrangements had been made to hold the reception there on its grounds. A magnificent magnolia tree dominated the garden, towering high and wide, a few silky white petals fallen from its branches scattered across the redbrick courtyard.

Zack allowed the honeyed scent of the tree to linger in his nostrils for an extra moment as he stepped outside. He'd have a beer, he decided, or whatever alcoholic concoction they were serving; then he'd be on his way.

"Zack? Is that you?"

He turned his head to the right, and there she stood, as beautiful and bloodless as ever, the bride herself. He wished he already had his hands on that drink.

"It really is you," she declared, the heels of her dyed-to-match shoes clicking against the bricks as she rushed to greet him. "You came. I don't believe it."

"I don't much believe it myself," he muttered, avoiding the embrace she tried to press upon him. He saw her stiffen, then smile, as he drew back, pretending she hadn't noticed his withdrawal.

"Were you here in time for the ceremony?" she asked.

He nodded. "I drove over from Sanibel Island. I've been here vacationing for the last few days." He didn't want her to think he'd come all this way solely on her account. "I suppose I ought to offer best wishes. Congratulations, Georgia; maybe this time it'll last."

The warmth of her smile dipped a degree or two, but again she recovered rapidly. She'd long since given up correcting him for using her first name. "I know it will. Harold's a wonderful man and I'm lucky to have found him. You must come and meet him. It looks like he's catching up with some friends right now, though." She paused. "Beth isn't with you by any chance?"

"No," he said, his eyes hardening in grim suspicion. "You didn't invite her, did you?"

"No, I didn't invite her. You can relax, Zack. I haven't had any contact with your sister, exactly as we agreed." She sighed. "Frankly, I'm surprised to see you, especially since you don't seem terribly happy to be here. Why did you come?"

"Honestly?"

"Yes, of course."

"Probably for the same reason you sent the invitation to me. Curiosity. Beyond that, I haven't a clue."

"I sent the invitation to you because you're my son."

"A fact you've made a career forgetting whenever it's suited your purpose."

She flushed. "This is my wedding day. I'd hoped, at the very least, that we could put aside the bitterness for a few hours and be a family."

"Since when were we ever a family? You're right, though; this is no occasion for arguments. I should leave."

"No." She put out a hand, catching him on the shoulder. "Don't go. I want you to stay. Come on, you must be hungry. Men are always hungry."

After a moment of indecision, he relented. "I missed lunch. I suppose I could eat, as long as it's more than finger sandwiches."

"There's a whole roast beef ready to be carved, and mounds of steamed shrimp. Will that do? You used to love roast beef."

He still loved roast beef, and shrimp, although there'd rarely been money for either one when he was a child. "Sounds okay."

She settled him at the buffet table, departing only after she'd made him promise not to leave until he'd met his new stepfather. Zack kept from rolling his eyes at that thought. He could hardly wait.

Soon she drifted off to circulate and accept best wishes from the fifty or so guests in attendance, stepping into the part of gracious bride with the dignified ease of a queen. If only they knew the truth about her. He wondered if Harold did.

Resentful and irritated, he helped himself to generous servings of both entrées, pinning the man carving the roast with a hard eye when the guy hesitated over serving him an extra large portion. In no mood for company, Zack found an empty table and sat down to eat.

As his hunger lessened, so did the rougher edges of his bad mood. That was when he began to watch Georgia and her new husband.

It could all be an act, he decided, and very probably was, but as she stood next to Harold, laughing and chatting, dancing the traditional dance, Zack glimpsed a difference in her, a softness around the eyes that he'd never seen before. It made him wonder, as incredible as the idea might be, if she actually loved the poor sap.

The fact that Harold adored her was more than obvious.

Zack watched the pair of them clown for their audience as they cut the cake, gleefully mashing slices into each other's faces. *Nah,* he reminded himself, his mother loved only one person, and that person was her. He'd be an idiot to ever believe otherwise.

Still, she was growing older; there was no denying that fact, despite all the extraordinary measures she used to stave off the inevitable.

On the verge of fifty, she could still pass for thirty-five in the right light. But the clock kept right on ticking, and she wouldn't be able to hold back its effects for much longer. Maybe it was more than age. Maybe she was afraid she might end up alone. Was that why she kept finding men to marry? He'd always thought it was the money, but perhaps it was fear—and the money.

Old and alone.

Madelyn had talked about that, wanting to find someone to spend her life with. Someone who wouldn't mind the inevitable lines on your face or a little tremor in your hand when you reached up to push back a stray wisp of white.

He imagined Madelyn white haired and frail, old, and knew he wouldn't mind.

"Zack? I'd like you to meet Harold." His mother walked forward with her new husband. "Darling, this is my son, Zack Douglas."

Manners kicking in, Zack stood, towering over the shorter, older man. He held out his hand. "Pleased to meet you."

"Same here," Harold declared, taking his hand in a firm, exuberant shake. "When Georgie told me her boy'd shown up, I didn't expect a full-grown man like you. Of course, I should have, if I'd done the math. Then again, she looks so young I never imagined." He beamed fondly over at her. "You must have been a baby yourself when you had him."

"Very nearly," she murmured, lips curving.

Harold angled his chin toward Zack. "You've got the look of her, though, no doubt. Especially around the eyes."

What else did he have of her? Zack thought sourly. Is that why he'd come here? To prove to himself that he and his mother were nothing alike? Or to prove that they were?

"So what business are you in?" Harold inquired.

"Advertising. I'm an art director with Fielding and Simmons."

"Oh, sounds impressive. Big firm?"

"Big enough."

"Here in Florida?"

"No, New York. I came south to enjoy a warm holiday . . . and for the wedding," he added, oddly reluctant to appear rude in front of the other man. "What about you, sir? What keeps you occupied?"

"No 'sirs' here; that's a name for old stiffs and generals. Call me Harold."

"All right, Harold."

"Well, happens I'm in dry cleaning. Surprised your

mom didn't mention it to you. I've managed to build up quite a respectable little line of stores over the years. Yes, indeed, a very respectable line of stores. Fifteen of them now, scattered here and there around these parts. If you've got any laundry stacked up that needs doing, you swing by one of my shops, and we'll take care of you fast and on the house."

"That's very generous, and I'd be pleased to accept if I wasn't headed home tomorrow." Actually he'd been planning to stay another three days. When had he suddenly changed his mind?

"Oh well, next trip, then. You come down and stay with us. Georgie and I, we'll show you the sights, won't we, Georgie?" Harold tossed an arm around her shoulders and gave a jovial squeeze.

"Of course," she replied smoothly, "that would be lovely."

For a moment, Zack met her eyes, recognizing the same translucent green that stared back at him every time he looked in a mirror. Was it wistful resignation he read in hers now? He couldn't be sure.

Georgia broke eye contact, then turned to straighten her husband's tie, giving his chest a gentle pat. "I'm just going to visit with Zack another minute or two; then I think we need to start saying our good-byes. Otherwise, we'll miss our plane."

Harold glanced at the gold Rolex on his wrist. "Oh, you're right, and planes don't wait. Honeymoon in Aspen," he volunteered. "This one wants snow for Christmas. Great to meet you, Zack."

"Great to meet you, Harold," he said, surprised to actually mean it. They exchanged one more handshake; then the groom strolled away.

"Thank you," she murmured.

He lifted a single dark brow. "For what?"

"For Harold. For being so decent to him. It was kind."

"It wasn't meant to be kind. I simply had no reason not to be decent . . . to Harold."

"Touché." She sighed. "Well, I hope you got what you came for today. And I hope things work out between you and whoever this woman is who's set you to brooding."

"What makes you say I'm brooding? I don't recall mentioning any woman," he said, brows locking in a fearsome scowl.

"You didn't have to mention her." Her smile held a wisdom ages old. "I may not have been much of a mother, I admit, but I am one hell of a woman, a woman who knows men. And you, my dear son, are a man with woman trouble written all over him."

"Now I suppose I'm expected to confide in you? Ask for your precious hallowed motherly advice?" he said sarcastically.

"No, and even if you did, I wouldn't give you any. I've made too many mistakes in my life to hand out advice. Some of those mistakes I regret, a few deeply and for the rest of my life. Others I've come to accept as lessons well learned. I have only one comment, one question. If you let this woman go, this one you obviously love, will you look back and see her loss as a lesson learned or as a lifetime regret?"

For a moment he couldn't speak, aware of the funny

little pain that pinged inside his chest whenever he thought of Madelyn.

Impatient, Georgia twitched her fingers as if longing for a cigarette. "It's been interesting to see you, Zack, and I'm truly glad you came to my wedding. Of course, I know you won't, but give your sister my love. And take care of yourself. I'll drop you a postcard sometime."

CHAPTER TWENTY

"I just heard, and you don't have to say a word." Peg stalked into Madelyn's office, as ruffled as a mother hen whose favorite chick has been slighted by the other barnyard fowl.

"I'm taking you to lunch right now," she continued. "A long lunch, to revive your spirits. I already called the girls and they're going to meet us at the restaurant. And if management doesn't approve of us taking a few much-needed extra minutes, well, they can stick it up their pipes and smoke it."

"I believe the phrase is 'stick it *in* their pipes,'" Madelyn said. "And you know smoking's against company policy, at least inside the building."

"How can you joke? You must be furious. Devastated. I know I would be, especially after all the hard work you've put in, especially losing out to *him*."

"It isn't what you think—"

"Of course it's what I think. What else could it be?

You're very brave, trying to put such a good face on it, but there's no disguising the truth. As if it isn't bad enough their handing the entire Giatta account back to Zack, but then to promote him on top of it. Oh, Madelyn, how dreadful for you. I'm really sorry. You deserve better." She tapped a carefully filed, pale pink nail against the leg of her slim black pantsuit. "And to think I invited him to my wedding. Makes me feel like a traitor."

"Thanks for the support, but it isn't necessary, really. You shouldn't blame Zack. The decision wasn't up to him."

"I suppose not, but—"

"Giatta was returned to him, but they offered the promotion to me. I declined it."

"You *what*?" Peg squeaked, loudly enough to turn the heads of two suits from accounting who were passing in the hall. She waited until they walked on. "I couldn't have heard you right. Repeat that, please."

"They offered me the promotion—senior art director—but I turned it down."

Peg's mouth dropped open. "Why? It's everything you've dreamed of for the past five years. Everything you've worked for, and now you're passing on it? I don't understand."

"I haven't wanted to tell you. I know you'll be sad, maybe even angry, and it's been a difficult decision to make, but, well, I've ... I've decided to leave the company. I'm quitting. It's the right thing to do. I resigned this morning."

"Now I need to sit down." Peg sat, hard.

Madelyn looked away and gazed out the window as she searched for a way to explain, one that wouldn't sound like a complete lie, even if it was.

She sighed and turned back. "It's time for me to move on, try new opportunities, test my options. I'm getting married in a few days. This seems like a good time to make a new start."

"But why would you want to jump ship? Especially now. Is it James? Is he making you quit?"

"No, of course he isn't making me quit. He wants me to do whatever makes me happy. But I have to admit, he's offered to back me financially, to help me start my own firm. It's a great opportunity, one I think I'll be damned good at. Give me a few months and I'll be calling you with an offer to defect and come work for me."

"If you do, I'll be there in a heartbeat—you know that. I could probably talk Todd into coming on board too." Sober faced, Peg studied her, a frown lining the smooth skin of her forehead. "And there's nothing else?"

"No, of course not." Peg's concern and doubt shone in her eyes, as transparent as glass.

Madelyn knew she needed to convince her friend that she was happy about her decision. Otherwise the prying might begin.

She planted a big, exuberant smile on her face. "I'm really excited. Starting my own firm is going to be the best move I've ever made. And when the time comes and I decide to get pregnant, I won't have to worry about putting someone like Larry into cardiac arrest over my impending maternity leave."

"You're right about that," Peg said with a laugh. "And you don't mind? About Zack getting your promotion?"

"A little, but they offered the job to me first, and knowing that is what's important. Don't worry. I'll make sure Mr. Douglas knows he came in second." She tossed Peg a smug victory wink.

"When are you leaving, then?"

"Steady yourself for another shock. Tomorrow's my last day. With Christmas and the honeymoon, it seemed best."

"Lord, Madelyn, when you heap it on, you really heap it on. Well, Suzy and Linda are holding a table for us and we're late. I guess our commiseration lunch will have to be a going-away party."

At midmorning on Christmas Eve, Zack walked into the employee lounge on the slim chance he might find a home-baked treat or two that some benevolent soul had brought in to share with the rest of the staff. He'd missed breakfast this morning and hunger was whittling a hole in his belly.

Todd March stood before a long countertop that ran nearly the entire length of the left side of the room, a well-used blue-and-white-striped ceramic mug in hand.

He turned his head toward Zack. "I didn't expect to see you today. I'd heard you were off enjoying the beaches and the babes down Florida way until after Christmas."

Todd poured himself a coffee from the pot and added two generous spoonfuls of sugar to cover the bitter twang certain to be there.

"I was, but I had too much work," Zack told him. "I needed to come back early."

Zack lifted the lid on a box of leftover doughnuts and studied the remains. One jelly that oozed red like an open wound and half a dried-out chocolate. Not at all what he'd hoped for. Untempted, he let the lid flap shut. If he wanted anything decent, he supposed he'd have to brave the cold and run over to the deli across the street.

"We're definitely on skeleton staff today," Todd said. "I wouldn't be here either if I'd had any vacation time left, but taking a three-week honeymoon kind of tapped me out."

"How was the honeymoon, by the way?"

A smug, lascivious grin curved Todd's lips. "Fabulous. Everything a man could want and more. Vacation time's not the only thing that got tapped out, if you know what I mean."

Amused, Zack returned the grin. "Glad to hear it."

Todd snapped his fingers. "Speaking of things I heard, congratulations on your promotion."

"Thanks."

"Guess that's the reason you had to rush back early, to pick up the slack and then some until they can find a replacement for Madelyn. Man, did that news come out of left field. Peg's been moping around ever since she heard. You'd think Madelyn was dying, not moving."

Zack's ears perked up. "What do you mean, a replacement for Madelyn?"

"I figured you knew. She quit. Resigned as of yesterday."

"She quit?" he repeated, thunderstruck.

"Yeah, Peg told me she has plans to start up her own firm, bankrolled by that millionaire fiancé of hers. She said that's the reason Madelyn turned down the promotion they—"

"The promotion they what?" Zack crossed his arms

over his formidable chest and waited for the younger, shorter man to respond, a grim expression on his face.

Todd set down his mug, careful not to slop hot coffee over the edge and burn himself. "The . . . um . . . the promotion they gave to you." He coughed. "They offered it to her first. At least that's what she told my wife. People are wondering, though, if Madelyn said that, you know, to save face. It isn't like her to make up stories, but on the other hand if they really did offer her the senior slot, then why'd she quit?"

Zack knew exactly why, the only reason there could be. She'd quit to get away from him.

December twenty-seventh.

Her wedding day.

Madelyn awakened, a sick knot of dread twisted in the bottom of her stomach. She put her hands over her eyes as she lay against the sheets and wished she could disappear.

Holy crap, what had she done? Why had she ever agreed to marry James? If she went through with the marriage, it would be a terrible mistake. If she didn't . . . she couldn't even contemplate the fallout if she didn't.

Three hundred and fifty friends, relatives, and business associates were readying themselves even now for the ceremony due to take place in less than five hours. How could she disappoint them all?

Embarrass herself and her family?

Devastate James?

Picturing his reaction made her shudder.

Last night at the rehearsal dinner he'd been so happy. And two days before, Christmas Day, there had been a twinkle of undisguised delight in his summer blue eyes as he'd watched his two families, the one by blood, the other by bond, come together to celebrate and rejoice as one.

How could she even consider taking that from him? How could she consider shattering his hopes, destroying the dreams they'd made for their future?

No, cowardice had led her to this point; bravery would see her through. She'd made a promise, and it was far too late to break it now. Her current fears probably amounted to nothing more than bridal jitters, nerves that would pass away once she forced herself out of bed, into action. Once she was up and doing, all would be well.

But the nerves did not pass, her hands and feet chilled to the temperature of ice. Her skin paste white beneath layers of foundation and blusher, eyelids contoured with a careful blending of blue and brown shadow, her mouth stained translucent peony pink. She studied herself in the mirror, once the professional stylist finished with her hair and makeup, and thought she resembled a gaily painted doll, pretty yet lifeless underneath.

She moved and spoke and acted as if nothing were amiss, though she couldn't choke down a bite of breakfast. Not even a glass of juice.

By the time she reached the anteroom of the church, where she would wait until the ceremony was ready to begin, her head was swimming as if she might faint. Her hands trembled as though palsied.

She sat and willfully hid them within the skirt of her exquisite wedding gown.

"Madelyn, are you all right?" Brie bent close, caught in the band of sunlight streaming through a tall casement window.

As maid of honor, she looked a picture in a long, elegant dress of blush rose satin, her short golden hair curling around her narrow, often too serious face.

Madelyn met her sister's concerned eyes, then raised her chin and mustered a smile. "Of course. Why wouldn't I be?"

"You haven't seemed yourself this morning. Mother and I are wondering if you're ill."

"No, I'm fine, just nervous. It's perfectly normal to be nervous on your wedding day, isn't it?" She heard the words as they tumbled from her lips and knew they'd sounded defensive.

"I wouldn't know, since I haven't had a wedding yet." She laid a hand on Madelyn's shoulder. "You're trembling, a lot. Do you have a fever? What's wrong?"

Madelyn veered away. "Nothing. Nothing's wrong, I told you. I know you only want to help, but please, please leave me alone."

She glanced up and saw two of her six bridesmaids, Peg and Ivy, hovering in the doorway, worry etched on their faces.

"What?" she demanded, hysteria rising in her voice. "What are you both staring at? I didn't sleep well last night. I'm tired, okay? You'd think today of all days I could have five minutes to myself, five minutes' peace. Is that too much to ask? Get out! Go away! All of you, just go away!"

Abruptly, she burst into a flood of tears.

"You heard her, ladies." Laura Grayson strolled calmly into the center of the storm. "Madelyn needs a bit of breathing space and she'll be fine. Why don't you all go down the hall, give your hair and makeup a final check?"

Brie patted Madelyn's hand through the folds of her skirt, then left with the others as she'd been directed, closing the door behind her.

Madelyn tried to quit crying, but the tears wouldn't stop; they only flowed faster. She wiped at her face with her fingers and pressed the heels of her hands against her cheeks.

"Here, dear." Laura passed her daughter several tissues.

Grateful, Madelyn accepted them, blowing her nose, blotting her eyes.

Laura seated herself beside her daughter. She waited until the worst of Madelyn's tears slowed. "Now, why don't you tell me what's wrong?"

Madelyn shook her head and balled the tissues into her fist. She sniffed. "I can't." Another tear raced down her cheek.

"Of course you can. I'm your mother. You should know by now you can tell me anything, anything at all."

"Not this."

"Anything."

"You'll hate me."

"I could never hate you."

"You will once I tell you, because I can't . . . I can't go through with the wedding," she whispered in horror.

She waited for the explosion.

But her mother sat quiet and patient instead.

Madelyn took a shaky breath. "I know it's what you all want. It's what I thought I wanted too. What I'd convinced myself was for the best. But I can't, I just can't marry him. I'm sorry, oh God, I'm so sorry. How will I ever face him again? And all the guests, the expense. Oh Lord, this is so awful."

She began crying again, burying her face in the tissues again as she waited for her mother to speak, expecting, almost hoping, to be told to pull herself together and quit being ridiculous.

Laura sighed heavily. "If you feel that strongly, then you mustn't marry him."

"What?" She sniffed.

"This is my fault. I've sensed . . . well . . . for a while that something wasn't right. You haven't been happy, not like you should have been. I tried to make myself talk to you about it once or twice, but I suppose I was afraid of what I might hear. I love you and James, and I've always wanted to see you together. I let myself believe if I kept silent, it would turn out all right in the end. I was wrong and I'm sorry."

"No, this is entirely my doing." Madelyn blew her nose again, straightening her back. "I should have had the courage to call it off long ago." She hung her head, her voice low. "I should never have agreed to marry him in the first place."

"Why did you agree?"

"Because it made him happy. It made all of you happy, and I thought eventually, if I tried hard enough, I'd feel the same. Only I didn't, and the harder I tried, the worse it became." She sighed. "I do love him, you know."

"I know. Just not that way."

"No. Not that way."

Laura hesitated. "Madelyn, is there someone you do have those feelings for?"

Madelyn's eyes flew to meet her mother's.

"Yes, I suspected," Laura said. "I suppose I didn't want to find out about that either."

"James didn't—"

"No. You hid your feelings very well, perhaps too well. I don't believe anyone else had a clue. So what of this other man? Why isn't he the one waiting out there today, ready to take vows with you?"

"Because he doesn't believe in vows, not the wedding sort anyway. He's been hurt before and doesn't want to be hurt again. I let my own fear and pride drive him away. If he'll take me back, I've decided I'm going, on his terms this time."

"And will that be enough?"

"Yes. He's what I want. Being with him makes me happy."

"Well, if anyone can bring him around, it'll be you." Laura took a deep breath. "First, though, there's a wedding to cancel. Shall I tell James for you?"

Color burst in Madelyn's cheeks. "No. I'm the one who's made a mess of everything. I'm the one who should break the bad news."

Zack stomped harder on the accelerator to increase his speed, checking the hour on the dashboard clock.

Too late.

Even if the directions he'd been given to the church were perfect and he made no mistakes following them, he was still cutting it far too close. Any minute now, Madelyn would be walking down the aisle, placing her hands into those of another man, repeating the solemn words that would legally bind her to that man.

He should have gone to her days ago to plead his case and persuade her to have him after all. Or driven to her parents' home to interrupt their pretty Christmas and declare himself, proclaim the love he could no longer deny.

But he hadn't. He'd been too stubborn. Too stupid. And most of all too afraid.

It wasn't as if Madelyn hadn't given him plenty of chances already. He'd had more than sufficient time to change his mind. Instead, he'd kept silent, letting her believe she wasn't worth the risk. What if he'd rejected her once too often? What if she told him no?

This morning he'd awakened twisted inside sheets drenched damp and cold with his own sweat, shivering as panic weighed upon his chest, anvil heavy. He'd known in that moment he had to try, one last time, before she was gone from his life forever. And she would be gone. She'd seen to that when she'd resigned her position at F and S.

Until she'd made that final break, there'd still been the chance of contact between them. Even if it amounted to nothing more substantial than a glimpse of her at the end of a hallway. Or the hint of her sweet scent lingering in the air where she'd passed.

She'd told him to stay away and he'd abided by her wishes. By resigning, she'd told him good-bye in the most permanent way she could. There was a very real chance he might never set eyes on her again.

This morning he'd realized he couldn't let that happen. He could not let her go.

The traffic signal at the intersection ahead turned yellow.

Zack floored the gas pedal and flashed through, figuring if he picked up an unwanted police escort it might help him reach the church that much sooner. He'd deal with any fines and tickets later.

But he arrived without any difficulty and brought his car to an abrupt halt not far behind the long black limousine that waited at the base of the church's front steps.

Wedding guests were milling around the grounds, gathered into groups of two or more, some with coats, some without, as they ignored the chill breeze that refused to warm despite the clear, bright sunshine in the sky.

Was the ceremony over? Were they all waiting to shower the newlywed couple with rice and best wishes? Or had the wedding yet to start? Did he still have time? Zack sprinted from his car, not even bothering to lock the doors as he took the stone church steps two at a time, the tails of his unbuttoned coat flying behind him.

He spotted Peg and Todd standing together near the wide double-door entrance.

"Is she married?" he demanded. "Is it over?"

Astonished, Peg blinked. "Zack? Where'd you come from?"

"New York."

"This morning?"

"Yes, this morning. Now, tell me, is she married? Is Madelyn married?"

"No, but—"

"Where is she?"

"Still in the church, I think, but—"

"Where?" He darted a look inside but couldn't see much beyond the vestibule.

"Down the rear hall, to the right, in one of the anterooms. But I don't understand why you're here. What do you want with Madelyn?"

"I want to make her my wife, if she'll still have me."

Unwilling to waste another second, he raced into the church, forgetting all about the stunned couple he'd left behind.

He tried four different rooms, entering each after a brief rap that barely announced him. In the first two rooms he found nothing; in the third he startled a trio of bridesmaids who sat gossiping together in a circle. The last room was cluttered with brooms, mops, and buckets. The janitor's closet.

Where is Madelyn?

Frustrated, desperate, he raced ahead, rounding one final corner that led down a short hallway and ended with a thick, carved cherrywood door. Sprinting toward it, he knocked twice then turned the knob.

"Madelyn?"

He saw her immediately, a vision swathed in yard upon yard of soft, billowy white. Her hair was a mass of coppery curls that cascaded down her shoulders, along her back, its color more luminous than the ribbon of sunlight shining through a narrow casement window at her back.

In all his life, he'd never seen anything or anyone as beautiful and knew he never would. He came fully into the room and closed the door so they could be alone. He walked closer, noticing a faint puffiness around her eyes; her lids were swollen as if she'd been crying. He said her name a second time.

She turned her head. "*Zack?* What are you doing here?"

For a moment he couldn't speak, his throat tight with emotion. "I couldn't stay away. I couldn't let you go, not without telling you first." In a rush, he crossed the space that separated them and grasped her hands, pressed them to his chest.

"Without telling me what?" she repeated in amazement.

"That I've been a fool, a stupid fool who almost let the best thing that's ever happened to me slip away. I know I've done this badly, waited until the last possible second to speak. But you haven't married him yet, so it's not too late. Say it's not too late, Madelyn. Say you'll marry me instead. I love you. I can't bear the thought of spending the rest of my life without you." He took her into his arms. "Please, sweetheart, please say you'll be my wife."

Madelyn blinked. It was like a dream, a wonderful, dazzling dream, the kind from which she never wished to wake. How many times in the past had she ached to hear him say such wonderful, lovely things to her? And how she'd despaired she never would. Yet here he was, saying the words. Her lips parted, "yes" trembling upon them, ready to be given voice. But fairness prevented her from uttering it. First she had to tell him the truth, had to let him know what he obviously still did not realize.

She placed her hands against the firm warmth of his chest and gazed into his eyes. "I am yours. I always have been. But you don't have to marry me, Zack. I've already called off the wedding. I told James a few minutes ago that I couldn't marry him. I think I broke his heart."

Zack hugged her tighter. "He's a big boy. He'll recover."

"I pray you're right."

She thought of James's face. The pasty white shock.

The shine of unshed tears in his eyes. The look of stunned, anguished betrayal. She'd begged his forgiveness. He'd given her silence as his reply before he'd turned and walked away.

"You're really not going to marry him?" Zack asked.

"No, I'm really not. I couldn't, not feeling the way I do about you. I've tried so hard not to love you, but it seems you're stuck in my heart."

"Good, because you're stuck in mine too."

He kissed her then and sent the room and the world spinning away. It was a long time before he let her come up for air.

"Take me away from here," she begged. "Take me away where we can be together, alone."

"I'll take you anywhere you want to go, as soon as you agree to marry me. We could even do it today. I think there's still time. You're all done up for the occasion, looking so beautiful you take my breath. Your family's here and the minister; we could go ahead right now."

"I already told you, you don't have to marry me. I'm not going to insist this time. I love you and I want to be with you; the rest isn't important."

He brushed a knuckle across her cheek. "So you don't mind if we just live together, *hmm*? No ties? No commitments?"

"That's right. No ties. No commitments."

"For as long as it lasts?"

"Yes," she repeated, "for as long as it lasts."

He smiled. "That's a sweet offer, Red, except for one thing."

Her heart gave a great thump of fear. "What thing?"

"The fact that I expect nothing less from you than

forever—kids and pets and a house in the burbs included. And you should accept nothing less from me in return. So you see, you might as well give up now and agree to marry me."

"But you don't want to marry me," she sputtered.

"Who says I don't?" He shot her a fierce scowl. "Can't a man change his mind at least once in his life?"

She studied him for a long moment, while the idea sank in that he really meant what he'd said. He really, truly wanted to marry her. He loved and trusted her enough to take the risk and build a life for them—together. She hadn't thought it was possible, and yet now . . .

She twined her arms around his neck, smiling. "All right, you can change your mind this once. But after we're wed, never, ever again."

He set his hands on her waist and lifted her off her feet, twirling her in a circle.

He began to laugh. "After we're wed, I won't want to change my mind. I'll want you, my dearest Madelyn, and only you until death do us part. I swear."

"I love you," she said, joy shimmering in her blue eyes like a perfect cloudless day. "Always."

She met his lips and sighed at the sweet, sweet touch. She'd missed it so much. She'd missed him. She closed her eyes and lost herself in the wonder of his embrace.

He was pressing her mouth wider to take a deeper drink when she unexpectedly pulled away.

"Oh, I just remembered something," she declared.

"Remembered what?" he said, trying to kiss her again.

"My job. I quit my job."

His eyebrows arched. "Ah, and so you did."

"And gave my promotion away to you."

He grinned. "So you did."

She pinned him with a dangerous look. "You should give it back. You're the only reason I turned it down, you know."

"I could give it back. But I won't. After all, how would we explain?"

She frowned.

"Don't worry," he said reassuringly. "I'll think of a way to make it up to you."

"You'd better think hard, then, and make it good."

"Oh, don't worry." He leered, running a hand over her bottom to press her closer. "It'll be good and hard."

She glared at him for a moment, then laughed. "You are incorrigible, but I love you anyway. And we'll just see who makes creative director first."

"So long as it goes to a Douglas, my dear, that'll be just fine with me."

Then he pressed his lips to hers again and made her forget everything but him and the strength of their love.

Read on for a sneak peek at
Tracy Anne Warren's next
contemporary romance,

THE MAN PLAN

Available in August 2014 from Signet

"Good evening, sir." The doorman, who moved with fluid grace to open the front door, was resplendent in his gray and black uniform, his steel gray hair and crisp British accent lending him even greater distinction.

James Jordan nodded. "Good evening, Barton. I hope you had a pleasant day."

"Yes, very pleasant. Thank you for asking, sir."

Rather than striding on toward the elevator, James paused. "Did Ms. Grayson get moved in?"

Barton smiled. "Indeed, yes, she did. Some friends of hers helped with her belongings. She seems a delightful young woman, a very welcome addition to the building."

James smiled. "Ivy's a special girl."

Once inside the elevator, James punched the button for the fifteenth floor instead of inserting his pass key and going directly to his penthouse. Since he owned the building and had made the arrangements for Ivy's move, he knew exactly which apartment was hers.

It will be nice to see her again, he thought.

Two years ago Christmas—that's how long it had been since he'd stood in the same room with Ivy. He'd accepted her parents' long-standing invitation that year because her sister, Madelyn—his ex-fiancée, who had jilted him at the altar—and the man she'd jilted him for and then married had been absent from the family festivities. They'd been visiting Douglas's sister for the holidays or some such.

Ivy'd been there with a date, a thoroughly smitten college boy whose brown eyes had followed her every move, whose every action was designed to please her. Just as James had predicted, she'd outgrown her childish adoration of him, her anguished, lovesick proposal to him all those years ago nothing but a forgotten memory.

The elevator gave a soft *ding*. He stepped out, walked briskly down the well-lit hallway with its attractively painted pale blue walls and neat gray carpet. Her apartment was the last door on the left—a cozy end unit.

Reggae music pulsed like an aching tooth, reaching his ears long before he neared her door, which was propped wide open with a packing box. More boxes were stacked inside; piles of them ranged in every direction.

He peered inside, rapped his knuckles on the door. "Ivy?"

No answer.

He moved inside, called again. "Ivy, are you here?"

He stopped and set his briefcase on the floor beside the living room sofa.

Nothing, only the beating rhythm of the music, which grew louder the farther into the apartment he went. He followed the noise, striding down a hallway and past a guest bath to the bedroom doorway. He stopped on the threshold, eyes widening at the sight that greeted him.

Snugged into a pair of tight plaid cotton shorts, a woman stood bent headfirst into a huge clothing wardrobe. The entire top half of her body was concealed beneath masses of hanger-hung clothes as she quite obviously searched for something on the bottom.

Friend of Ivy's?

A grin of pure male appreciation spread across his mouth.

What a pair of legs, he thought with a silent wolf whistle. They were smooth and golden, with a supple length that went up—all the way up. As for her rear end, a man couldn't help but get ideas when such round, tight, squeezable lushness was put within reach.

He tucked his suddenly itchy palms into his pockets and reminded himself to act like a gentleman. Still, gentleman or not, it didn't mean he couldn't enjoy the show. Only a saint could have looked away, and he made no claims to such perfection. Unable to tear his eyes away, he watched her backside do a provocative dance, wiggling up and down, side to side, as she strained to reach whatever it was that eluded her.

He stifled a groan, and was trying to decide on the politest way to announce himself when she lost her balance, her legs splaying wide.

A small screech echoed from inside the wardbrobe's depths.

Acting on instinct, he rushed forward and grabbed her hips to keep her from toppling all the way in.

She screeched again, louder this time, then jerked and

stiffened. Her bottom arched backward, pressing for a long, electrified moment smack-dab against his fly. He sucked in his breath and his stomach as if he'd been seared by a live brand, heat scalding his groin.

Fighting the urge to grind her against his sudden arousal, he hauled her up out of the wardrobe. Dresses, shirts, and skirts exploded across the floor as her head popped free.

He released her and took a hasty step back.

"Who is it? Who's here?" the woman demanded in a fierce voice as she spun around, fists clenched. She was clearly ready to fight despite the sea of long blond hair covering her face.

"Don't worry, I'm not going to hurt you!" he shouted over the blaring music.

She froze and peered out through her cloud of hair with a pair of curiously familiar blue eyes. "*James?*"

His jaw slackened. "*Ivy?*"

She shoved her hair out of her eyes. "James! Where'd you come from? You scared the living bejesus out of me."

He could say the same, but for different reasons, as he was still trying to wrap his mind around the fact that the mystery woman, whose spectacular ass had just been pressed against his crotch, was Ivy. Little Ivy, who he'd known since she was a baby.

Clearly she wasn't so little anymore, and not just because of her height.

"Yeah, well, you shaved a good year off my life too," he said, going on the attack to hide his lingering discomfort. "What in the hell did you think you were doing standing on your head in that wardrobe?"

"Unpacking," she said simply.

Suddenly her expression changed, a huge smile spreading over her mouth. "Let's argue later. Right now I just want to say hello." She raced forward and threw her arms around him in a fierce hug. "Oh, James, it's so great to see you! It's been so long. Way too long."

He stiffened momentarily in her embrace before he brushed aside the last of his earlier reaction and hugged her back.

Even so, he was the first to pull away.

Once free, he moved across the room to put some much-needed distance between them. "You suppose you could turn that noise down?" he asked once he turned to face her again.

"What?" she called loudly, giving her head a little shake.

"The music." He motioned with a hand. "Turn. It. Down."

She nodded in sudden understanding and moved to click off her sound system.

Silence swept like a refreshing wave through the room. "Don't you like reggae music?" she asked.

He shook his head. "Not this far north of the Caribbean, I don't. Sounds a lot better on a beach with a tall rum punch in hand. Numbs the misery."

She grinned and met his eyes, blue against blue. "To each his own. Bob Marley and me"—she crossed a pair of fingers—"we're tight, if ya know what I mean, *man*," she said in a bad Jamaican accent.

He laughed.

"But, hey," she said, reverting to her normal voice, "what are you doing here? I thought you were out of town on business."

"My meetings wrapped up early, so I flew back a day

ahead," he said. "And what do I find when I stop by to welcome you to your new place? Your door standing wide open, inviting anyone to stroll right on in. You ought to know better. What if I'd been a thief or a lunatic?"

This time she was the one who laughed. "Please, this is the last place I'd be in danger. The security here is as good as at Fort Knox."

"Actually, it's better. It ought to be, since my company is the one that financed the design of the army's latest security system upgrade. But you aren't supposed to know anything about that and I never mentioned it."

She stared for a moment. "Of course not. I have no memory of anything you just said."

He grinned.

"As for my leaving the door open," she went on, "I needed to air things out. I painted the spare room, the one I'm going to use for my studio, and it still smells of latex, even though I used the low-VOC kind." She wrinkled her nose. "I opened a couple windows and the front door to get a cross breeze."

"Airing paint fumes out of an artist's studio? I'd think an artist would love the smell of paint."

"The smell of oil paint for canvas, definitely, but not wall paint," she said. "Linseed oil's like a fine wine—you never get tired of the bouquet. Latex is just stinky plastic. Plus, it's healthier to air things out."

James crossed his arms over his chest. "Well, whatever the reason, I want you to promise me that you won't leave your door open again when you're alone. Safe building or no safe building."

She planted her fists on her hips. "And if I don't?"

"I'll tell your mother, of course," he replied in a serious tone.

"You wouldn't."

"Try me."

She made a face and stuck her tongue out at him.

For the first time since he'd walked into the room, he relaxed, recognizing his old Ivy.

Only she wasn't his old Ivy, not anymore.

Studying her once again, he found it as impossible to ignore the physical differences in her from the front as he had from the back.

Her heart-shaped face, with its high cheekbones and angular chin, had a newfound maturity, all her familiar youthful softness winnowed away into clean, refined lines. Her mouth was a full, womanly pink, and her deepset blue eyes contained wisdom and determination he'd never glimpsed in her before.

Then there was her body—lovely, slender, and tall.

As a man whose height was just over six feet two, he liked tall women; they didn't intimidate him the way they could other men. Still, he wasn't used to standing next to a woman who could turn her head and nearly look him in the eye. Particularly not when the female in question was his little friend Ivy Grayson.

Disturbing—that's what it was. Not just her height but the whole dynamic package.

Disturbing and sobering and unwanted.

I bounced her on my knee, for God's sake.

He'd played peekaboo and got-your-nose with her when she was a gurgling toddler. The thought of her sitting on his knee now . . .

He cleared his throat and glanced around at the stack of packing boxes. "Looks like you have your work cut out for you."

"You got that right." She shot him a hopeful look. "Wanna help?"

Her question caught him off guard. Professionals always did his packing and unpacking; he'd never had the need or inclination to bother with such mundane domestic chores. A quick phone call and he could have someone over here to help Ivy, but somehow he didn't think she would care for the idea.

He had work to do tonight, but then, he always had work to do, and Ivy looked so hopeful. Maybe helping her for a couple of hours wouldn't be so bad.

"Sure," he said, "assuming I'm allowed to have dinner first. Have you eaten?"

She shook her head. "I kept meaning to take a break and run out to get something, but I just kept working instead."

"Then let me treat you to dinner. How about Per Se? I know them there and they can usually squeeze me in even on a crowded night."

She bent to pick up a few of the clothes scattered across the carpet, then crossed to hang them up in the walk-in closet. "That sounds wonderful, but would you mind terribly if I asked for a rain check? I've been on the run since five this morning and I'm pooped." She plucked at her shorts and T-shirt. "Plus, I'd have to shower and change and fix my hair. I'd rather stay casual tonight. You understand, don't you?"

He did understand actually. There were many times

he wished for just such an evening and the chance to stay casual.

"Okay," he agreed. "Why don't we order something in, then? How about Chinese or Italian? I know good places for both that deliver."

She tossed him a smile. "Now you're talking. You call in our order; then I'll point you toward a packing box while we wait for the food to arrive."

James groaned in mock agony before pulling out his cell phone to dial.

Ivy put a last bite of Szechuan beef in spicy ginger sauce into her mouth and chewed.

Delicious, she thought, her tongue tingling with fiery heat. She swallowed, then leaned back in her chair, replete and content.

She looked across the small table she and James had cleared earlier of packing paraphernalia and watched him finish his meal. His elegant fingers maneuvered the chopsticks with easy grace; his masculine jaw and the beautiful lines of his strong throat as they worked were something her artist's eyes couldn't help but admire.

Warmth settled low and spread through her belly, thighs, and in between, physical reactions that had nothing to do with the spiciness of her meal. Just watching him made her want. His simplest movements were dynamic, compelling, appealing.

When she'd first seen him—after she'd gotten over the shock of their actual first encounter, when he'd grabbed her hips to pull her out of the wardrobe (she could still feel the *wow* from that even now)—part of her had hoped the old feelings would be gone. The sensible side of her had wished she wouldn't experience the rush of love for him that had consumed so many years of her life, that they would be friends—no more, no less.

But nothing had changed, at least not for her.

From the moment she'd touched him, she'd known—all the emotions, all the love surging back like an unstoppable wave rushing to shore. As she'd hugged him, pressing her body to his, she'd breathed him in, savoring the clean, male scent of his skin that was so uniquely his own.

And she'd clung, wanting to never let go again.

But he'd pulled away far too soon, stepping back to place a distance between them, to reestablish the barriers and silent borders of platonic friendship that were never to be crossed.

She skimmed her eyes over his urbane, classic beauty. His thick, close-cut golden hair and his eyebrows, which were two pale slashes across his stubborn, patrician forehead. His nose was straight and sized to suit his handsome face, while his masculine lips retained just enough softness to invite a woman's kiss.

She wondered what he'd do if she leaned across the table and planted one on him. A big, hot, wet smooch that would rock them both all the way to their toes.

Knowing James, he would probably pat her on the head and tell her to find a nice boy her own age, exactly as he had all those years ago.

Only she didn't want a boy her age; she wanted a man.

She wanted James.

And by God, I'm going to have him, no matter what it takes.

She'd have to take it slowly, though, she realized. She'd have to work hard in order to make him see her in a new light—a mature, desirable light.

Could she do it?

Of course I can, she assured herself.

No dream was impossible if you wanted it badly enough. Isn't that what had given her the courage to pursue a career as a painter despite the astronomical odds against success? Wasn't that what had brought her to New York City to strike out on her own, even though the chances were good she'd fall flat on her face?

But if she wasn't daunted by the riskiness of her career choice, then why should she be daunted by the unlikelihood of winning James? All she needed was a plan of action and some good insider information. But who was close enough to him to give her the inside skinny about his private life and habits—and any current girlfriend competition, of course?

In the next second, she knew exactly who.

Of course! she thought, doing a happy little dance inside.

Outwardly, she sipped her lukewarm China tea and smiled at James.

Unsuspecting, he smiled back.

ALSO AVAILABLE FROM
NEW YORK TIMES BESTSELLING AUTHOR

Tracy Anne Warren

THE TROUBLE
WITH PRINCESSES

A Princess Brides Romance

Just before receiving her inheritance, Princess Ariadne
decides to defy convention and take a lover instead of a
husband. And when renowned bachelor Rupert Whyte
agrees to give her a few lessons in lust, their forbidden
liaison will lead them too far astray to turn back...

<u>ALSO IN THE SERIES</u>
The Princess and the Peer
Her Highness and the Highlander

"Tracy Anne Warren is brilliant."
—*New York Times* bestselling author
Cathy Maxwell

Available wherever books are sold or at
penguin.com

facebook.com/LoveAlwaysBooks

s0514